Changeling Press LLC

ChangelingPress.com

Tempest/ Reclaiming Venom Duet
A Dixie Reapers Bad Boys Romance
Harley Wylde

I0668926

Tempest/ Reclaiming Venom Duet
A Dixie Reapers Bad Boys Romance
Harley Wylde

All rights reserved.
Copyright ©2025 Harley Wylde

ISBN: 978-1-60521-949-3

Publisher:
Changeling Press LLC
315 N. Centre St.
Martinsburg, WV 25404
ChangelingPress.com

Printed in the U.S.A.

Editor: Crystal Esau
Cover Artist: Bryan Keller

The individual stories in this anthology have been previously released in E-Book format.

No part of this publication may be reproduced or shared by any electronic or mechanical means, including but not limited to reprinting, photocopying, or digital reproduction, without prior written permission from Changeling Press LLC.

This book contains sexually explicit scenes and adult language which some may find offensive and which is not appropriate for a young audience. Changeling Press books are for sale to adults, only, as defined by the laws of the country in which you made your purchase.

Table of Contents

Tempest (Dixie Reapers MC 21) 4
    Chapter One..5
    Chapter Two 14
    Chapter Three...24
    Chapter Four 34
    Chapter Five..44
    Chapter Six..52
    Chapter Seven...64
    Chapter Eight..73
    Chapter Nine...83
    Chapter Ten...92
    Chapter Eleven 104
    Chapter Twelve 116
    Chapter Thirteen...128
    Chapter Fourteen 138
    Chapter Fifteen..150
    Chapter Sixteen 161
    Chapter Seventeen...171
    Chapter Eighteen 182
    Chapter Nineteen...192
    Chapter Twenty...201
    Epilogue...209
Reclaiming Venom (Dixie Reapers MC 22) 216
    Prologue...217
    Chapter One...222
    Chapter Two 237
    Chapter Three..249
    Chapter Four 259
    Chapter Five...269
    Chapter Six...278
    Chapter Seven..290
    Chapter Eight...299
Harley Wylde..309
Bad Boys Multiverse 310
Changeling Press LLC...311

Tempest (Dixie Reapers MC 21)
A Dixie Reapers Bad Boys Romance
Harley Wylde

In the heart of the South lies the Dixie Reapers MC -- an unbreakable brotherhood bound by loyalty and secrets. But when a fierce storm brews both outside and within the club, all bets are off.

Kasen -- I've spent my life hiding in the shadow of my father, Tank, the previous Sergeant-at-Arms for the Dixie Reapers. He'll never understand my crush on Tempest, the current SAA, so I've kept it to myself. But until recently, I thought Tempest only saw me as a child. Now that I know he wants me the way a man wants a woman, I have to decide if I have what it takes to be his woman. Belonging to the Dixie Reapers' Sergeant-at-Arms isn't for the faint of heart.

Tempest -- I may be the Sergeant-at-Arms, but one pint-sized half-Hispanic woman has me tied in knots. I shouldn't want Kasen. She's off-limits -- one of Tank's little princesses. Yet I can't get her off my mind. When she's kidnapped, I feel the rage taking over. They've dared to touch what's mine, and now I'm going to make them pay. Once I have Kasen back by my side, I'll make sure she's never out of my sight again. I'm done hiding how I feel.

Get ready for a tumultuous ride of love, loyalty, and fierce retribution.

Chapter One

Tempest

The sight of Kasen sitting with an unknown man at the café across the street made my blood boil. I gripped the handlebars of my Harley Davidson Road King, knuckles turning white as I fought the urge to storm over there.

Who the fuck was this guy? I watched them laughing and talking like old friends. Every fiber of my being screamed at me to intervene, to protect what was mine.

But Kasen wasn't mine. Not really.

I inhaled sharply, trying to regain control. My fingers flexed, itching to throttle something. Someone. The tension coiled in my muscles, ready to spring into action at a moment's notice.

My eyes narrowed as the stranger leaned in closer to Kasen. Too close.

"Easy," I muttered to myself, though the growl in my voice betrayed my inner turmoil.

I had no claim on Tank's daughter, no matter how much I wanted her. How much I'd always wanted her, even when I shouldn't have. But seeing her with another man awakened a primal possessiveness I could barely contain.

The roar of my bike's engine would be so satisfying right now. A warning. A challenge.

I resisted. Barely.

My gaze remained locked on Kasen, drinking in the sight of her. The curve of her smile. The toss of her hair. Memorizing every detail as if it might be the last time I saw her.

Because if I gave in to this rage, it just might be.

Kasen's laughter rang out again, a melodic sound

twisting something deep in my gut. She leaned forward, gesturing animatedly as she spoke to the stranger. Her eyes sparkled with mirth, her whole face lighting up in a way I'd rarely seen.

"Damn it," I muttered, my teeth grinding together. The sight of her so carefree, so open with this unknown man, felt like a knife to the ribs.

Who the hell was he? Some clean-cut pretty boy, by the looks of it. No patches, no ink visible. Nothing like the MC life Kasen had grown up around.

My mind raced, possibilities flashing through like gunfire. A boyfriend? A date? Just a friend?

Each option stoked the fire of jealousy burning in my chest. I shouldn't care. Kasen wasn't mine to claim. But logic had no place in the storm of emotions threatening to overwhelm me.

"You're off-limits," I growled under my breath, though whether I was talking to Kasen or myself, I couldn't say. "Tank's daughter. A club princess. Untouchable."

But God, how I wanted to touch her. To stake my claim. To show this interloper and the whole damn world that Kasen belonged with me.

The rational part of my brain, buried deep beneath layers of possessive fury, knew I needed to take a step back. She wasn't mine. But watching her laugh with another man felt like a betrayal of something I'd never even had.

As Sergeant-at-Arms, it was my job to protect the club and its family. Kasen was both. The urge to march over there, to drag her away from potential danger, rushed through my veins like wildfire.

I let out a soft growl, trying to reason with myself. This little prick wasn't a threat. Too damn soft. I could probably break the fucker with one hand. I needed to keep my ass right where I was -- watching from a distance.

The consequences of overstepping would be severe. Tank would have my head if I made a scene over his little girl. And the club... well, they'd start asking questions I wasn't ready to answer.

I tore my gaze away from Kasen, trying to focus on anything else. The café's outdoor seating area bustled with life. Servers weaved between tables, trays balanced precariously. Laughter and chatter filled the air, a stark contrast to the tension coiled within me.

The street was no better. Cars crawled by in the mid-afternoon traffic. Pedestrians hurried along the sidewalks, wrapped up in their own little worlds.

All of it -- the noise, the movement, the life -- felt distant. Unreal. My entire universe had narrowed to a single point -- Kasen, who was completely oblivious to my presence.

My heart slammed against my ribs. I felt like a caged animal fighting for release. I gritted my teeth so tight I thought my teeth might shatter. This wasn't me. I didn't lose control, didn't let emotions rule my actions. But something about Kasen...

"Fuck," I growled, low and guttural.

I shouldn't care. She wasn't mine, had never been mine. Just a kid with a crush, off-limits in every way that mattered. But watching her now, all grown up and laughing with some stranger, it felt like a sucker punch to the gut.

My fingers twitched, aching to reach for a cigarette, anything to occupy my hands and calm the storm raging inside me. But I couldn't risk losing sight of her, not even for a second.

Then it happened. Kasen leaned forward, her delicate hand brushing against the man's arm. It was casual, probably meaningless, but it sent a jolt of electricity through my body. My vision tunneled, narrowing to that single point of contact.

"Jesus Christ," I hissed, my heart thundering so loud I was sure the whole damn street could hear it.

The bike beneath me vibrated, responding to the tension in my body. I forced myself to breathe, to loosen my death grip on the handlebars. But I couldn't tear my eyes away from Kasen, from the easy way she touched that man.

It shouldn't matter. It *didn't* matter. But try telling that to the green-eyed monster clawing its way up my throat.

My mind raced, weighing options. I could storm over there and show this nobody who he was dealing with. But the consequences...

"Fuck," I muttered.

Tank would rip me apart if he thought I was sniffing around Kasen. No one dared touch his triplets. Hell, I hadn't even been aware any of them had been on date before. Did he know where his precious daughter was right now? Who she was with? Would he approve of her being with someone like this kid?

But the sight of her, laughing and carefree, made my blood boil. What if this guy wasn't what he seemed? What if Kasen was in danger? He didn't look like he had enough muscle to do much harm, but that didn't mean he wasn't the brains behind some sinister operation.

I flexed my fingers, fighting the urge to reach for the knife at my belt. "Get it together," I muttered to myself. "You're the Sergeant-at-Arms, not some lovestruck teenager."

The title sat heavily on my shoulders. I had responsibilities, a duty to the club that came before everything else. Even my own wants. Even Kasen.

But as I watched her lean in closer once more to the stranger, something primal roared to life inside me. My protective instincts warred with club loyalty, leaving me frozen in indecision.

"Goddamnit, Kasen," I whispered, my voice rough with emotion. "What are you doing to me?"

I kept my eyes locked on Kasen and her companion, cataloging every gesture, every laugh. The way she tucked a strand of hair behind her ear. The slight tilt of her head as she listened. I was gathering intel, I told myself. Nothing more.

Suddenly, Kasen's gaze swept across the street. Our eyes met, and the world seemed to freeze. Electricity sparked through the air between us, charged with unspoken words and hidden desires.

Her eyes widened slightly, recognition flashing across her face. I saw her breath catch, saw the slight tremor in her hand as she reached for her drink.

"Tempest?" I saw her mouth my name, barely a whisper.

For a heartbeat, I forgot how to breathe. Then the moment shattered as her companion said something, drawing her attention back. But the damage was done. My resolve crumbled like ashes in the wind.

Did she know? Could she feel this magnetic pull, this invisible tether drawing us together? I couldn't confront her now, not with that unknown bastard sitting there. But later... later, I'd get her alone. I'd make her explain what the hell was going on.

My mind raced, plotting out scenarios. I'd catch her leaving the cafe, or maybe outside her place. Somewhere private, where I could let this simmering rage and confusion boil over without risking the club interfering.

With a sharp inhale, I made my decision. The Harley roared to life beneath me, a beast awakening. The engine's growl matched the storm of emotions churning in my gut -- anger, jealousy, desire, all tangled up in a knot I couldn't unravel.

I cast one last look at Kasen, committing her face to memory. Then, with a twist of the throttle, I peeled away from the curb, leaving nothing but the echo of thunder in my wake.

The wind whipped past as I tore through the streets, my mind a chaotic mess of conflicting thoughts. Kasen's face haunted me, her wide-eyed look of recognition burned into my retinas. I pushed the bike faster, harder, trying to outrun the storm inside me.

The clubhouse loomed ahead. I pulled in, killing the engine with a savage twist. The sudden silence felt oppressive.

"Yo, Tempest!" Thunder called from the picnic table. "You look like you're about to murder someone."

I ignored him, striding toward the clubhouse door. "Where's Tank?" I growled.

Thunder's eyebrows shot up. "Inside. Everything okay?"

I shouldered past him without answering. The cool dimness of the clubhouse interior did nothing to calm the fire in my veins. I scanned the room, zeroing in on Tank's hulking form by the bar.

"We need to talk," I said, my voice low and tight. "Now."

Tank's eyes narrowed, assessing. He nodded once. "So, talk."

I reached behind the bar for a mug and poured myself a beer, downing it in one go. Then I slammed the mug down.

"What's got you so worked up?" Tank asked, his tone deceptively casual.

"Your daughter."

"Which one?" he asked. "In case you forgot, I have three."

"Kasen."

Tank's expression hardened. "What about her?"

"She's out there, with some guy. Some nobody."

Tank's eyes narrowed. "And?"

"And I thought you should know," I said, struggling to keep my voice even. "Didn't look like the type to be in a club."

Royal snorted into his drink. "Since when do you care about the girls' social lives, Tempest?"

I shot him a glare that could have melted steel. "It's called looking out for family, asshole."

Tank stood slowly, his imposing frame towering over me. "Kasen's a grown woman. She can see whoever she wants. Within reason. But I'd be fine if she never wanted to leave home."

"But --"

"But nothing," Tank cut me off. "Unless you've got a damn good reason why I should be concerned, I suggest you drop it."

The challenge in his voice was clear. I clenched my fists, torn between spilling everything and keeping my mouth shut. "I thought you'd want to know," I muttered finally, backing down.

Tank studied me for a long moment, his expression unreadable. "Thanks for the heads-up," he said finally. "Now why don't you go cool off? You look like you're about to explode."

I nodded stiffly, turning on my heel and stalking toward the door. I stormed out of the clubhouse, my boots echoing on the concrete. The sun beat down, intensifying the heat of my anger. I needed to hit something. Hard.

The newly built gym beckoned. I stripped off my cut, tossing it over a chair as I entered the stuffy room. The punching bag swayed slightly, taunting me.

I lashed out, my fist connecting with a satisfying *thud*. Again. And again. Each punch carried the weight of my frustration, my jealousy, my impotent rage.

Kasen's face flashed in my mind. Her smile, directed at that stranger. My knuckles split, leaving smears of red on the bag.

"Fuck!" I roared, unleashing a flurry of blows.

I don't know how long I stood there, pummeling the bag until my arms burned and sweat soaked my shirt. The pain in my hands was a welcome distraction from the ache in my chest.

"You trying to kill that thing?"

I whirled around, fists ready. Royal stood in the doorway, eyebrows raised.

"The fuck you want?" I snarled.

He held up his hands. "Easy, brother. Just checking you haven't lost your mind completely."

I turned back to the bag, landing another solid hit. "I'm fine."

"Yeah, you look it." Royal snorted. "This about Tank's kid?"

I froze, then slowly faced him. "What?"

Royal shrugged. "You come in looking murderous, asking for Tank. Then you're in here beating the shit out of that bag. Doesn't take a genius."

"You don't know what you're talking about," I said.

"Maybe not," he conceded. "But whatever's going on, you need to get your head straight. We can't afford our SAA losing his shit over some piece of ass."

Red clouded my vision. Before I realized what I was doing, I had Royal pinned against the wall, my forearm across his throat.

"Don't you ever talk about her like that," I said, my voice more growl than anything else. I sounded, and felt, like a feral beast.

Royal's eyes widened, then narrowed. He shoved me back, hard.

"Jesus Christ," he muttered. "You've got it bad, don't you?"

I turned away, running a hand through my sweat-soaked hair. "It's not like that."

"Bullshit," Royal shot back. "Look, man, I get it. She's hot. But she's Tank's daughter. You really want to go there?"

I slumped against the wall, suddenly exhausted. "It doesn't matter what I want."

Royal was quiet for a moment. Then he sighed. "Shit. You're in deep, aren't you?"

I didn't answer. I didn't need to.

Chapter Two

Kasen

I sat across from Connor, my fingers tapping a nervous rhythm on the café table. The chatter of other patrons faded to white noise as my gaze darted to the opposite sidewalk. There he was. Tempest. His dark eyes bored into me, intense and unwavering. I'd spotted him not too far into my date with Connor, except at the beginning, I hadn't really thought of it that way. He'd made it clear after a few minutes this was more than friends meeting.

"So, how's your dad doing?" Connor asked, his voice cutting through my distraction.

I snapped my attention back, forcing a smile. I'd forgotten I'd told him about my dad's motorcycle accident. "He's... improving. Slowly."

My heart raced. Tempest hadn't moved. I could feel the heat of his stare. I glanced that way again and saw him pull out onto the street and ride away. My heart felt like it dropped to my stomach.

You're seriously screwed up, Kasen. Here I was with this super sweet guy, and all I could think about was the biker I shouldn't want.

"That's good to hear," Connor continued. "I was thinking maybe we could --"

I nodded, barely registering his words. My mind drifted. I'd been in love with Tempest for a long time. Puppy love at first, but over the years, it had grown into something more. Not that I thought he'd ever see me that way.

"Kasen? You okay?" Connor's brow furrowed.

"Yeah, sorry." I shook my head. "Just tired."

Lies. I was wide awake. Every nerve on edge. Why had Tempest been watching me? It wasn't the first time I'd noticed. There had been other times I'd been in town and spotted him in the distance. Almost as if I had a personal bodyguard. I just didn't understand why. Unless my dad had asked him to keep an eye on me.

Connor leaned forward. "As I was saying, there's this new restaurant --"

I forced myself to focus. Nodded again. Smiled. But I couldn't pay attention to Connor no matter how hard I tried. He just wasn't... exciting. I doubted he'd ever ridden on a motorcycle or driven over the speed limit. I liked a man with rough edges. Probably because I'd grown up around them.

"Sounds great," I managed, though I had no idea what I was agreeing to. I took a sip of water. Nearly choked.

Connor's lips kept moving. I caught fragments. "Friday... pick you up... seven?"

"Sure," I replied automatically. My mind elsewhere.

With the man who'd been watching over me. The one I couldn't have.

The one I couldn't stop wanting.

I somehow made it through the rest of my so-called date. I'd been so distracted I had no idea what we'd even talked about it. Which made me feel awful. Connor deserved better.

I stepped out of the café and saw my best friend waiting for me. Akira, Wraith's daughter, waved at me. I walked over and smiled at her.

"You weren't waiting long, were you?"

Akira shook her head. "Just got here."

The honking of horns and the buzz of conversation surrounded us as Akira and I weaved through the crowded sidewalk. My heart still raced from the encounter at the café.

"I can't take it anymore, Akira," I blurted out, my voice strained. "Tempest was there, watching me the whole time I was with Connor."

She held up a hand. "Wait. Connor is the guy you knew in high school, right? The one who just came back to town?"

"Yeah. Remember? I told you I ran into him at the bookstore, and he invited me to the café for lunch."

"Right. Now back to what you were saying about Tempest," she said.

"It's like he's everywhere."

Akira raised an eyebrow, her hand resting on her slightly swollen belly. "And that's a problem because…?"

I sighed, frustration bubbling up. "Because he's Tempest! He's intense and dangerous and… God, I want him so badly it hurts."

"Then go for it," Akira said, nudging me with her elbow. "You're not a kid anymore, Kasen. You can handle him."

I scoffed, sidestepping a rushing businessman. "You make it sound so easy."

"It is easy," Akira retorted, her eyes sparkling with mischief. "You want him, he clearly wants you. What's stopping you?"

"Everything!" I exclaimed, earning a few curious glances from passersby. I lowered my voice. "The club, my dad, his reputation…"

Akira rolled her eyes. "Excuses. Trust me, if your mom managed to tame your dad, you can handle Tempest. We grew up overhearing those stories. Both our dads were total players before they met our moms."

My stomach fluttered at the thought. "But what

if --"

"No what-ifs." Akira cut me off sharply. "You're a strong woman, Kasen. It's time you showed Tempest that."

I bit my lip, considering her words as we navigated the bustling street. Maybe she was right. Maybe it was time to face this head-on.

We ducked into a quiet coffee shop on the corner, settling into a secluded booth away from prying ears. The aroma of fresh coffee enveloped us, but it did little to calm my nerves.

"It's not just about me and Tempest," I confessed, my voice barely above a whisper. "Dad's still recovering. I can't pile on more stress with my... personal drama."

My fingers traced the worn edge of the table, memories of Dad's pale face in the hospital bed flashing through my mind. The fear of losing him still haunted me. He was home, and mostly healed, but what if he got into another accident? What if I lost him?

Akira reached across, her warm hand covering mine. "Kasen, your dad's tough. He wouldn't want you putting your life on hold."

I met her gaze, seeing the understanding in her eyes. She knew the weight of the MC world better than most.

"When Logan and I first got together," Akira began, a soft smile playing on her lips, "I was terrified. Not just of him, but of what it meant for my family, for my future."

I leaned in, hanging on her every word.

"But you know what?" she continued, her voice strong. "Loving him was worth facing those fears. It still is, every single day."

Her hand drifted to her belly, and I saw the love

and certainty in her eyes.

"The club life isn't easy," Akira admitted. "But neither is denying what your heart wants. Trust me, I've been there."

I swallowed hard, her words hitting home. "How did you know it was right?"

Akira's laugh was light, but her eyes held a depth of emotion. "I didn't. I just knew I'd regret it forever if I didn't try. Even if it meant defying my dad, and you know how scary he can be."

I nodded slowly, letting her words sink in. The chaos in my mind began to settle, like dust after a storm. "Maybe... maybe you're right."

Akira's eyes lit up. "Of course, I am. You've been pining for Tempest since you were sixteen, Kasen. It's time to do something about it."

My heart skipped. "But what if --"

"I told you. No what-ifs," she cut me off, her tone firm but kind. "You're stronger than you think. I've seen it."

I took a deep breath, feeling a spark of resolve ignite in my chest. It was small, but it was there. "Okay. I'll... I'll talk to him."

Akira grinned, triumphant. "That's my girl."

Suddenly, she leaned over and poked me in the ribs, making me yelp. "Life's too short to be a chicken, Kase."

I laughed despite myself, swatting her hand away. "Hey! I'm not a chicken, I'm... cautious."

"Cautious, my ass." Akira snorted, her eyes dancing with mischief. "You're the daughter of Tank. The ex-Sergeant-at-Arms for the Dixie Reapers. Since when do you play it safe?"

I couldn't help but smile, feeling the tension dissipate. "Fair point."

"And as for your dad, he's been through worse than watching his daughter fall in love." Akira winked. "If my dad can come around and welcome Logan into the family, your dad shouldn't have an issue with Tempest. As least he's part of the club."

I winced at the word "love," my heart racing. "It's not just that. You know how protective he is. If things go wrong with Tempest..."

"Then Tank will deal with it," Akira said firmly. "Look, I know firsthand how the club works. Your happiness matters to your dad more than anything. Although, I'm sure he has an odd way of showing it sometimes. I think that just comes with being the daughter of a Reaper."

I chewed my lip, considering her words. "How do I balance it, though? My needs and his?"

Akira leaned forward, her dark eyes intense. "You talk to him. Be honest. Tank's not made of glass, Kasen. He can handle the truth, and he deserves to hear it from you."

Her words hit home, and I felt a weight lift from my shoulders. "You're right. God, when did you get so wise?"

She patted her belly with a wry smile. "Apparently, growing a human gives you superpowers. Who knew?"

We both laughed, the sound echoing in the quiet coffee shop. As our laughter faded, I reached out and squeezed Akira's hand. "Thank you. For everything."

She squeezed back, her smile warm. "Anytime, girl. Now go get your man."

I glanced around. "We haven't even ordered yet."

She waved me off. "Go. I'll order a smoothie or something and wait for Logan to get off work."

As I stood and walked off, I felt a new determination coursing through me. The fear was still there, a quiet whisper in the back of my mind, but it no longer paralyzed me. I took a deep breath, tasting possibility on the air.

"I'm doing this," I mumbled to myself.

The city blurred around me, the kaleidoscope of noise and color barely registering. My mind raced, replaying every moment with Tempest, every stolen glance, every time his presence had set my heart racing.

"Enough hiding," I muttered.

A car horn blared, jerking me back to reality. I'd nearly stepped off the curb into traffic. Shaking my head, I forced myself to focus on my surroundings. The familiar streets of my hometown stretched before me. I got in my car and headed home, straight for the Dixie Reapers compound.

My phone buzzed. Dad's face lit up the screen. I hesitated, then silenced it. *Later*, I promised silently. *I'll explain everything later.*

The clubhouse loomed ahead, its weathered exterior as familiar to me as my own reflection. Music pulsed from inside. I paused at the edge of the parking lot, my heart thundering in my chest.

Tempest's bike stood among the others, its chrome gleaming in the late afternoon sun. My breath caught. He was here.

"Now or never, Kasen," I whispered, wiping my sweaty palms on my jeans.

I took one step forward, then another. The clubhouse door swung open, spilling laughter and the acrid scent of cigarette smoke into the air. And there he was.

Tempest stepped out, his massive frame filling

the doorway. His eyes, hard as steel, scanned the lot before landing on me. I saw the flicker of recognition, the slight narrowing of his gaze.

My mouth went dry. Every instinct screamed at me to run, to hide, to go back to playing it safe.

I lifted my chin and met Tempest's stare head-on. "We need to talk." I called out, my voice steadier than I felt.

Tempest's eyebrow arched, a hint of surprise breaking through his intimidating facade. He took a step toward me, and I braced myself for whatever came next.

"Talk?" His voice was gravel and whiskey. "About what?"

I swallowed hard. "Us."

His eyes narrowed. "There is no us."

"Bullshit," I snapped, surprising myself. "You've been watching me. Following me."

"It's my job to keep an eye on things," Tempest snapped back.

"On me, you mean?" I stepped closer, emboldened by anger. "I'm not a child anymore, Tempest."

His gaze raked over me, leaving fire in its wake. "I know."

The admission hung between us, electric.

"Then why --"

"You're Tank's daughter," he growled. "Off-limits."

I laughed, bitter and sharp. "That's not your call to make."

I could see the battle raging behind his eyes. "Kasen," he warned, voice low. "Don't push this."

I closed the distance between us, close enough to feel the heat radiating off his body. "Or what?"

His control snapped. In one fluid motion, Tempest's hand cupped the back of my neck, pulling me against him. His lips crashed into mine, hungry and desperate.

I melted into the kiss, months of pent-up desire exploding between us. My fingers twisted in his shirt, anchoring myself as the world spun.

When we finally broke apart, both gasping for air, I saw the raw need in Tempest's eyes.

"Fuck," he breathed.

I nodded, unable to form words.

"This changes everything," he murmured.

I nodded, heart racing. "I'm counting on it."

Tempest's grip on my neck tightened, eyes blazing with conflicting emotions. Desire. Anger. Fear.

"You have no idea what you're asking for," he growled, his breath hot against my cheek.

I met his gaze unflinchingly. "Try me."

"This isn't a game, Kasen. The club, your father --"

"I don't care," I interrupted, my voice stronger than I felt. "I'm tired of pretending. Aren't you?"

Tempest's eyes darkened. In one swift motion, he pulled me around the corner of the clubhouse, away from prying eyes. My back hit the rough brick wall, his body caging me in.

"You want this?" he demanded, his voice low and dangerous. "You want to risk everything?"

I swallowed hard, pulse racing. "Yes."

Tempest's hand slid from my neck to cup my face, his touch surprisingly gentle. "There's no going back from this. You understand that?"

I nodded, leaning into his touch. "I've wanted this -- wanted you -- for years, Tempest. I'm not backing down now."

Something shifted in his eyes. Before I realized what was happening, his lips crashed into mine again, harder this time. Demanding. I matched his intensity, pouring years of longing into the kiss. My fingers tangled in his hair, pulling him closer.

Tempest groaned, the sound vibrating through me. His hands roamed my body, leaving trails of fire in their wake. I arched into him, desperate for more.

Suddenly, he pulled back. I whimpered at the loss.

"Not here," he panted, resting his forehead against mine. "Not like this."

Reality came crashing back. We were still outside the clubhouse. Anyone could walk by.

"Your place," I suggested, breathless. "Now."

Tempest nodded, his eyes dark with promise. "Lead the way, little girl."

As we untangled ourselves and headed for his bike, I knew there was no turning back. Whatever came next, I was all in.

Chapter Three

Kasen

I gripped the steering wheel, knuckles white, as Tempest's house loomed ahead. My heart thundered in my chest, threatening to burst. What the hell was I doing?

The rumble of his bike was a constant reminder he was right behind me. I couldn't shake the image of his piercing gaze, a mix of curiosity and concern etched on his rugged features.

"Get it together, Kasen," I muttered, willing my racing thoughts to slow.

But they wouldn't. They kept circling back to Tempest -- his intensity, his barely contained anger, the way he commanded respect with just a look. I'd been infatuated since I was sixteen, but this? This was madness.

The bike's engine roared louder as Tempest pulled up beside me. I stopped the car and rolled down my window.

"You okay?" His gruff voice carried over the rumble of the engine.

I nodded, not trusting my voice. I didn't give him a chance to ask anything else and took off. Tempest matched my speed effortlessly.

We were getting close now. Too close. Panic clawed at my throat. What if someone from the club saw us? What would they think? What would my dad think?

Tempest's house appeared around the bend. My palms were slick with sweat as I eased off the gas. This was it. No turning back now.

I pulled into his driveway, my breath coming in short gasps. Tempest circled around, parking his bike with practiced ease. As he dismounted, his eyes never left me.

This was either the bravest or dumbest thing I'd ever done. Probably both. Was I making a mistake? This was huge! He'd told me there would be no going back. The more I thought about it, the more worried I became.

I turned off the engine, my hand trembling as I reached for the door handle. Then I saw him. Viking. Across the street, hunched over a sleek black motorcycle, his massive frame impossible to miss.

My stomach dropped. Of all the people to be here, it had to be the Road Captain. I froze, one foot on the driveway, torn between fleeing and facing whatever storm I'd just walked into.

Viking's head was bent over the bike's engine, his long hair falling forward. He seemed oblivious to my presence, but for how long?

"Shit," I whispered, my heart hammering against my ribs.

I forced myself out of the car, my legs unsteady. Tempest was watching me, his expression unreadable. The air felt charged, snapping with unspoken tension.

"You came," Tempest said, his voice low and rough.

I nodded, unable to find my voice. My eyes darted back to Viking, then to Tempest. The conflict raging inside me was almost painful. I wanted this -- wanted him -- so badly it hurt. But the consequences... God, the consequences could be disastrous.

"I... I shouldn't be here," I managed, hating how weak I sounded.

Tempest took a step closer, his presence both thrilling and terrifying. "But you are."

I swallowed hard, fighting the urge to close the

distance between us. "If Viking sees --"

"Let him," Tempest growled, his eyes flashing with a familiar intensity.

My breath caught. This man would be the death of me, one way or another.

I couldn't think. The air felt thick with years of unspoken desire threatening to ignite. Tempest was mere inches away, close enough I could smell leather and motor oil, could feel the heat radiating off his body.

"Kasen," he said, my name a gravelly whisper on his lips.

My knees nearly buckled. "Tempest, I --"

He reached out, fingers barely grazing my arm. That slight touch sent shockwaves through me. I jerked back instinctively, the reality of our situation crashing around me.

"We need to slow down," I blurted, my voice trembling. "This... us... it's too fast."

There was a storm brewing behind his eyes. "What are you saying?"

I struggled to form coherent thoughts, overwhelmed by his proximity, by the weight of what we were risking. "I'm saying... I don't know if I can handle this. The club, the scrutiny. It's all so much."

Tempest's expression hardened, but I caught a flicker of something else -- hurt, maybe? -- before it vanished. "You think I can't protect you?"

"It's not about protection," I said, fighting to keep my voice steady. "It's about being ready for what comes with... with being yours."

The words hung between us, heavy with implication. Tempest's eyes bored into mine, searching for something. I held my breath, terrified of what he might see.

I couldn't bear it another second. Without waiting for his response, I spun on my heel and bolted for my car. My heart thundered in my chest, drowning out everything but the desperate need to escape.

"Kasen!" Tempest's voice boomed behind me, a mix of confusion and anger.

I fumbled with my keys, cursing under my breath as they slipped from my sweaty fingers. "Come on, come on," I muttered, snatching them up.

The car door clicked open and I threw myself inside, slamming it shut. My hands shook as I jammed the key into the ignition.

"Goddamnit, Kasen!" Tempest's fist pounded on the window. "Don't you dare run from this!"

I revved the engine, refusing to look at him. "I'm sorry," I whispered, knowing he couldn't hear me.

Tires squealed as I peeled out of the driveway. In my rearview mirror, I caught a final glimpse of Tempest. He stood rigid, his face a mask of frustration and something else I didn't want to name.

My chest ached. What had I done?

I burst through the front door, my vision blurred by unshed tears. The familiar scent of home -- lavender and leather -- hit me but brought no comfort. I raced up the stairs, taking them two at a time, desperate to reach the sanctuary of my room.

"Kasen? That you, honey?" Mom's voice drifted from the kitchen.

"Yeah, I'm -- I'm not feeling great," I choked out, praying she wouldn't come investigate.

I slammed my bedroom door, leaning against it as my legs gave out. Sliding to the floor, I hugged my knees to my chest, finally letting the tears flow. "Stupid, stupid, stupid," I muttered, banging my head against the door with each word.

Tempest's face flashed in my mind -- the hurt in his eyes, the tension in his jaw. God, how could I have been so impulsive? So cowardly? I stumbled to my feet, stripping off my clothes as I made for the bathroom. The shower hissed to life, steam quickly filling the small space. I stepped under the scalding spray, letting it sear my skin.

"What were you thinking?" I whispered, pressing my forehead against the cool tile. "He's the Sergeant-at-Arms, for Christ's sake. Dad would lose it if he knew."

The water pounded against my back but did nothing to wash away the memory of Tempest's touch, his intensity. I closed my eyes, remembering the way he'd looked at me -- like I was the only thing in his world that mattered.

"But at what cost?" I asked the empty bathroom. "The club is everything to him. To Dad. I can't... I can't be the reason it all falls apart."

Yet even as I said the words, my traitorous heart rebelled. The thought of never feeling Tempest's arms around me again, never seeing that smile he seemed to reserve just for me -- it felt like a physical pain in my chest.

"Damnit, Tempest," I growled, slamming my palm against the tile. "Why'd you have to make me fall for you?"

* * *

Tempest

The cigarette flared to life in my hand, a tiny inferno against the encroaching twilight. I inhaled deeply, the smoke a searing brand down my throat, acrid and bitter. My eyes narrowed, tracking the empty road where Kasen's taillights had vanished minutes ago.

"Fuck." The word was a gritty rasp on my tongue.

Frustration coiled through me, tension in every muscle. Kasen's wide, questioning eyes haunted me, her faltering words about needing space echoing in my head. *You knew this wouldn't be easy. She's Tank's daughter, damn it.*

The rumble of a motorcycle cut through the quiet, drawing my gaze across the street. Viking, fiddling with his engine. Had he seen her? The thought twisted in my gut, a cold knot of apprehension. She'd freaked over him seeing us together, and I'd told her it didn't matter. But now... I got her point and understood her worry over the situation. Didn't mean I had to like it.

Another drag, the smoke curling into the twilight. *She's not ready. Maybe she'll never be.*

But doubt gnawed at the edges of my conviction. The memory of Kasen's smile, the way she looked at me when she thought I wasn't watching -- it sparked something in me, a flicker of warmth in the frozen wasteland of my heart.

"Damnit, girl," I muttered, letting out a frustrated groan. "What are you doing to me?"

I flicked the cigarette, watching embers scatter like dying fireflies on the concrete. My jaw muscles worked beneath the skin like restless demons.

The club would have opinions. Loud, unwelcome ones. Kasen was one of the club princesses. I might be an officer, but that wouldn't matter. As far as Tank was concerned, no one was good enough for his girls, which was probably why all three were still single.

I could already hear the whispers, feel the

prickling heat of judgmental stares. Tank's daughter and the Sergeant-at-Arms. It was a recipe for disaster, a powder keg waiting for the spark of gossip to ignite.

But I'd meant it when I said if we took that next step, that was it. Neither of us would be able to take it back, and I didn't think I wanted to. Now that I'd set my sights on her, I was having a hard time letting her go. For one, it wasn't in my nature. For another, I'd finally given myself permission to have the one thing I'd wanted for a while -- Kasen. Now I was giving her the space she needed, and I fucking hated it. She didn't think she could handle being mine, and while there was a chance she was right, I also knew she was stronger than she realized.

But a small voice in my head kept whispering *what if she's not*? Being the woman of the Sergeant-at-Arms wasn't for just anyone. She'd need nerves of steel. Her mom was one of the sweetest people I'd ever met. If Emmie could stand by Tank, then I figured Kasen shouldn't have an issue being by my side. It all depended on her, and how much she decided to believe in herself. And whether she'd allow herself to be happy without worrying about what everyone else thought.

The roar of a passing bike shattered the silence, making me straighten instinctively. It was just Thunder heading to his house. I gazed across the street at Viking again, but he still wasn't paying me any attention. Staring off in the direction Kasen had left, my eyes narrowed. "I need a partner. Not a liability."

I crushed the cigarette under my boot, the sound a satisfying crunch that echoed the breaking of my own doubts. My gaze fixed on the horizon, where the setting sun painted the sky in shades of blood and fire, a canvas of chaos mirroring the turmoil within me.

"Ball's in your court, Kasen," I murmured, the words barely audible but heavy with meaning. "Show me you can handle this life, this dance on the razor's edge. Then we'll talk. Then we'll see if the fire in your eyes can truly withstand the storm."

Viking's voice sliced through my brooding. "Girl problems?"

"None of your damn business."

"Might be the club's business," Viking countered, wiping his hands on a rag as he stepped closer. "That was Tank's kid, wasn't it?"

I turned to meet Viking's steady gaze, heat pooling in my chest. "And if she is?"

He shrugged, but his eyes sharpened like daggers. "Just saying, brother. You're playing with fire."

"I can handle the heat," I growled.

"Can she?" His question hung in the air, heavy with implication.

"She's stronger than she looks."

"She'd have to be," Viking said, "to stand beside the Sergeant-at-Arms."

The truth of his words stung more than I cared to admit. If Kasen couldn't handle a chance encounter with a brother, how the hell would she cope with the constant scrutiny and danger that came with my position? She'd grown up the daughter of the previous Sergeant-at-Arms, but we all knew Tank coddled his girls.

"She just needs time," I muttered, more to myself than to Viking.

Viking clapped me on the shoulder. "Time might be a luxury you don't have, brother. Word travels fast in this club."

As he walked away, I stared down the empty

road. I'd waited years for Kasen, watched her transform from a fiery teenager into a woman who ignited my blood. But Viking was right -- time had been slipping away.

I needed to know if Kasen was all in because half-measures wouldn't cut it. Not in this life. Not with me.

I stalked into the house, slamming the door behind me. The walls seemed to close in, suffocating me with their familiarity. I needed air, space to think.

Before I even realized what I was doing, I turned and headed for my bike. The engine roared to life. I tore out of the driveway and raced to the gate. Sam saw me and threw it open before I hit it head-on.

The wind whipped past as I pushed the bike faster, harder. Each turn was a razor's edge between control and chaos. Just like my feelings for Kasen.

I found myself on the outskirts of town, pulling into a dingy bar. The neon sign flickered weakly, promising escape in bottom-shelf whiskey.

Inside, the air was thick with smoke and regret. I claimed a stool at the far end, signaling the bartender.

"Whiskey. Neat."

The amber liquid burned going down, a welcome distraction from the storm in my head. I stared at my reflection in the grimy mirror behind the bar.

"What the hell are you doing, old man?" I muttered.

The door creaked open, and I tensed instinctively. In the mirror, I watched Sticks walk in, his presence commanding.

"Thought I saw your bike outside," he said, sliding onto the stool next to me.

I grunted, downing the rest of my drink.

Sticks ordered his own, then turned to face me.

"Viking called. Said you might need a friendly ear."

I snorted. "Friendly, my ass. More like nosy bastards, the lot of you."

"Maybe," Sticks conceded. "But we're also family. And family looks out for each other."

I met his gaze, seeing the concern there. "Even when one of them is eyeing the old SAA's daughter?"

Sticks' expression hardened. "Especially then."

Chapter Four

Kasen

My phone buzzed, jolting me from my daydream. Connor's name flashed on the screen, along with a message: *Looking forward to our date tonight! See you at 7?*

I stared at the text, my finger hovering over the reply button. Tempest's face flashed in my mind, his intense eyes boring into me. I shook my head, trying to dispel the image.

"Get it together, Kase." I tapped out a quick *See you then* before I could change my mind.

I tossed the phone on my bed and stood, catching my reflection in the mirror. My hair was a mess, and I looked like I hadn't slept in days. Which wasn't far from the truth.

As I rifled through my closet, my thoughts drifted back to Tempest. The way his jaw clenched when he was angry, the raw power in his stance. I shivered, remembering how it felt to be near him.

"Stop it," I muttered, yanking a dress off its hanger. "This date is about clarity, not Tempest."

But even as I slipped on the dress, I couldn't shake the nagging feeling that I was making a mistake. What if Tempest found out? The thought of his anger, that barely contained rage directed at me, sent a thrill down my spine.

I applied my makeup with shaking hands, trying to focus on Connor. Sweet, safe Connor. He was everything Tempest wasn't -- stable, predictable, uncomplicated.

So why did that thought fill me with disappointment?

I grabbed my purse, pausing at the door. It

wasn't too late to cancel. To stay home, to avoid the mess I was surely walking into.

But I needed answers. And maybe this date would provide them.

With a deep breath, I stepped out into the night, the weight of my decision settling on my shoulders like a lead blanket.

I pushed open the restaurant door, the cheerful hostess greeting me a stark contrast to the knot in my stomach. My eyes swept the room, scanning faces, searching. For what, I wasn't sure.

The door. My gaze lingered there, half-expecting Tempest to burst through, all barely contained fury and raw intensity. I could almost see him, leather-clad and scowling, demanding to know what the hell I was doing here.

"May I help you?" the woman asked.

"Um, I'm meeting someone."

"Kasen!"

I jumped, spinning to face Connor's warm smile. He stood, waving me over to a corner table.

"Hey," I managed, forcing a smile as I slid into the seat across from him. "Sorry if I'm late."

"Not at all," Connor replied, his easygoing nature on full display. "I just got here myself. How are you?"

I nodded, my mind already drifting. "Fine, thanks. You?"

As Connor launched into a story about his day, a waitress approached. I ordered a latte on autopilot, barely hearing Connor's own order.

"So," he said once we were alone again, "I was thinking after this we could --"

The restaurant door swung open. My head snapped up, heart racing. But it was just a young couple, laughing as they entered.

"Kasen?" Connor's voice pulled me back. "Everything okay?"

I blinked, focusing on his concerned face. "Yeah, sorry. Just... thought I saw someone I knew."

Connor's easygoing smile returned, and I felt a pang of guilt. He was nice, genuinely nice. The kind of guy who'd remember your coffee order and text you good morning. Nothing like Tempest's brooding intensity, the way his presence filled a room with electric tension.

"So, tell me about your week," Connor said, leaning forward with interest. "Any exciting plans coming up?"

I opened my mouth to respond, but my mind conjured an image of Tempest instead. What the hell was wrong with me? I was the one who'd run out on him.

"Oh, you know," I heard myself say, the words coming out automatically. "Just the usual. Work, family stuff."

Connor nodded, seemingly satisfied with my vague answer. "Speaking of family, how are your sisters doing? You mentioned they were thinking of moving, right?"

I blinked, forcing myself to focus. "Yeah, they're... good. Still deciding."

Not that my dad would let them move out easily. Which was why all three of us still lived at home.

My gaze drifted to the window, half-expecting to see a motorcycle roaring past. Tempest's bike, all sleek lines and raw power. Just like him.

"And what about you?" Connor's voice broke through my reverie. "Any big decisions on the horizon?"

I turned back to him, guilt twisting in my gut. Here was this sweet guy, genuinely interested in my life, and all I could think about was a man who probably saw me as a flake, a pain in the ass, and a child who'd run away.

"I'm… still figuring things out," I admitted, and it wasn't entirely a lie.

Connor reached across the table, his touch gentle as he squeezed my hand. "Hey, that's okay. We've all been there."

I nodded, trying to smile, but all I could think was how different it would feel if it were Tempest's calloused hand gripping mine. The intensity, the danger, the thrill.

I cleared my throat, determined to give Connor a fair chance. "So, tell me about your work. Any exciting projects lately?"

Connor's face lit up, and he launched into a description of his latest architectural design. I nodded along, trying to focus on his words, but my mind wandered. I couldn't help but imagine how Tempest would react in this situation.

He'd probably scoff, those intense eyes narrowing. "Buildin' fancy houses for rich folks? Waste of time," I could almost hear him growl. "Real men build with their hands, not fancy computers."

The restaurant buzzed around us, the clatter of dishes and hum of conversation a stark contrast to my inner turmoil. A server told someone at a nearby table about the specials, her voice sharp and clear, cutting through the din. It reminded me of how Tempest's commands always rang out over the chaos of the clubhouse.

I glanced around, taking in the sleek modern decor, all clean lines and muted colors. It was nice, objectively speaking, but it felt… sterile. Nothing like the raw, lived-in feel of the Dixie Reapers' clubhouse. There, every scuff and dent told a story. Here, everything felt too polished, too perfect.

A couple at the next table laughed, the sound grating on my nerves. I shifted in my seat, suddenly hyperaware of how out of place I felt. This wasn't my world. These weren't my people.

"Kasen?" Connor's voice snapped me back to reality. "You okay? You seemed a million miles away for a second there."

I forced a smile, guilt gnawing at me. "Yeah, sorry. Just… lost in thought, I guess."

A server came over and took our order. It wasn't long before our food and drinks arrived at the table. But I could barely taste anything.

I nodded mechanically as Connor launched into another story about a project he'd just finished. His words washed over me, barely registering. If Tempest were here listening to this, he'd probably be drumming his fingers on the table, impatient. Those dark eyes scanning the room, always on alert. Maybe he'd lean in close, his voice a low rumble. "This place ain't us, darlin'. Let's ride."

"… and then the client decided to change the entire floor plan!" Connor chuckled, oblivious to my wandering thoughts.

"Mm-hmm," I murmured, fighting to keep my expression neutral. The realization hit me like a punch to the gut. My heart wasn't in this. It wasn't fair to Connor, and it definitely wasn't fair to me.

Silence fell between us, heavy and awkward. I fidgeted with my napkin, tearing it into tiny pieces. The tick of the wall clock seemed impossibly loud.

"I should…" I started, then faltered. How could I

explain? That every second here felt wrong? That my entire being ached to be somewhere else, with someone else?

Connor tilted his head, concern flickering across his face. "Everything all right?"

I opened my mouth, closed it again. The words wouldn't come. I was stuck, caught between politeness and the overwhelming urge to bolt.

Connor cleared his throat, breaking the tense silence. "Listen, Kasen, I've really enjoyed tonight. How about we do this again next week? Maybe that new Italian place downtown?"

My stomach tightened. The suggestion hung in the air, demanding a response. I could feel my pulse quickening, trapped between two impossible choices.

"I…" I started, my voice barely above a whisper. Tempest's face flashed in my mind, but then guilt crept in. Connor was nice, normal. Safe. Everything Tempest wasn't.

"Sure," I heard myself say, the word feeling foreign on my tongue. "That sounds… nice."

Connor beamed, oblivious to the war raging inside me. "Great! I'll text you the details."

I nodded, forcing a smile even though it felt more like a grimace. "Looking forward to it," I lied, the words tasting bitter.

As Connor chatted about the restaurant, my mind drifted. I pictured Tempest, probably at the clubhouse right now. Would he be thinking of me? Did he even care that I was out with someone else?

I knew, with a certainty that scared me, no matter how many dates I went on with Connor or anyone else, my heart belonged to Tempest. It always had. But I needed time -- time to figure out if there was any hope for us, or if I was just chasing an impossible dream. I didn't feel brave enough to face my father, or the rest of the club. And I wasn't sure I was strong enough to stand beside the club's Sergeant-at-Arms.

"Kasen?" Connor's voice snapped me back to reality. "You seem distracted."

I plastered on another fake smile. "Just tired," I said. "It's been a long week."

I stood up, grabbing my purse. "Thanks for tonight, Connor. It was… nice." The word felt hollow, but I forced it out anyway.

Connor rose, his smile genuine. "I had a great time, Kasen. Can't wait for our next date."

My stomach twisted. I nodded, not trusting myself to speak. We walked to the restaurant exit, the cool night air hitting my face as we stepped outside.

"Let me walk you to your car," Connor offered.

"No need," I said quickly. "I'm just over there."

I gestured vaguely, already backing away. Connor looked disappointed but didn't push it.

"All right, drive safe. I'll text you."

"Sure thing," I mumbled, turning away.

With each step toward my car, Tempest's image grew clearer in my mind. His brooding eyes, the tension in his jaw, the raw power he exuded. My heart raced, and it had nothing to do with the man I'd just left behind.

I collapsed into the driver's seat, letting out a shaky breath. The silence in the car was deafening.

"What the hell am I doing?" I whispered, gripping the steering wheel.

I closed my eyes, seeing Tempest's face. The way he looked at me when he thought I wasn't paying attention. The electricity crackling between us whenever we were close.

But then reality crashed in. He was the club's

Sergeant-at-Arms. Dangerous. Volatile. My dad would lose it if he knew how I felt.

I started the engine, my mind a battlefield of desire and doubt.

"I can't keep living like this," I muttered, pulling out of the parking lot.

As I drove home, all I could think about was Tempest. I needed to talk to him, but what would I say? After the way I'd run off, what if he'd decided he was done with me? It would break my heart if he rejected me, even though I'd essentially done that to him the day I'd driven off from his house. Technically, I'd said we needed to slow down. Then he hadn't done anything more than follow me around. Not once had he tried to talk to me about our relationship. Living in this limbo was slowly killing me.

I turned toward the clubhouse. Whatever happened next, I needed to know where I stood with him. If I'd completely blown it, or still had a chance. The familiar rumble of motorcycles grew louder as I approached the clubhouse. It looked like Owen was showing off his new ride to Atlas and Reed. Naturally the three had to rev their engines, trying to see who had the bigger dick.

My hands shook on the steering wheel. What was I doing? This was insane.

I parked, heart pounding. The lot was full of bikes. Music and laughter spilled from inside. Looked like the guys were cutting loose.

I stepped out, legs unsteady. A few Prospects lounged by the door, eyeing me curiously. They'd only recently joined. Lucas, Caden, and Landon. All three were a bit younger than me. Since it was club business, I wasn't entirely sure why they'd been allowed to prospect, but I wondered if it was the club's way of making sure the Dixie Reapers would never die out.

I lifted my chin, striding past them with more confidence than I felt.

Inside was chaos. Bodies everywhere, drinking, laughing, yelling over the blaring music. The air thick with smoke and tension. Looked like more than just Reapers were present tonight. I saw a few people I didn't recognize, and they weren't wearing cuts, which meant they'd likely come from town. But if they were allowed inside, then Wire or Lavender had vetted them and Tempest had given his permission for them to come through the gates.

My eyes scanned the crowd, searching. There -- by the bar. Tempest.

He stood alone, nursing a beer. His posture rigid, eyes alert. Always on guard.

I pushed through the throng, pulse racing. Tempest's gaze locked on me. His eyes widened, then narrowed.

"What are you doing here?" he asked as I approached.

I swallowed hard. "We need to talk."

He set down his beer, grabbing my arm. "Not here."

He led me through the crowd, and out the door. The cool night air hit my flushed skin.

Tempest released me once we'd gone a few feet from the building, crossing his arms. "Talk."

I opened my mouth, but words failed me. How could I explain the storm of emotions inside me?

"I can't do this anymore," I finally blurted. It hadn't come out the way I'd meant, which I knew when he spoke.

"Yeah, you made that clear when you took off the other day. Go home, Kasen. Before someone tells your daddy you're here talking to me."

Before I could say anything else, he went back inside, leaving me alone in the parking lot. I hadn't even had the chance to explain what I meant. The ache in my chest grew, and I had a feeling I'd just destroyed my relationship with him before it even began.

Chapter Five

Tempest

I pushed through the heavy doors of the sports bar, the sound of the TVs and chatter so loud it made my damn head hurt. My eyes locked onto Kasen immediately, her hair catching the dim light as she leaned in close to Connor, laughing at something he'd said.

Red clouded my vision as I strode toward their table, patrons scattering out of my path. The crowd parted like the Goddamn Red Sea, whispers and curious glances following in my wake.

"Fuck," I mumbled under my breath, trying to rein in the jealousy threatening to explode out of me.

Kasen. I kept reminding myself she was Tank's daughter, and totally off-limits. But seeing her with another man made my blood boil.

I balled up my fists. The urge to grab Connor by the throat and throw him across the room was almost overwhelming.

"Get it together," I muttered to myself, drawing in a deep breath.

But it did nothing to calm the storm raging inside me. Every step closer to their table stoked the flames of my anger higher. By the time I reached them, I was a powder keg ready to blow.

I slammed my hand on the table, making their drinks jump. "Connor," I spat, my voice sharp as a blade. "Didn't expect to see you here."

I wouldn't have had a fucking clue who this prick was, except I'd done a little digging. After I'd seen Kasen with him more than once, I'd decided it was best to find out who the hell she was hanging out with. We'd run across too many guys who looked like upright citizens only to find out they were total scum.

The kid's eyes widened, fear flashing across his face. Good. He should be afraid.

Kasen's head snapped up, her blue eyes meeting mine. For a split second, surprise flickered in their depths before being replaced by a steely defiance that made my blood sing. She leaned back in her chair, crossing her arms over her chest.

"Tempest," she said, her voice steady despite the tension I could see coiling in her shoulders. "What brings you to this neck of the woods?"

I ignored her question, keeping my gaze locked on Connor. "You got business here, boy?"

My fingers itched to wrap around his scrawny neck. I flexed them against the tabletop instead, the wood creaking under my grip.

Kasen's eyes narrowed. "He's here because I invited him. Do you have a problem with that?"

The challenge in her voice sent a jolt through me. Part of me admired her fire, while another part wanted to throw her over my shoulder and carry her out of here.

I leaned in closer, my voice dropping to a dangerous growl. "Yeah, I got a problem with that."

Connor squirmed in his seat, his Adam's apple bobbing as he swallowed hard. Sweat beaded on his forehead, and he couldn't seem to meet my eyes. The kid knew he was out of his depth.

"I... uh... I didn't mean any disrespect," he stammered, his voice barely above a whisper.

I ignored him, my focus zeroing in on Kasen. Her defiance only stoked the fire in my gut. I leaned in close, my breath hot against her ear.

"You're Dixie Reapers' property," I growled, each word dripping with possessiveness. "And it's time everyone knew it."

The words hung in the air, heavy and charged. I felt Kasen stiffen beside me, her breath catching. For a moment, the world narrowed to just us two -- the heat of her body, the scent of her perfume, the sexual tension sizzling between us.

"I'm not anyone's property," Kasen hissed back, but I caught the slight tremor in her voice.

I fought the urge to grab her, to show her exactly what she meant to me, to the club. Instead, I straightened, my gaze never leaving hers. "We'll see about that," I said, my voice low and full of promise.

The tension in the air snapped like a live wire. Conversations around us stuttered to a halt, leaving an eerie silence in their wake. I could feel dozens of eyes boring into us, hungry for drama.

A glass clinked against wood, the sound echoing in the sudden quiet. Chairs scraped across the floor as patrons shifted for a better view. The air grew thick with anticipation, making it hard to breathe.

From the corner of my eye, I caught sight of Viking and Sticks at a nearby table. Viking's massive frame was relaxed, but his eyes were sharp, taking in every detail. Sticks twirled a drumstick between his fingers, a smirk playing at the corners of his mouth. Fucker carried those things everywhere these days. After not playing in forever, he'd taken the hobby back up several months ago.

"Well, well." Viking's deep voice carried easily across the room. "Looks like our Sergeant-at-Arms is laying down the law."

Sticks chuckled, his eyes dancing with amusement. "About damn time, if you ask me."

I met Viking's gaze, seeing the approval there. He gave me a slight nod, the gesture speaking volumes. Despite our talk the other night, it looked like he'd back me if I decided to go after Kasen. Good to know.

My gaze swept the room. Most patrons quickly looked away, but I could still feel the weight of their attention. I turned back to Kasen. The fire in her eyes only fueled my determination. This wasn't over -- not by a long shot.

Kasen's chair screeched against the floor as she shot to her feet. "Who the hell do you think you are?" Her voice cut through the silence, steady but filled with anger.

My blood boiled, but I held my ground. "You know damn well who I am, Kasen."

"Oh, I know exactly who you are, Tempest," she spat, leaning in close. "You're the asshole who's ignored me for years, and now you think you can just waltz in here and claim me like some piece of property?"

I fought to keep my voice level. "I believe I already made my move. You're the one who turned tail and ran."

"I know that! Then I tried to explain things to you. Then you were the one who walked off."

"What the hell are you talking --"

Kasen's laugh was sharp, bitter. She cut me off before I could finish my sentence. "Yeah, and you didn't exactly chase after me. From where I'm standing, you've made it pretty clear how little I matter to you."

The words stung more than I cared to admit. My chest tightened, a mix of anger and something dangerously close to regret. "You've always mattered, Kasen. More than you know."

Her eyes widened for a fraction of a second

before narrowing again. "Bullshit. You can't just decide I'm yours when it's convenient for you."

I leaned in closer, my voice dropping to a dangerous growl. "This ain't about convenience. This is about keeping you safe."

"Safe?" Kasen's voice rose, drawing more attention. "I don't need your protection, Tempest. I need you to back the hell off and let me live my life!"

The tension between us felt volatile. Despite the fact I knew everyone was hanging on our every word, all I could focus on was Kasen, her chest heaving with anger, her eyes challenging me to make the next move.

I squared my shoulders, meeting Kasen's fiery gaze head-on. "This ain't a game, Kasen. You're Dixie Reapers, whether you like it or not. That means something."

"It means I'm trapped," she spat, her words laced with venom. "Trapped by a club that thinks it can control my every move."

"It's for your own good. You don't know what's out there."

Kasen's laugh was hollow. "And you do? You think you can protect me from the big, bad world?" She leaned in, her voice dropping to a whisper only I could hear. "Or are you just scared of what I might find if I look elsewhere?"

The insinuation hit me like a sucker punch. I fought to keep my expression neutral, but inside, I was seething. "You're playing with fire, little girl."

"I'm not a *little girl* anymore, Tempest," Kasen retorted, her chin jutting out defiantly. "And if you think you can scare me into submission, you've got another thing coming."

She straightened, her voice rising so everyone could hear. "In fact, I think I'll go on that date with

Connor after all. And maybe I'll find a few more guys to keep me company while I'm at it."

The words hung in the air, a challenge I couldn't ignore. My vision blurred red at the edges, but I forced myself to stay still. "You don't mean that."

Kasen's eyes glittered dangerously. "Watch me."

I caught Viking's eye across the room. His expression was a mix of amusement and concern, one eyebrow raised as if to say, *You've really stepped in it now, brother.* Beside him, Sticks tapped his drumsticks on the table, his nervous tic matching the tension in the air.

The entire place was watching and waiting, eager to see how the Dixie Reapers' Sergeant-at-Arms would handle this challenge to his authority. Part of me wanted to tell them all to fuck off, but they weren't important right now. Kasen was.

I turned back to Kasen, my voice low and dangerous. "You think this is a game? The club isn't something you can just ignore when it's convenient."

She stood her ground, fire in her eyes. "And I'm not a possession you can claim whenever you feel like it."

My knuckles turned white with the effort of restraining myself. The urge to grab her, to shake some sense into her, was almost overwhelming. But I knew it would only push her farther away.

"This isn't over," I growled, stepping closer until we were nearly nose to nose. "You want to play with fire? Fine. But don't come crying when you get burned."

Kasen's breath hitched, but she didn't back down. "Is that a threat, Tempest?"

"It's a promise," I said, my voice barely above a whisper. "You're ours, whether you like it or not. And sooner or later, you'll realize that's exactly where you want to be."

Kasen's eyes blazed with defiance. Without another word, she spun on her heel and strode toward the exit, her posture rigid with anger and hurt pride. I wasn't even sure if she noticed she'd left her precious Connor behind.

I watched her go, my chest tight with a mix of rage and something dangerously close to longing. The sway of her hips as she walked away was like a taunt, reminding me of everything I couldn't have -- not yet, anyway.

"Fuck," I muttered under my breath, running a hand through my hair.

The bar door slammed shut behind Kasen, the sound echoing like a gunshot. I fought the urge to go after her. To grab her and make her understand.

Connor cleared his throat, reminding me of his presence. "I should probably go…"

I whirled on him, my voice a low growl. "Yeah, you should. And if I catch you sniffing around Kasen again, we'll be having a very different conversation."

He scrambled out of his seat, nearly tripping over his own feet in his haste to leave. The bar patrons parted for him, their eyes darting between me and the door.

Viking's hand landed heavy on my shoulder. "Easy, brother. You made your point."

I shrugged him off, my skin crawling with pent-up energy. "Did I? Because from where I'm standing, all I did was push her away."

Sticks piped up, twirling a drumstick between his fingers again. "Maybe that's not such a bad thing. Give her some space, let her cool off."

I rounded on him, teeth bared. "And let her run

off with every Tom, Dick, and Harry in town? Not fucking likely."

Viking stepped between us, his bulk forcing me back a step. "Think, Tempest. You go after her now, you'll just make things worse. Let her stew for a bit. She'll come around. Besides, did you notice the way she lit out of here? She didn't even pause to look back at that kid. He wasn't even on her radar."

I wanted to argue, to push past him and hunt Kasen down. But the rational part of my brain knew he was right. I took a deep breath, forcing the tension out of my shoulders. The fact she hadn't given Connor a second glance did soothe my anger a bit.

"Fine. But I'm not letting this go. She needs to understand her place."

Viking's eyes narrowed. "Just remember, brother. She's not some club whore. She's Tank's daughter. Tread carefully."

The reminder was like a bucket of ice water. Tank. Shit. If he found out about this...

I nodded curtly, already plotting my next move. This game of cat and mouse with Kasen was far from over. And I intended to win.

Chapter Six

Kasen

I drummed my fingers on the coffee shop table, heart pounding. The door chimed. Not him. My eyes darted back to my phone, scrolling mindlessly as I tried to quell the butterflies in my stomach. Was I really doing this? Three dates in one day. Part of me knew this was childish, but I hadn't been able to stop myself from moving forward with my plan. If for no other reason than I wanted to see what Tempest would do.

The memory of his intense gaze sent a shiver down my spine. I squared my shoulders. No turning back now.

"Kasen?"

I looked up, plastering on a smile. "Jake? Hi!"

He grinned, all boyish charm as he slid into the seat across from me. "Great to finally meet you in person. You look even prettier than your profile pic."

"Thanks," I mumbled, heat rising to my cheeks. Yes, I'd found some men to date online. I knew this could go horribly wrong, but that's why I'd made sure to meet them at a busy location and not let them pick me up. No way I was getting into a car with any of them. I might be a little naive at times, but I wasn't stupid.

Jake launched into small talk about the unseasonably warm weather. I nodded along, gaze drifting to the entrance every few seconds.

"So, what do you do for work?" Jake asked.

I snapped my attention back to him. "Oh, I'm a receptionist for a dental office. You?"

"Software engineer. Love it, but the hours can be brutal."

My phone buzzed. I snatched it up, pulse quickening. Just a text from one of my sisters.

"Everything okay?" Jake's brow furrowed with concern.

"Yeah, sorry. Just… expecting an important call." The lie tasted bitter on my tongue. "It was just my sister. I can call her back later."

Jake smiled. "No worries. Hey, want to grab a refill?" He gestured to my nearly empty mug.

"Sure," I said, forcing enthusiasm into my voice. As Jake headed to the counter, I exhaled slowly. What was I thinking? Tempest probably didn't care who I dated. Sure, he'd blown up last night, and yet again, he'd let me walk off without coming after me. Every time my mom tried to storm off, Dad would pick her up and carry her off to their room. My sisters and I had learned early on when that happened, we needed to make ourselves scarce.

As Jake returned, a small part of me still hoped to see a furious Tempest burst through that door.

The bell above the door chimed. My heart leapt into my throat as Tempest strode in, his presence electric. The bustling cafe seemed to still, conversations hushing as heads turned. Yeah, everyone noticed when he entered a room. Women fawned over him, and the men wanted to *be* him.

My breath caught. Tempest's piercing gaze swept the room, landing on me with laser-like focus. A shiver raced down my spine.

Jake's voice faded to a distant hum as Tempest approached, each step deliberate. His expression was unreadable, but his eyes… God, his eyes burned with an intensity that made my skin prickle.

"Kasen?" Jake's concerned tone barely registered. "Are you all right?"

I couldn't tear my gaze from Tempest as he reached our table. Without a word, he planted himself beside me, radiating raw power. The message was clear: Mine.

My heart thundered. I gripped my mug, knuckles white. "T-Tempest," I managed. "What are you doing here?"

"Thought I'd grab some coffee." His voice was low, dangerous. "Didn't expect to find... this."

Jake shifted uncomfortably. "Um, I'm Jake. And you are..."

Tempest's gaze never left me. "Leaving. With Kasen."

This was exactly what I'd wanted, wasn't it? So why did I feel like I'd unleashed something I couldn't control? And to think this was only step one of my plan for today. What would he be like after he saw me on two more dates?

I swallowed hard, torn between the thrill of Tempest's possessiveness and an urge to assert my independence. Jake cleared his throat, clearly uncomfortable.

"So, uh, Kasen," he attempted, voice wavering, "you were saying about your work..."

I nearly laughed. Poor guy was trying too hard to ignore the huge biker beside me. I had to give him points for taking it all in stride.

Tempest's presence loomed larger, his body angled toward me, effectively cutting Jake out. The tension was palpable, snapping in the air between us.

I stood abruptly, chair scraping against the floor. "I'm sorry, Jake. I should go."

Jake's bewildered expression tugged at my conscience. "But we just --"

"Thanks for coffee," I rushed out, grabbing my

purse. To Tempest, I hissed, "Outside. Now."

Without waiting for a response, I strode toward the exit, heart pounding. The cool air hit my flushed cheeks as I stepped onto the sidewalk.

Tempest was right behind me, his hulking frame casting a shadow as he followed me around the corner of the building. I spun to face him, anger and excitement warring inside me.

"What the hell was that?" I demanded.

His eyes narrowed. "Could ask you the same thing. What are you playing at, Kasen?"

"Playing? I'm not playing anything. I'm living my life."

Tempest took a step closer, looming over me. "With some random asshole?"

"Jake's not an asshole. He's nice." At least, the short time I'd spent with him, he'd *seemed* nice.

"Nice," Tempest spat the word like it tasted foul. "You don't need nice. You need --"

"What?" I challenged, tilting my chin up. "What do I need, Tempest?"

For a moment, I thought he might actually answer. His gaze dropped to my lips, and my breath caught. Then his expression hardened.

"You need to stop this bullshit," he growled. "No more dates."

I bristled. "You don't get to decide that."

"The hell I don't." His hand shot out, gripping my arm. Not painfully, but firmly. "You're coming with me."

"I have plans," I protested, even as my body thrilled at his touch. "I'm not your property. You don't get to decide what I do or who I see."

I yanked my arm free and went to my car, getting in and speeding away before Tempest could catch up to me. I'd wanted my plan to succeed, but not like this.

* * *

Four hours later, I sat in a dimly lit movie theater, the rom-com on screen a blur of colors and meaningless dialogue. Mark, my second date of the day, munched popcorn beside me, oblivious to my distraction. In his defense, I'd chosen a movie specifically so we wouldn't have to talk. After all, I wasn't here because I was interested in really dating him. I felt bad, but at the same time, he probably wasn't here to find a girlfriend. Like most guys, he was likely just hoping for a hookup.

My mind raced, replaying Tempest's stormy expression, the possessive fire in his eyes. What was I doing here? This game suddenly felt childish, dangerous.

"You okay?" Mark whispered, leaning close. "You seem a million miles away."

I forced a smile, guilt gnawing at me. Shit. So he'd noticed after all. "Just... thinking about work. Think I forgot something important before I left yesterday," I lied, my gaze drawn to the theater entrance. Part of me still half-expected Tempest to appear, to claim me again with that burning intensity.

As the movie droned on, a familiar prickling sensation crawled up the back of my neck. My breath caught. I knew, without turning, he was here.

Slowly, I shifted in my seat, peering over my shoulder. There, a few rows back, sat Tempest. I didn't know how he'd gotten in without me noticing. His eyes, shining with an intensity that made my insides liquefy, were fixed on me. A shiver raced down my spine.

"Hey," Mark whispered, his breath warm against

my ear. "Want to share some popcorn?"

I nodded absently, not really hearing him. My attention was split, torn between the flickering images on screen and the man who refused to let me go. Tempest's body coiled with tension even as he sat perfectly still.

"This part's hilarious." Mark chuckled, oblivious to the silent drama unfolding around him.

"Mm-hmm," I mumbled, my heart racing. How had Tempest known where to find me? Sure, I'd hoped he would, but it wasn't like I'd advertised where I was going. The questions swirled in my mind, but beneath them all, a thrill of excitement pulsed through my veins.

I risked another glance back. Tempest's eyes hadn't left me, his gaze a tangible weight on my skin.

"Kasen?" Mark's voice cut through my thoughts. "You sure you're okay?"

I turned back to him, forcing a smile. "Yeah, sorry. Just… thought I saw someone I knew."

As I settled back in my seat, I could still feel Tempest's eyes burning into me, his possessiveness settling over me. And despite everything, a part of me reveled in it.

The credits rolled. House lights flooded the theater.

Tempest was on his feet in an instant, striding toward the exit. My heart leapt into my throat.

"That was fun," Mark said, stretching. "Want to grab a coffee?"

I barely heard him. My eyes were locked on Tempest's retreating back. The pull was magnetic, undeniable.

"I… I'm sorry, Mark. I have to go." The words tumbled out.

Confusion creased his brow. "Everything okay?"

"Yeah, just... remembered something urgent." I was already standing, gathering my purse.

Mark's disappointment was palpable, but I couldn't bring myself to care. Yeah, I knew it made me a bitch, but I wasn't ready to admit I'd used him. I hadn't walked into this even thinking of giving him a chance. Hopefully, he'd find what he was looking for with his next date.

Tempest was disappearing through the doors. I hesitated for a split second. Following him was playing right into his hands. But the alternative -- letting him walk away -- was unbearable.

"Sorry again," I mumbled to Mark, then bolted.

I'd thought for sure he'd be waiting for me. But when I reached the street, he was nowhere to be found. My heart pounded in my chest, and I couldn't deny the disappointment I felt right then.

What the hell is wrong with you, Kasen? I wanted him, but... what? Did I want him to chase me? To force me to admit I needed him?

Or maybe deep down, what I really wanted was for him to act like just about every other Reaper. I wanted to see the caveman side of him. The Tempest who would throw me over his shoulder, tell me I was his, and not give me a choice in the matter.

Yep. It was official. Living with a bunch of alpha-holes had ruined me.

* * *

Three hours later, I sat across from Alex at Bella's, a cozy Italian place downtown. My third and final date for the day. Warm candlelight flickered, and the aroma of garlic and herbs filled the air. It should have been romantic.

Instead, my nerves were frayed. Every chime of

the door had me flinching, half-expecting to see Tempest's hulking frame fill the entrance.

"So, Kasen," Alex's voice cut through my spiraling thoughts. "What made you want to work at a dental office??"

I blinked, forcing myself to focus. "Oh, um, I just sort of fell into the job. I didn't really have any experience and they hired me anyway. I've been there about four years now."

Alex nodded, clearly interested. "It's great to stick with one employer for a while. Looks good on a resume when you're ready to move on."

"I'll probably stay as long as they'll have me. I enjoy it there."

As Alex launched into a story about his own work, my eyes drifted to the entrance again. Where was Tempest? The anticipation was killing me, a mix of dread and electric excitement coursing through my veins. He'd followed me to every date today. Was he finally giving up?

Alex's voice faded into background noise as I scanned the restaurant for the hundredth time. The waiter approached, notepad in hand.

"Are you ready to order?" he asked.

I nodded absently, barely glancing at the menu. "Chicken parmesan, please."

"And for you, sir?" the waiter turned to Alex.

As Alex deliberated over pasta choices, the bell above the door chimed. My head snapped up, heart racing, but it was just an elderly couple. I exhaled slowly, trying to calm my nerves. The waiter walked off, leaving me and Alex alone once more.

"Kasen?" Alex's concerned voice broke through my thoughts. "Is everything okay? You seem... distracted."

I forced a smile, hating how transparent I was being. "Sorry, I'm fine. Just… a little tired. It's been a hectic day."

Alex's brow furrowed. "Are you sure? We can call it a night if you're not feeling up to this."

"No!" I said, too quickly. "No, really, I'm good. Tell me more about your job."

As Alex resumed talking, our food arrived. The aroma of melted cheese and marinara sauce filled the air, but my appetite had vanished. I picked at my chicken, my stomach in knots.

Then I felt it. A shift in the air, the hair on my arms standing up from the crackle of electricity. A feeling I'd come to associate with Tempest being nearby. I didn't need to look to know. He'd arrived.

His presence filled the room, demanding attention without a word. I turned, our eyes locking across the crowded restaurant. His eyes were burning with a mix of anger and something else -- something that made my breath hitch.

He strode toward us, his gait purposeful, shoulders tense. In seconds, he was beside our table, looming over us like a storm cloud.

Alex looked up, confusion evident on his face. "Can we help you?"

Tempest ignored him, his gaze fixed solely on me. "Kasen," he growled, my name a command on his lips.

I swallowed hard, torn between defiance and the urge to follow him out of there immediately. "Tempest," I managed, my voice barely above a whisper. "What are you doing here?"

Alex's eyes darted between Tempest and me, his discomfort palpable. He shifted in his seat, the scrape of chair legs against tile cutting through the tension.

"I… uh, is everything okay?" Alex asked, his voice wavering as he started to stand.

The thrill of excitement coursing through me warred with embarrassment. My cheeks burned as I stood abruptly, nearly knocking over my water glass.

"I'm sorry, Alex. I have to go," I blurted, grabbing my purse. "Thanks for dinner."

Without waiting for a response, I brushed past Tempest, the heat of his body sending a shiver down my spine. I burst through the restaurant doors, gulping in the cool night air.

Heavy footsteps followed. Had I finally pushed him to the breaking point? I was equal parts excited and terrified.

"What the hell are you playing at, Kasen?" Tempest's voice was low, dangerous.

I whirled to face him. "Me? You're the one crashing my dates!"

His eyes flashed. "Dates. Plural. That's the third guy today."

"That's right," I shot back, chin lifted in defiance. "Got a problem with that?"

Tempest stepped closer, his presence overwhelming. "You know damn well I do."

My heart raced, anger and desire tangling in my chest. "Why? It didn't seem like you were interested. If you were, you would have…"

"Would have what?"

I remained silent, and he growled, closing the distance between us.

I backed up, my shoulders hitting the brick wall. Tempest planted his hands on either side of my head, caging me in.

"Tempest," I breathed, my resolve wavering.

His eyes burned into mine, emotions I couldn't

decipher swirling in their depths. For a moment, I thought he might kiss me.

Instead, he pushed away, running a hand through his hair. "This isn't over," he said, voice rough with frustration.

I watched him stalk away, my body trembling from the encounter. What the hell had I gotten myself into? And why was he leaving? I'd thought for sure something would happen this time.

I took a shaky breath and pushed off the wall, my legs unsteady as I started walking. The cool night air did little to calm the fire Tempest had ignited in me. My mind raced, replaying every heated glance, every terse word.

"Damnit," I muttered. I'd wanted his attention, but this... this was like playing with dynamite.

A low rumble of voices caught my attention. I glanced over my shoulder, spotting Bull and Wire leaning against their bikes across the street. They weren't even trying to be subtle. Bull's eyes met mine, his expression a mixture of amusement and concern. He nudged Wire, who looked up from his phone.

"You good, little one?" Bull called out.

I forced a smile. "Just peachy."

Wire snorted. "Yeah, looked real peaceful back there."

My cheeks burned. "You saw that?"

"Honey, the whole damn town probably saw that." Bull chuckled.

I groaned, covering my face with my hands. "Great. Just great."

"Your old man's going to love this," Wire said, earning an elbow from Bull.

I dropped my hands, fear replacing embarrassment. "You can't tell my dad!"

Bull's expression softened. "Not our place to tell, darlin'. But you might want to sort this out before it explodes in everyone's faces."

I nodded, my throat tight. As I turned to leave, Wire called out, "For what it's worth, I've never seen Tempest this worked up over anyone."

Their knowing laughter followed me as I hurried away, my heart pounding with a mix of dread and exhilaration. Whatever storm was brewing between Tempest and me, it was clear I wasn't the only one who'd noticed.

Chapter Seven

Tempest

I spotted Kasen stepping out of her house, and my blood instantly boiled. She was dressed to kill -- tight jeans, low-cut top, hair done up. But it wasn't her outfit making me clench my fists. It was the punk waiting for her, leaning against a motorcycle with a cocky grin.

Goddamnit. I thought she was done with these games. And who the fuck let the asshole inside the compound? Without thinking, I strode across the street, boots pounding the pavement. Each step fueled my rage. How dare she pull this shit again?

Kasen's eyes went wide as I approached. Good. Let her be surprised.

I watched indecision flicker across her face. She hesitated, glancing between me and her date. The punk straightened up, eyeing me warily. *Smart move, asshole.*

"Tempest," Kasen breathed, her voice a mix of shock and something else. I felt my chest tighten.

I stopped in front of her, close enough to smell her perfume. It took every ounce of control not to grab her and throw her over my shoulder. My gaze burned into hers. A maelstrom of emotions churned inside me -- anger, jealousy, desire. I willed myself not to reach for her.

"Going somewhere?" I asked, my voice low and dangerous. The words came out as a near-growl, laced with barely restrained fury.

Kasen's eyes flashed, a mix of defiance and uncertainty. She crossed her arms, a protective gesture I knew all too well. But I could see the slight tremble in her fingers, betraying her nervousness.

"It's just a date, Tempest," she retorted, her chin

lifting. "You don't own me."

Her words hit me like a punch to the gut. I took a step closer, invading her space. "Is that what you think this is about? Ownership?"

Kasen's resolve wavered, her voice less steady as she replied, "I… I can date whoever I want."

I could see the rapid pulse at her throat. My hands itched to touch her, to remind her of what we had. But I held back, my anger and hurt fueling my restraint.

"You're playing with fire, Kasen," I warned, my voice rough. "And you're gonna get burned."

I took another step closer, my presence looming over her. The little shit with the motorcycle shifted uneasily, his eyes darting between us. Good. Let him squirm.

"You think I don't know what you're doing?" I snarled, my words sharp as knives. "Trying to make me jealous?"

Kasen's eyes widened, her breath catching. I could see the conflict in her gaze, the way she fought to maintain her composure. But I knew her too well. I could read every micro-expression, every subtle shift of her body.

Her cheeks flushed, a mix of anger and embarrassment coloring her skin. I watched as her resolve crumbled under my intense scrutiny. Part of me wanted to back off, to give her space. But the larger part, the part consumed by jealousy and possessiveness, pushed me forward.

"Maybe I am," Kasen admitted, her voice barely above a whisper. She met my gaze, a challenge in her eyes despite the softness of her tone. "Maybe I want to see if you care."

Her words hit me like a sucker punch. Of course,

I cared. How could she not know? Hadn't I expressed that I wanted her to be mine? The urge to grab her, to show her exactly how much I cared, was almost overwhelming. But I held back, fighting for control.

My expression softened for a moment, a flicker of vulnerability breaking through my hardened exterior. I saw Kasen's eyes widen, catching a brief glimpse behind my walls. But I couldn't let it linger. I couldn't be weak, not now. "You know I do," I growled, my voice rough with emotion I couldn't fully contain. "But this isn't the way."

The words hung between us, heavy with implication. I watched Kasen's face, saw the conflict in her eyes. She opened her mouth to speak, but before she could, movement caught my attention.

The punk kid who'd dared to think he could take Kasen out, shifted uncomfortably. "Uh, I think I should..." he mumbled, backing away.

I didn't even spare him a glance. My eyes were locked on Kasen as the kid retreated, the sound of his footsteps fading into the night.

"Yeah, get your ass out of my compound," I said. "And don't even think of ever coming back."

Silence fell, thick and charged. Only the sound of his bike could be heard as he started it up and sped away. The air between me and Kasen buzzed like a livewire, with all the things we'd left unsaid for too long. I wanted to reach out, to touch her, but I held myself back. This moment felt precarious, like one wrong move could shatter everything.

Kasen's eyes searched mine, and I wondered what she saw there. Did she see the storm of emotions I was barely keeping in check? The jealousy, the anger, the fear... and underneath it all, the raw, undeniable need for her? Every time I thought we were starting to sort things out, she pulled this shit.

I couldn't take it anymore. The distance between us felt like a physical ache. Without thinking, I reached out, my hand brushing against Kasen's arm. The touch was electric, sending a jolt through my body. I struggled to keep my voice steady as I confessed, "I can't stand seeing you with anyone else."

The words came out raw, honest in a way I rarely allowed myself to be. My fingers tightened slightly on her arm, a gesture both possessive and tender. I watched Kasen's face, searching for her reaction, my heart pounding so hard I was sure she could hear it.

Kasen's eyes widened, and I saw the moment her defenses began to crumble. She swallowed hard, her gaze locked with mine. The silence stretched between us, taut as a wire. I could feel the heat of her skin beneath my fingers, could smell the faint scent of her perfume on the night air.

"Then what do you want, Tempest?" Kasen finally asked, her voice a mix of challenge and hope. The words hung in the air, heavy with possibility. "After that first night... you haven't tried to get that close again. What am I supposed to think?"

"I didn't try to get..." I pinched the bridge of my nose. "I followed you like a damn dog, tracking your every fucking move. It's not like you didn't see me."

My mind raced. I wanted her safe. I wanted her by my side. I wanted to erase the memory of every other man who'd ever touched her. But most of all, I wanted her to understand what she meant to me, even if I couldn't find the words to express it.

I took a deep breath, the cool night air filling my lungs. The decision crystallized in my mind with sudden clarity. I steeled myself for what came next.

"I want you with me, now and forever," I

declared. The words came out as a command, leaving no room for argument. My eyes bored into hers, challenging her to deny the electric current always sparking between us. "What the hell did you think I meant when I told you that first night that there was no going back?"

She opened and closed her mouth a few times. "You never came after me. I only said I needed to slow things down. Not put the brakes on entirely!"

"Jesus, Kasen." I had to remember I wasn't dealing with a thirty- or forty-year-old woman. Even at twenty-five, she was more immature than most women her age. Thanks largely to her dad, who babied all his girls.

Kasen's breath hitched. I watched the emotions play across her face -- surprise, uncertainty, desire. Her teeth worried at her lower lip as she hesitated, the weight of the decision visibly pressing down on her shoulders. When I'd told her before there would be no going back, I'd thought for sure she understood. Had all this fucked-up shit happened because we hadn't clearly communicated with one another?

I fought the urge to shake her, to demand an immediate answer. My nails dug into my palms, the familiar anger bubbling just beneath the surface, but I forced it down. This was too important to let my temper rule.

Kasen's gaze searched mine, and I let her see everything -- my desire, my fear, my determination. I'd never been so exposed, so vulnerable. It took every ounce of control not to look away.

Finally, her expression softened. "Okay," she agreed, her voice steady despite the tremor I felt in her arm. "Let's date and get to know one another better. Not as Tempest, Sergeant-at-Arms, and Kasen, daughter of Tank, but just... us. And I'm not ready to tell my dad just yet. Unless you want to do the honors?"

Relief flooded through me, followed quickly by a surge of possessive triumph. I nodded sharply, already planning our next move. Together. It was more than I'd dared hope for, but now that I had it, I'd be damned if I'd let anyone take it away.

The tension in my shoulders eased slightly, but my mind was already racing ahead. "Fuck, no, I don't want to tell Tank. Do I look like I have a death wish? Pack light. We need to move fast."

"Pack? Where are we..."

I held up a hand. "Not telling you. But I think we need out of here for at least a few days while we figure shit out."

Kasen nodded, her eyes wide with a mix of excitement and apprehension. As she disappeared into the house, I pulled out my phone quickly calling Viking. When the call connected, I didn't even give him a chance to speak.

"Viking, I'm taking Kasen out of town. Need you to cover the jobs assigned to me."

"What the hell, Tempest? We've got --"

"I don't give a fuck what we've got," I snarled, cutting him off. "Make it happen." The club would understand. Eventually. Right now, all that mattered was getting Kasen away from here.

The creak of the front door had me spinning around. Kasen stood there, a small duffel clutched in her hand. Her eyes met mine, a mix of determination and fear swirling in their depths.

"Ready?" I asked, reaching for her hand.

She nodded, her fingers intertwining with mine. The touch sent a jolt through me, igniting a fire I'd been fighting to control for too long.

I led her to my bike, the chrome gleaming in the fading light. I took her bag and stowed it in my saddlebags. I'd need to head over to my place and grab a few things as well. As I swung my leg over, I felt Kasen hesitate.

"Second thoughts?" I asked, unable to keep the edge from my voice.

She shook her head, climbing on behind me. Her arms wrapped around my waist; her body pressed against mine. "No," she said, her breath warm against my ear.

I kicked the bike to life, the engine's roar drowning out the doubts threatening to creep in. "Stopping by my place, then we'll head out."

I rode over to my house, and saw Viking watching from across the street, looking all kinds of pissed, but at least he wasn't heading over. I went inside and packed a few things, then carried the bag outside and shoved it into the other saddlebag. Getting back on my bike, I pulled down the drive and to the front gates.

The wind whipped past us, carrying away the last remnants of hesitation. Kasen's arms tightened around my waist, her body molding against mine as we leaned into a curve. The rumble of the engine beneath us matched the pounding of my heart.

I felt it then -- a sense of rightness settling over me like a second skin. This was where she belonged. Where we belonged.

"You okay back there?" I called over my shoulder, my voice gruff against the rush of air.

"Never better," Kasen shouted back, her laugh carried away by the wind. My lips curved up a little. The road stretched out before us, an endless ribbon of possibility. Whatever fallout waited for us when we returned -- none of it mattered right now.

"Tempest," Kasen's voice was close to my ear, "What about the club?"

I tensed, my hands tightening on the handlebars. "They'll understand," I growled, more to convince myself than her. "And if they don't... well, we'll cross that bridge when we come to it."

The truth was, I didn't know how this would play out. But with Kasen pressed against me, her trust evident in every mile we put behind us, I knew one thing for certain -- whatever came next, we'd face it together. And for now, it was enough.

The highway stretched endlessly before us, a dark ribbon cutting through the night. Kasen's arms tightened around my waist as we leaned into a sharp curve. The roar of the engine drowned out everything but the pounding of my heart.

I pushed the bike faster, relishing the rush of adrenaline. With each mile, the suffocating weight of expectations fell away. Out here, we weren't Tempest the Sergeant-at-Arms or Kasen, Tank's daughter. We were just us.

A sign for a motel flashed by. My muscles ached from hours of riding. Kasen's grip had loosened, her head resting against my back. Time to stop.

I pulled off at the exit and found the motel, then stopped in the parking lot, killing the engine. The sudden silence felt heavy. Kasen stirred, lifting her head.

"Where are we?" she mumbled, voice thick with exhaustion.

"Nowhere important," I replied, swinging my leg over the bike. "Just a place to crash for the night."

I held out my hand, steadying her as she

dismounted. She stumbled slightly, legs stiff from the ride. Without thinking, I wrapped an arm around her waist, pulling her close.

Kasen looked up at me, her eyes wide in the dim light. The air between us was so thick with tension it practically hissed and spat. For a moment, I considered closing the distance, claiming her lips with mine. But now wasn't the time.

"Come on," I said gruffly, releasing her. "Let's get some sleep."

The night clerk barely glanced up as we entered, sliding a key across the counter without a word. Smart man. The room was basic -- one bed, a rickety table, peeling wallpaper. But it was clean enough, and far from prying eyes. That's all that mattered.

Kasen hesitated in the doorway, her gaze fixed on the single bed. I felt a flicker of uncertainty. Maybe this was a mistake. Maybe I'd pushed too far, too fast.

"I'll take the floor," I offered, my voice rough.

Kasen's head snapped up, her eyes meeting mine. "Don't be ridiculous," she said, a hint of her usual fire returning. "We're both adults. We can share."

I nodded, not trusting myself to speak. As Kasen disappeared into the bathroom, I stripped down to my boxers and T-shirt, settling on one side of the bed. My body thrummed with awareness, every nerve ending on high alert.

When Kasen emerged, wearing an oversized T-shirt and little else, I had to clench my fists to keep from reaching for her. She slipped under the covers, her back to me, leaving a careful distance between us.

I had a feeling tonight was going to be a living hell, and I'd get little to no sleep.

Chapter Eight

Kasen

The roar of Tempest's bike died, leaving an eerie silence in its wake. I got off, my heart pounding. The beach house loomed before us, a silent sentinel against the darkening sky. When we'd woken earlier in the day, he'd suggested a trip to Florida. It was my first time coming here.

Tempest's eyes found mine. "You okay?"

I nodded, not trusting my voice. His presence, so close yet unreachable, set my nerves on fire.

He strode toward the house, muscles taut under his leather cut. I followed, drawn by an invisible thread. The door creaked open. Tempest's hand brushed my lower back as he ushered me inside. Electricity coursed through me. "Take a look around."

I stepped into the open living area, my fingers trailing along the back of a plush sofa. The ocean stretched endlessly beyond the windows, a canvas of blue and gold. My throat tightened. "It's beautiful."

Tempest grunted in agreement, his eyes never leaving me as I explored. I could feel the weight of his gaze, heavy and intense. I paused at a shelf lined with seashells, picking up a delicate spiral. "This place... it's so peaceful."

"That's the idea," Tempest replied, moving closer. "We can be whoever we want to be while we're here. I made sure to book a reservation in a place that didn't have any other clubs."

I turned, startled by his proximity. His scent -- leather and something uniquely him -- enveloped me. This trip was much needed, and I knew it would either bring us closer, or make us realize we weren't meant to be together. For a moment, the world narrowed to just us. Then Tempest cleared his throat, stepping back. "You should get settled in. I'll grab the bags."

As he strode out, I released a shaky breath. This sanctuary might feel like a safe haven, but who would protect my heart from Tempest?

The rhythmic crash of waves pulled me toward the sliding glass doors. I stepped onto the deck, the wooden planks warm beneath my bare feet. Salt-tinged air filled my lungs as I gripped the railing, drinking in the endless expanse of ocean.

Tempest's presence materialized behind me, a silent shadow. He didn't touch me, but I felt the heat radiating from his body. My skin prickled with awareness.

"Beautiful." His voice was rough, barely audible over the surf. "It's your first time seeing the ocean, right?"

I nodded, not trusting myself to speak. Whatever was happening between us, it made the very air feel scorching hot.

"Come on," Tempest said, gesturing to a pair of Adirondack chairs. "Let's sit."

We settled in, the chairs creaking softly. The breeze tousled my hair, carrying away some of the nervous energy thrumming through me. Silence stretched between us, surprisingly comfortable.

Tempest shifted, his gaze fixed on the horizon. He'd asked if this was my first time at the ocean, but he hadn't said it was his. I wondered when he'd gone to the beach before. I didn't know as much about Tempest as I'd thought I did. Only what I'd observed myself or overheard when no one thought I was paying attention.

"What do you want, Kasen?" The question caught me off guard. "I mean, what are your dreams?

Your hopes?"

I stared at him, pulse quickening. Was this really happening? The man I'd been infatuated with for years, asking about my aspirations?

"I…" I swallowed hard. "I'm not sure anyone's ever asked me that before."

Tempest's eyes snapped to mine, intensity burning in their depths. "I'm asking now."

I took a deep breath, the salty air steadying me. "I want…" The words caught in my throat. Tempest waited, his gaze unwavering. "I want to be my own person. And I'd really like to find a way to make things work between the two of us. I'm tired of letting other people decide who I can be with, what types of jobs I can work, or where I can go."

"You like your job," he said.

Not quite what I meant, but he wasn't wrong. Still… the rest of my admission hung between us, heavy with implications. I rushed on, the dam finally breaking. "I'm tired of being Tank's daughter, or just one of the triplets. I want to make my own choices, forge my own path. But I'm scared too. What if I fail? What if I disappoint everyone? I also understand why the others left. None of them were going to find happiness in this town, not with the entire club watching their every move. You saw how hard Akira had to fight to be with Logan."

Tempest's jaw tightened, a muscle twitching. For a moment, I feared I'd said too much. Then he spoke, his voice low and gravelly. "I get it. More than you know."

I blinked, surprised. Tempest shifted in his chair, leaning toward me. "Being Sergeant-at-Arms… it's not just a title. It's a weight. Every decision I make affects the club, affects lives." His eyes met mine, filled with an unexpected vulnerability. "Sometimes I wonder if I'm cut out for it. If I can balance the violence, the duty, with… with who I want to be. I already had anger issues. And it's no secret I haven't trusted women. Not after I got fucked over a long time ago. But I want to be different, for you."

My breath caught. This was a side of Tempest I'd never seen, never even imagined existed beneath his intimidating exterior. "How do you handle it? The pressure."

He gave a humorless chuckle. "One day at a time. Some days better than others." His hand twitched, as if he wanted to reach out but thought better of it.

The realization hit me like a physical force. Here was Tempest, the man I'd put on a pedestal for so long, sharing his own insecurities. We were both trapped by expectations, struggling to find our true selves.

I felt a connection forming, deeper than the crush I'd nursed for years. This was something real, something raw and honest. And for the first time, I allowed myself to hope maybe Tempest saw me as more than just someone he needed to protect.

I couldn't help but laugh, the tension easing from my shoulders. "Remember when you taught me to ride?"

Tempest's eyes crinkled at the corners, a smile softening his features. "You mean when you nearly ran over your mom's prized rosebush? That was the first and last time you were allowed to ride a motorcycle on your own."

"Hey!" I protested, but I was grinning. "I was sixteen, and that bike was huge."

"You were fearless," Tempest said, his voice low and warm. "Still are. I wasn't sure at first, not after the way you ran off that night."

The compliment sent a flutter through my chest. I leaned back, letting the ocean breeze cool my flushed cheeks. "What about you? Any embarrassing teen stories to share?"

Tempest's laugh, a deep rumble, seemed to vibrate through the air between us. "Oh, I've got plenty. There was this one time…"

As he launched into a story about a spectacularly failed attempt to impress a girl at a county fair, I found myself captivated. Not just by the tale, but by the way his whole demeanor changed. The ever-present tension in his shoulders eased, his hands gesturing animatedly as he spoke.

I'd never seen him like this -- relaxed, open, almost… playful. It was intoxicating.

The sun began its descent, painting the sky in brilliant hues. Our laughter faded into a comfortable silence. I glanced at Tempest, only to find his intense gaze already fixed on me. The air between us seemed to thicken, charged with an electricity I couldn't quite name.

My heart raced. Was this the moment I'd dreamed of for so long?

Tempest's hand moved suddenly, reaching for mine. His callused fingers enveloped my smaller ones, the touch both gentle and firm. My breath caught in my throat.

"I need to tell you something."

I swallowed hard, barely able to breathe. "What is it?"

His thumb traced small circles on the back of my hand, sending shivers up my arm. "These feelings I have for you… they're not new. But they've grown stronger than I ever thought possible. I denied them for a long time, knowing you were too young and someone I should never hope to be with. Then you became this incredible woman, and I found it hard to look away."

My heart pounded so hard I was sure he could hear it. Tempest's eyes, usually guarded, now flared, the intensity both thrilling and terrifying me.

"I've tried to fight it," he continued, his words carrying the weight of long-held emotions. "Told myself it wasn't right. That I should stay away. But I can't anymore. You're all I think about. Your smile, your laugh, your strength. Everything about you draws me in."

I sat frozen, hardly daring to believe what I was hearing. This man, who I'd idolized from afar for so long, was baring his soul to me. The vulnerability in his expression was different from the fierce protector I knew him to be.

"Say something," he urged, a hint of his usual impatience creeping into his tone. "Please."

I took a shaky breath. "I… I've been in love with you since I was sixteen," I blurted out, the words tumbling free after years of silence. "But I never thought… I mean, you're you, and I'm just --"

"You're everything," Tempest interrupted fiercely. "Don't you see that?"

The tension between us crackled like lightning, electric and dangerous. Tempest's grip on my hand tightened, his rough fingers a stark reminder of the violence they were capable of. Yet his touch remained gentle, at odds with the storm I saw brewing in his eyes.

I leaned in, drawn by an invisible force. Tempest's breath hitched, his body going rigid. For a heartbeat, I thought he might close the distance.

Instead, he released my hand and stood abruptly. "We should head inside," he said, his voice rough. "It's getting cold."

Disappointment crashed over me, but as Tempest helped me to my feet, I caught the look in his eyes. A silent promise burned there, along with barely restrained desire. He was holding back, I realized. For me. The last time we'd kissed, I'd run away. It seemed this time he was giving me time to accept what was happening.

We retreated into the beach house, the warmth enveloping us like a cocoon. Tempest strode to the kitchen, his movements taut with unresolved tension.

"I'll make us something to eat," he said, yanking open the fridge. "You like pasta?"

"Wait. How is this place stocked?" I asked.

"I paid extra to have them meet the Instacart driver. Placed an order when I booked the place."

I nodded, settling onto a bar stool to watch him work. "Pasta is fine. Need any help?"

"Nah, I got this," Tempest replied, his back to me as he gathered ingredients. "So, tell me about the art project your friend is working on. The one with the motorcycles?"

As I launched into an explanation, the rhythmic sound of his knife on the cutting board punctuated my words. The normalcy of the moment felt surreal after our charged conversation outside.

"Sounds badass," Tempest commented, glancing over his shoulder with a hint of a smile. "Maybe we can check it out together when she's finished."

"I'd love that." I couldn't believe he'd remembered that. He'd overheard me telling Owen about it and had asked what we were talking about, but that had been a month ago.

The pasta's aroma filled the air as we settled onto the couch, plates balanced on our laps. Through the expansive windows, stars winked into existence, mirroring the twinkling lights of distant ships on the horizon. We ate and watched TV, falling into a comfortable silence.

When we finished, we took our plates to the kitchen and rinsed them in the sink before placing them in the dishwasher. Tempest led me over to the sliding glass door again, and we stared out at the night sky.

Tempest's arm draped around my shoulders, a casual gesture that set my nerves on fire. I leaned into him, relishing his solid warmth.

"You see that constellation? That's Orion." He pointed with his free hand.

I squinted. "Where?"

His chuckle rumbled through his chest, and he shifted, stepping behind me, one hand on my arm, the other pointing to the sky again. "Right there, those three bright stars in a row. "And that's Orion's Belt."

As he traced the pattern, I found myself focused more on the rough feel of his fingers than the celestial display. My heart hammered.

"You know a lot about stars?" I asked, desperate to maintain conversation.

Tempest shrugged. "Picked it up along the way. Helps pass the time when I'm on a job."

Silence fell between us, charged with unspoken possibilities. The rhythmic crash of waves against the shore seemed to echo the pounding of my pulse.

"I want you to know --"

I held my breath, torn between hope and fear. He wanted me to know what?

He exhaled sharply. "I respect you. And your

family. Whatever this is between us, we take it at your pace. No pressure. But if we decide to do this, to become a couple, your dad is probably going to lose his shit. That's something we'll both have to face when the time comes."

Relief and disappointment warred within me. "I know."

As the night deepened, exhaustion crept in. Tempest offered his hand. "C'mon, time for bed."

At my door, he paused. His gaze roamed my face, intense and unreadable. "Goodnight, Kasen," he murmured, voice rough with restrained emotion.

"Goodnight," I whispered back, my hand on the doorknob.

For a heartbeat, neither of us moved.

I slipped inside and closed the door, my heart racing. Through the wood, I heard Tempest's heavy exhale and the soft thud of his forehead against the frame. My fingers hovered over the handle, tempted to throw it open, to act on the spark I felt between us.

But I didn't.

Tempest's footsteps retreated down the hall, each one echoing with the weight of unsaid words. I pressed my ear to the door, listening as they faded.

In the silence that followed, I could almost feel him standing there, wrestling with tumultuous emotions threatening to overwhelm me. The air felt thick with anticipation.

My mind raced with possibilities. What would tomorrow bring? How long could we dance around this growing attraction before one of us snapped?

I pictured Tempest's face, the intensity in his eyes when he looked at me. The way his jaw clenched when he held back. He was a powder keg of barely contained passion, and I was the match, ready to ignite.

But he'd promised to respect my boundaries, to let me set the pace. The thought both thrilled and terrified me.

I took a deep breath, steadying myself. Whatever challenges lay ahead, we'd face them together. And for the first time in my life, I felt ready for the unknown.

Chapter Nine

Kasen

I couldn't sleep. The sheets twisted around me like a straitjacket, trapping the heat of another restless night. With a frustrated sigh, I kicked them off and padded to the window. Moonlight spilled across the beach, painting the sand silver. The ocean whispered, beckoning.

What the hell. A walk might clear my head.

The cool sand sifted between my toes as I made my way down to the water's edge. Waves lapped gently at the shore, a soothing rhythm. I closed my eyes, inhaling the salty air.

My thoughts were chaotic. I appreciated the fact Tempest wanted to take things slow, but at the same time, I yearned for more. I understood why he was waiting. I really did. Didn't make it any easier.

A flicker of movement caught my eye. Had he noticed I'd left the house and followed me?

"Hello?" I called, peering into the shadows. Silence answered.

My heartbeat quickened. I suddenly felt rather foolish for being out here alone. I had no idea what time it was, but it was late enough I didn't see another soul around. I'd allowed the peaceful setting to lull me into a sense of safety. Something told me I might have made a horrible mistake coming out here without telling Tempest.

Get a grip, Kasen. You're imagining things.

Another flash of motion. Closer this time. Then again, maybe it wasn't my imagination.

Fear clawed up my throat as dark figures emerged from the gloom. Their eyes gleamed with predatory intent.

"Who are you? What do you want?" My voice shook.

They didn't answer. Just kept coming.

Run. The command exploded in my mind, but my legs wouldn't move. I was a deer in the headlights, frozen as death approached. Everything my dad had taught me was utterly useless in the face of danger.

Oh God. This can't be happening.

Tempest's face flashed through my mind. I'd never see him again. Never tell him... Why had I done such a stupid thing? I knew the dangers in the world and knew how to defend myself. And yet, I stood here, frozen in complete fear. A tear slid down my cheek as I realized how much trouble I was in.

A strangled cry escaped me as rough hands seized my arms.

Panic exploded through me, and I was suddenly unfrozen. I thrashed against the iron grip of the man holding. Kicking with all my might, but not able to connect.

"No! Let go!" I screamed, my voice raw and desperate. His fingers dug into my flesh, bruising.

I kicked out wildly once more, connecting with something solid. A grunt of pain. It was a small victory, but I'd take it.

"Shut her up!" a harsh voice hissed.

A meaty hand clamped over my mouth, muffling my cries. The acrid taste of sweat and dirt flooded my senses. I bit down hard, tasting blood. If only I'd managed to run before it was too late! I might have made it to the house, or gotten close enough Tempest would have heard me scream for help.

"Bitch!" The man snarled but didn't let go.

My eyes darted frantically, searching for escape, for help. But the beach stretched empty in both directions. Why had I come out alone?

One of them produced a zip tie. The plastic cut into my wrists as they bound them behind my back. Tears of frustration and terror streamed down my face.

God, please. Someone. Anyone.

* * *

Tempest

My head snapped up, every muscle tensing. A scream, distant but unmistakable, shattered the night's quiet.

"Fuck," I growled, already in motion. I stopped by Kasen's room and saw it was empty. Rushing through the house, I scanned every room but couldn't find her anywhere. My feet pounded against the wooden stairs as I tore down to the beach, adrenaline surging through my veins like liquid fire.

Sand flew beneath me as I sprinted toward the sound out on the water, my heart thundering in my ears. Who the hell was out there? And why did I have a sinking feeling I knew exactly who it was? With Kasen not anywhere to be found inside the house, worry ate at me. Had it been her I'd heard scream?

"Kasen!" I roared, my voice raw with fear and fury. "Where are you?"

A boat's engine roared to life, a harsh intrusion on the peaceful night. I skidded to a halt at the water's edge, my chest heaving. Too late. Always too fucking late. I saw a small form held by two men, fighting to break free. And I knew…

"No!" I bellowed, my voice cracking. "Kasen!"

But she was already disappearing into the darkness, a small figure struggling against larger shapes on the rapidly retreating boat. The moonlight glinted off the wake, mocking me with its beauty.

Helplessness crashed over me, quickly replaced by a tsunami of rage. I wanted to tear something apart, to make someone bleed.

Instead, I fumbled for my phone, cursing as my trembling fingers struggled with the lock screen. Wire. He'd know what to do. He always did. I didn't give it a shit if it meant Tank would find out I'd brought his daughter here, didn't care if he wanted to beat the hell out of me. I'd let him. I fucking deserved it.

The call connected after an eternity of rings.

"Wire," I barked, my words tumbling out in a frantic rush the moment I heard him pick up. "They took her. Kasen. Fucking traffickers, I think. Speed boat, headed southeast from the Gulf Coast of Florida. Track her phone, now!"

I hoped like hell she'd had it on her, but I feared she'd left it behind. I hadn't thought to check, and I didn't want to leave the beach just yet. Not until I could no longer see any sign of the boat.

"Whoa, slow down," Wire's voice said through the speaker. "Who took --"

"There's no time!" I roared, pacing like a caged animal. "Every second counts. You hear me? If we lose her, I'll --" I choked on the words, the reality of the situation hitting me like a sledgehammer.

"I'm on it," Wire said, his tone sharpening. "Give me two minutes."

I stared out at the inky blackness of the ocean, my heart pounding in my chest. "Hang on, Kasen," I whispered. "I'm coming for you. I swear to God, I'm coming."

I could hear Wire's fingers flying over his keyboard, the rapid-fire clicking a counterpoint to my ragged breathing. "Got a ping," he said, his voice tight with concentration. "They're moving fast, but I've got a trajectory. Heading southeast, toward the Keys."

I pictured the route. "How far out?"

"About ten miles and gaining. But Tempest..." Wire paused, and I could almost see him frowning at his screens. "There's a lot of islands out there. Lots of places to hide. And there's a chance they aren't aiming for the Keys at all. Could be going to Cuba."

My fist slammed into a nearby palm tree, bark splintering under the impact. "Then we search every fucking one!"

"Easy, brother," Wire cautioned. "I'm triangulating cell towers, trying to narrow it down. Thankfully they're close enough to land I'm able to get a signal from her phone. If they were farther out... Give me a few more minutes."

I paced the beach, each step leaving a deep furrow in the sand. My mind raced, conjuring images of Kasen -- terrified, hurt. The thought of those bastards laying a hand on her made my vision go red.

"I should've been watching her," I growled, more to myself than Wire. "I didn't even fucking hear her leave the damn house!"

"You can't blame yourself," Wire said, his typing never slowing. "Focus on getting her back."

I took a deep breath, trying to channel the rage into something useful. "What's our play? We can't go in half-cocked. And when Tank finds out I lost his daughter..."

"Working on it," Wire replied. "I've got a few ideas, but we'll need backup. Let me make some calls. And yeah, you're probably fucked when it comes to Tank. He's going to lose his shit."

I nodded, even though he couldn't see me. "Do it. Whatever it takes. I'm not losing her, Wire. Not Kasen."

The fierce protectiveness in my voice surprised even me. When had the girl who'd always looked at me with those big, adoring eyes become so important? I already knew the answer. She always had been. I'd just been too blind to see it until recently, or at least, that's when I'd allowed myself to admit it.

"We'll get her back," Wire said, his tone leaving no room for doubt. "I promise you that, brother."

I stared out at the horizon. "Yeah," I growled. "And God help anyone who gets in our way."

"Shit," Wire muttered. His fingers flew across the keyboard, the sound echoing through the phone. "They're heading toward Cuba, just like I feared. But I've got a fix on their exact coordinates. For now."

"How long?" I snapped.

"At their current speed, they'll hit Cuban waters in about two hours."

"Fuck!" I slammed my fist into my thigh, welcoming the burst of pain. "We need to intercept them before that happens."

"Already on it," Wire said. "I'm calling in some favors. The Devil's Boneyard MC can get to your location the quickest. There's also a group in Miami called Twisted Tides. I've dealt with them a few times in the past. I'm going to call their President, Tiger. He can probably have boats in the water within the hour."

I nodded, my mind racing. "Good. Tell them to arm up. These fuckers won't give her up without a fight."

"What about you?"

I was already sprinting back toward the house. "I'm grabbing my gear and heading to the airstrip down the highway. Privately owned, but if I pay enough, maybe they'll fly me to Miami. Tell the Twisted Tides I'm heading their way."

"Tempest." Wire's voice was hesitant. "We should call Tank."

My stomach twisted. "No. Not yet. Not until we have her back safe. He's still recovering. This is the last thing he needs."

"He deserves to know --"

"I said no!" I roared, then took a deep breath. "Look, I'll take whatever beating he wants to dish out. But right now, I need to focus on getting Kasen back. You hear me?"

A pause. "All right. But you better pray we find her fast. And for the record, if you weren't our Sergeant-at-Arms, I'd still tell Tank whether you liked it or not."

I hung up without responding, my mind already mapping out the rescue. As I burst into the house, a cold, deadly focus settled over me. Those bastards had no idea what was coming for them.

Hold on, Kasen. I'm on my way.

I tore through the house, grabbing my go-bag and weapons. Things I always kept stashed in my saddlebags. My hands shook as I checked the clip in my Glock. Focus. I needed to be sharp. For Kasen.

The drive to the airstrip was a blur of screeching tires and ignored speed limits. I parked haphazardly, running toward the small office building. A sleepy-eyed man looked up as I burst through the door.

"I need a plane. Now." I slammed a wad of cash on the counter. "Miami. It's an emergency."

He blinked, taking in my wild eyes and the visible gun at my hip. "Sir, I can't just --"

I leaned in close, my voice a low growl. "Listen carefully. A girl's life is at stake. Either you get me a pilot and a plane in the next five minutes, or I'll take one myself. Your choice."

Something in my expression must have convinced him. He swallowed hard and nodded.

Twenty minutes later, I was in the air, my knuckles white as I gripped the armrests. The pilot, a grizzled veteran who'd seen some shit, didn't ask questions. Just nodded grimly when I told him to push it as fast as the plane could go.

My phone vibrated. Wire.

"Talk to me," I barked.

"Twisted Tides is mobilizing. They'll rendezvous with you at their clubhouse. I've sent coordinates to your phone."

I grunted acknowledgment. "The traffickers?"

"Still on course for Cuba. But, Tempest..." Wire hesitated. "There's chatter. These guys aren't amateurs. They've got connections."

Ice settled in my gut. "How bad?"

"Bad enough that even the Twisted Tides are nervous. We're talking cartel-level shit."

I closed my eyes, picturing Kasen's terrified face. "Doesn't matter. We're getting her back."

"I know. Just... be careful, brother."

The plane touched down in Miami, and I hit the ground running. A sleek black motorcycle was waiting, courtesy of the Twisted Tides. I gunned the engine, weaving through traffic like a man possessed.

The clubhouse loomed ahead, a fortress of brick and steel. As I skidded to a stop, the massive gate swung open. A group of hard-faced men stood waiting, their cuts adorned with the Twisted Tides' emblem -- a kraken wrapped around a skull.

Their President, Tiger, stepped forward. His scarred face was grim. "Wire filled us in. We've got boats fueled and ready."

I nodded, my throat tight. "Thank you."

Tiger's eyes narrowed. "Don't thank us yet. This is going to get ugly."

"I'm counting on it," I growled.

Chapter Ten

Tempest

The phone felt like it was going to crack under my grip, Wire's voice a staticky storm in my ear. "39.2576° N, 74.5746° W. That's where they're holding her."

My heart felt like it would pound through my ribs as I barked the coordinates to Tiger. His grim nod was the only answer I needed. The engine roared to life, the speedboat a hungry beast slicing through the inky water.

Shoving the phone into my pocket, I was caught in a maelstrom of thoughts. *Kasen.* Her name was a mantra in my head, a prayer on my lips. I had to get to her. Make this right.

"How long?" I snapped at Tiger.

"Twenty minutes, pushing it," he replied, eyes fixed on the horizon, a mirror of my own relentless stare.

I checked my Glock once more, the familiar weight a comfort in the chaos. Full magazine. Good. My fingers danced over my cut, an inventory of weapons. Knife at my ankle. Backup at my lower back.

I would have liked more men with us, but the Devil's Boneyard couldn't get here fast enough. Hopefully, the few men Tiger had brought with him would be adequate. More remained at the docks waiting for us to return, or to send in reinforcements if we didn't come back.

The wind whipped my face, salt spray stinging my eyes. I didn't blink. Didn't flinch. My gaze remained locked on the horizon, searching for any sign of the traffickers' boat. I felt the ache of her absence like a phantom limb.

"We'll get her back." Tiger's voice cut through the engine's roar.

"Damn straight we will."

Her face flashed in my mind. Her smile. The way she'd look at me, thinking I wasn't watching. I always was. Always cared. And now, because of my carelessness, she was in danger.

The boat slammed into a wave, jolting me back to the present. *Focus.* I had a job to do. People to hurt.

"Wire say anything about their firepower?" I asked, my voice tight. I wasn't sure what he'd told the Twisted Tides President when he'd enlisted their help.

Tiger shook his head. "Nothing solid. We assume the worst. This crew has been causing trouble up and down the Florida coast for years. A lot of tourists tend to go missing. Always young women and teens."

"I'm in the mood for a fight. I don't give a shit how rotten they are, or how tough. I'm going to take the fuckers down." The words tasted like steel on my tongue, a promise and a threat. For Kasen, I would become the storm.

The traffickers' boat materialized on the horizon, a hulking shadow against the star-dusted expanse of the night sky. At some point, they'd switched to a much larger vessel. Which meant they'd likely had it docked out in the water out of sight from where they snatched Kasen. My muscles coiled beneath my skin, ready to spring into action.

"Cut the engine," I hissed, my voice barely audible over the gentle lapping of the waves against our own hull.

Tiger complied, the sudden silence pressing in around us like a tangible entity. We glided closer, the enormous vessel looming larger with each passing moment. My eyes raked the deck, searching for movement, for any hint of a threat.

Nothing.

My heartbeat hammered in my ears. Too easy. Was it a trap? A cruel game designed to lure us into their clutches? Or did these assholes think they were so invincible they didn't dare think someone would come after them? Then again, unless Kasen had talked to them, they'd have no idea who they'd taken, or the fact I'd be coming for them.

Octo, one of the Twisted Tides members, moved with the fluid grace of a panther in the night, securing our boat to the larger vessel with practiced efficiency. The soft *clink* of metal on metal sent a shiver down my spine. I glanced up, waiting to see if anyone on board had noticed. After a few heartbeats, I knew they weren't coming to investigate.

"Ready?" Stinger whispered, his voice barely a breath in the stillness.

I gave the Twisted Tides SAA a curt nod, my jaw tight. "I go first. Watch my six."

I knew I was on their turf, but this was my mission. My woman. Since they'd let me call the shots so far, it made me think Wire had asked them to give me the freedom to do what I felt was necessary.

Hauling myself over the railing, I felt my senses sharpen, every nerve ending buzzing with awareness. The deck creaked beneath my feet like a mournful sigh, the sound echoing in the oppressive quiet. I froze, listening intently for any telltale sign, any hint of movement in the shadows.

Octo and Stinger followed, their movements silent. "Spread out," I ordered, my voice low and tight. "Find Kasen. Anyone gets in your way --"

"We know the drill," Octo interjected. His tone made me want to punch him. "Not our first time doing something like this."

My eyes narrowed. "This isn't a game. These fuckers took one of mine."

"We've got this, boss," Stinger said, his voice reassuring but laced with sarcasm. Noted. I may be somewhat in charge of this mission, but I was the outsider here.

I took a breath to keep calm and clear-headed. "Then let's move. And remember --"

A distant shout ripped through the silence, shattering the eerie calm. I whipped around, adrenaline surging through my veins, my predatory instincts kicking into overdrive.

"Showtime," I said, a feral grin twisting my lips. The rage I'd been holding in check roared to life, demanding release, demanding blood. It was time to unleash the beast within and reclaim what was rightfully mine.

The ship's dim lights cast creepy shadows that danced across the deck, making the whole scene feel like something out of a horror movie. A figure emerged from the gloom -- the first guard.

I didn't hesitate. My fist connected to his temple, the sound of his body hitting the deck echoing in the night air. The rise and fall of his chest told me he still lived. Should have hit him harder.

"One down," I muttered, my breath ragged. The familiar thrum of violence pulsed through me, but I shoved it down. *Focus. Find Kasen.*

I pressed on, hugging the shadows. The ship's corridors were a maze, each turn a potential threat. Or Kasen. The thought of her, scared and alone, sent a fresh wave of anger crashing over me.

"What the fuck is this thing?" I whispered to Stinger.

"Luxury yacht. Not something authorities would assume to be carrying enslaved women." He shrugged. "Dealing in humans is profitable. Doesn't make it right."

Suddenly, voices. I froze, my ears straining to catch every word.

"… the boss wants her moved before sunrise," a gruff voice said.

"Why the rush?" another replied. "She ain't going nowhere."

Kasen. It had to be. I inched closer, peeking around the corner. Four men stood in a loose circle, cigarette smoke swirling around them like ghosts. Their attention was focused on something I couldn't see.

My fingers itched for my gun. One squeeze of the trigger and --

No. Too risky. Too loud. I needed information first.

Patience. Soon.

My eyes narrowed, calculating the distance, the angles, the precise choreography of violence that was about to unfold. Then, I exploded into motion.

I slammed into the first trafficker with the force of a freight train, my fist driving into the soft flesh of his solar plexus. His eyes bulged, and he doubled over, gasping for air. I didn't waste a moment, pivoting on my heel as my elbow connected with the second man's jaw. The sickening crack of bone echoed in the cavernous room.

"What the f --" The third man's curse was cut short as my boot found its mark in his groin. He crumpled to the ground, whimpering like a kicked puppy.

The fourth trafficker, adrenaline-fueled and

desperate, reached for a weapon tucked beneath his jacket. But I was faster. I snatched his wrist in a vise-like grip, twisting it until I felt the satisfying *snap* of tendons giving way. The gun clattered to the floor, a useless piece of metal.

"Where is she?" I snarled, my face inches from the terrified man. His eyes were wide, reflecting the flickering lights overhead. His lips trembled, forming words that wouldn't come.

My fist connected with his jaw, silencing him. Behind me, Octo materialized from the shadows, his grin splitting his face like a jagged scar. "Damn, brother." He whistled low. "Save some for the rest of us."

I ignored him, focusing on the zip ties I was using to bind the unconscious men. If we were in Reapers' territory, I'd have slaughtered them all. My heart hammered in my chest, adrenaline singing in my veins. I fought to keep my rage in check, knowing I needed a clear head to find Kasen.

"You good?" Octo asked, his voice laced with concern.

I nodded curtly. "Let's go."

We plunged deeper into the ship's bowels, the air growing thick with the stench of fear and desperation. Each step fueled my fury, threatened to consume me.

A door burst open ahead, revealing two more traffickers, their eyes wide with terror. One fumbled for his gun, his hands shaking. Had to be someone new to this type of work. Hell, they all seemed too inept.

I didn't hesitate. I lunged forward, a whirlwind of controlled violence. My fists connected with their targets in rapid succession -- jaw, ribs, temple. The first man crumpled to the ground, unconscious. The second tried to raise his gun, but Octo was there, a swift knee to the gut followed by an elbow to the base of the skull.

"Clear," Octo called, his voice calm and collected.

But I barely heard him. My mind was focused on one thing: finding Kasen. Each second felt like an eternity.

"Tempest." Octo's voice cut through my fog of rage. "We need a plan."

I spun around. "The plan is to tear this fucking ship apart until we find her."

We moved further and came to a door. Something told me Kasen would be behind it. Or at the very least, it would lead me to her.

My fist slammed against the door, the impact shooting a jolt of pain up my arm. *Son of a bitch*! The fucking thing hadn't looked like metal. There wasn't much I hadn't been able to bust my way through over the years. I narrowed my eyes.

"Stand back," I growled to Octo, my voice a low rumble that echoed in the tight space.

With a thunderous crash, my boot connected with the door. Metal screeched, hinges groaning in protest. Another kick. The lock splintered, sending shards of metal flying.

The door swung open, revealing a dimly lit hold that reeked. My breath caught in my throat.

There, huddled in the corner, was Kasen. Bound, terrified, but alive. Around her, other women cowered, their eyes wide, yet still filled with hope.

"Kasen," I breathed, my voice rough with emotion. The sight of her, so vulnerable, ignited a fire in my chest, a primal mix of protectiveness and something deeper, something I couldn't quite grasp.

I moved swiftly, kneeling beside her. My hands,

so often used for violence, were suddenly gentle as I worked to untie the ropes that bound her.

"I've got you," I murmured, forcing my voice to stay steady, "You're safe now."

Kasen's eyes met mine, shimmering with unshed tears. The helplessness in them tore at me, a stark contrast to the fiery spirit I knew burned within her.

"We need to move." Octo's voice cut through the tense silence, his words carrying the weight of urgency. "More could be coming."

I nodded, my focus razor-sharp. "Can you stand?" I asked Kasen, my voice soft, a stark contrast to the growl I'd used moments before.

She nodded, her voice barely a whisper. "Y-yes."

"Good girl," I said, helping her to her feet. I turned to the other women, my voice firm but reassuring. "We're getting you all out of here. Stay close."

There was a flicker in their eyes, a fragile flame that I was determined to protect. We had a fight ahead, but for now, we were free. And as long as I had breath in my lungs, I would keep them safe.

My eyes met Kasen's, the connection between us sparking like a live wire in the dim hold. Her face, etched with fear just moments before, softened with relief as my fingers worked with practiced ease, untying the last of her bonds.

"You… you came," Kasen whispered. I couldn't remember ever hearing her sound so… breakable.

I squeezed her hand, a silent reassurance. "Always will, Kas. Did you ever doubt I'd track you down?"

Her feet trembled slightly as she stood, and I gathered her close, the warmth of her body a comfort against the cold metal of our surroundings. The urge to pull her closer, lose myself in the moment, was a tempting siren song, but the urgency of our situation was a cold splash of water on burning coals.

"We have to go," I growled, scanning the shadows for any sign of our captors. "Can you move?"

She met my eyes, the fear replaced by a resolute glint. "Yeah, I'm okay."

Turning to the other women huddled behind us, I lowered my voice. "Stay close. Follow me."

Each step felt like we were walking on eggshells, every creak of the ship a potential alarm. Kasen clung to me, the pressure of her hand against my back a grounding force in the midst of the chaos.

The cool night air washed over us as we reached the deck. My eyes swept the scene, taking in everything, calculating, planning.

"They're over there." I pointed to where Octo, our escape route to freedom, was securing the speedboat. "Let's go."

The adrenaline pulsed through me, my body coiled tight, ready to strike at any threat. I helped Kasen into the small boat, my fingers lingering on her arm just a moment, the warmth seeping under my skin.

"Tempest…" she breathed, her eyes locking with mine, a silent question hanging heavy in the air.

I swallowed the lump in my throat. "Later," I promised, pushing away the yearning in her eyes and turning to help the remaining women aboard.

With everyone safely tucked into the boat, I took one more look at the dark hulk of the traffickers' ship. Still. Silent. A monument to their defeat. The satisfaction of victory was a bittersweet aftertaste in my mouth. Didn't change the fact my woman had been taken from under my nose, or that I'd damn near lost her forever. I still wanted to torch the damn thing. But that might draw the wrong kind of attention. Not to mention, we weren't in Reapers' territory. None of the Twisted Tides had made a move to kill any of them. It made me think they weren't quite as lawless as my club had once been, and in the case of assholes like these human traffickers, we still were.

"Go," I ordered. Tiger started the engine, the sound ripping through the night, carrying us away from the nightmare, toward the uncertain but hopeful future that lay ahead.

The roar of the engine vibrated through my bones as the speedboat sliced through the obsidian water. Tension radiated down my spine. My every muscle thrummed with it, a symphony of anticipation and fear.

"Any sign of them?" I barked at Tiger, his hands steady on the wheel, his face etched with grim determination.

"Nothing yet," he called back, his voice calm, a stark counterpoint to the storm brewing inside me.

My mind raced, a chessboard of possibilities laid out before me. Get them to shore. Secure their safety. Deal with the consequences, whatever they may be. My fingers twitched near the gun at my hip, a constant reminder of the threat that lurked just beyond the horizon.

This had been far too easy, which told me it likely wasn't over yet. I just didn't know if my club or the Twisted Tides would be the ones caught in the cartel's sights. They'd discover the missing women and retaliate. It was just a matter of who they decided to blame. I didn't think we'd left any trace of ourselves on the yacht. With some luck, they'd think some local thugs decided to steal their cargo for extra cash.

Kasen huddled close, her voice barely audible over the engine's roar. "Thank you."

I glanced down, surprised by the intensity in her eyes, the moonlight catching them. For a moment, the world narrowed to just her, her face etched with a vulnerability that tugged at something deep inside me. I swallowed hard, the words catching in my throat.

"Don't thank me yet," I growled, forcing my gaze back to the inky expanse ahead. "We're not safe until we hit land."

The other women huddled together, their voices a mix of relief and fear, their whispers painting the air with uncertainty. I strained to hear anything that didn't belong, my senses on high alert.

"ETA?" I demanded, needing the reassurance of a timeline.

Tiger's voice cut through the night, calm and steady. "Ten minutes, maybe less."

I nodded, a sliver of relief piercing the tension that had me in its grip. "Good. The sooner we're off this Goddamn water, the better."

As the shoreline emerged from the darkness, a jagged silhouette against the night sky, the knot in my chest loosened slightly. Almost there. Almost safe.

My boots thudded against the weathered wood of the dock. Turning, I offered Kasen a hand. Her fingers, cool and trembling, slipped into mine, her eyes wide and searching the shadows. I pulled her close, steadying her as she stepped onto solid ground.

"You okay?" I asked, my voice gruff.

She nodded, lips parting as if to speak, but no words escaped. The adrenaline finally ebbing, I exhaled, a long, shuddering breath. My eyes scanned the deserted dock, a habit ingrained through years of battle. Though the muscles in my shoulders remained coiled tight, a sense of calm settled over me.

"Octo, Stinger," I barked. "Get these women to a safe house. If you don't have one, I can ask Wire to find one. Then get them home, where they belong. Explain to them why going to the police is a bad idea."

They hustled the rescued women toward the waiting vehicles, leaving me rooted in place. The weight of the night's violence pressed down on me, a heavy cloak threatening to suffocate me.

"Tempest?" Kasen's voice, soft and hesitant, cut through my thoughts.

I met her gaze, struck by the mix of fear and something else -- a flicker of admiration? -- in her eyes. There were times I could still see the little girl I'd watched grow up, but it was always brief, overshadowed by the beautiful woman she'd become. *My* woman.

"I'm fine," I growled, the words harsher than I intended. "It's not over. You understand that, right?"

My gut told me this was going to come back to bite us in the ass. I didn't know how it would happen, but I'd always relied on my instincts. And right now, they were screaming that something bad was heading our way.

Her eyes met mine, a spark of determination igniting within them. "I know," she whispered. "But you'll be there, won't you?"

A silent promise formed in the tight set of my lips. I watched as she hurried toward the bikes near the two vehicles the women were loading into. Someone pointed out the bike I'd used to get here, and she climbed on, waiting patiently for me. The night's immediate danger had passed, but this was just the beginning.

Chapter Eleven

Kasen

The door crashed open, banging against the wall. Tempest burst in, cradling me against his chest. His heartbeat thundered beneath my ear, matching the frantic rhythm of my own. He'd seemed calm enough on the plane, but now that we were alone, it felt like he'd gone into overprotective mode.

"Hold on, sweetheart," he said, voice low and fierce.

I clung to him, inhaling the scent of leather and sweat. My body ached, but his arms were an anchor in the chaos.

Tempest strode to the couch, his movements fluid despite carrying my weight. He lowered me gently onto the cushions, his touch careful as if I might shatter.

"Are you hurt?" His eyes, usually hard as steel, lit with concern as they raked over me.

I shook my head. My throat felt raw from screaming. "You already asked."

"Yeah, but that was before we got on the plane. That was a while ago. So now I'm asking again."

Tempest's hands ghosted over my arms, my legs, checking for injuries. His fingers trembled slightly, betraying the intensity of his emotions.

"Talk to me," he demanded, cupping my face. "Where does it hurt? There's no way you…"

I leaned into his touch, craving the warmth. "I'm okay," I managed to whisper. "Just… shaken. All those lessons from my dad, and I couldn't defend myself when it counted."

A muscle ticked in his jaw. "I should've gotten to you sooner. If they laid a finger on you, I swear --"

"You came," I interrupted, surprising myself with the strength in my voice. "That's what matters."

Tempest's gaze softened for a fraction of a second before the anger returned, simmering beneath the surface. He stood abruptly, pacing like a caged animal. "When we get home, we're going to start training. I need to know if something happens again, you won't freeze up."

I watched him, marveling at how he could make even agitation look graceful. My heart raced, and not just from the aftermath of the rescue. Being this close to Tempest, alone, sent electricity coursing through my veins.

He turned back to me. "You're safe now. I won't let anyone hurt you again."

The intensity of his words stole my breath. I'd dreamed of Tempest noticing me for years, but I never imagined it would be like this -- raw, primal, protective. "I know," I whispered, meaning it with every fiber of my being.

Our gazes locked, and the world seemed to slow. The weight of what we'd just been through hung between us, heavy and charged. My chest tightened as I saw the storm of emotions in Tempest's gaze -- relief, anger, and something deeper I couldn't quite name.

"Kasen," he growled, his voice low and rough. "I need to check you over properly."

I nodded, unable to find my voice. Tempest moved with swift efficiency, retrieving a first-aid kit from a nearby cabinet. His movements were precise, practiced -- a stark contrast to the barely contained fury I could see in the set of his shoulders.

He knelt beside me, so close I could feel the heat radiating from his body. "This might sting," he warned, his fingers gentle as he examined a scrape on my arm I hadn't even noticed.

I hissed as he cleaned the wound, more from surprise than pain. Tempest's touch was surprisingly tender, at odds with his intimidating presence.

"Sorry," he muttered, his focus unwavering.

"It's fine," I managed, watching his face. The way he focused as he worked, as if I were the most important thing in his world, sent a shiver down my spine. "Tempest, I --"

"Don't," he cut me off, his voice tight. "Just... let me take care of you right now."

I fell silent, mesmerized by the careful movements of his hands and the way his brow furrowed in concentration. This was a side of Tempest I'd never seen before, and it made my heart race in an entirely new way.

As he worked, Tempest's voice dropped even lower, a rumble that seemed to vibrate through me. "You're safe now. I've got you." His words washed over me, soothing the jagged edges of my fear. I didn't know why he kept repeating himself, unless he needed to say the words as much as I apparently needed to hear them.

I took a shaky breath, feeling the tension slowly bleed out of my muscles. "I know," I whispered, surprised by how much I meant it. With Tempest here, I did feel safe. Protected. While part of me had wondered if he'd ever find me, if I'd ever see him or my family again, I knew that he would have torn the world apart to search for me. It was just the Dixie Reapers' way.

His eyes flicked up to mine for a moment, dark and intense. "No one's gonna hurt you again. I swear it."

The conviction in his voice made my chest

tighten. Without thinking, I reached out, my fingers brushing against the corded muscle of his forearm. "You already said that. I'm really okay now, Tempest. I'm back with you, and those men can't hurt me. You don't have to keep reassuring me everything is okay."

Tempest went still at my touch. The air between us suddenly felt charged, electric. His gaze locked onto mine, and I saw something flare in those depths -- something that made my heart stutter and my breath catch.

For a long moment, neither of us moved. I could hear the pounding of my own pulse in my ears, feel the warmth of his skin beneath my fingertips. The world beyond this moment ceased to exist.

His eyes never left mine as he spoke, his voice low and rough. "I can't do this anymore."

My heart plummeted. "Do what?" I whispered, fear creeping back in.

He shook his head, frustration etched in every line of his face. "Pretend. Act like I don't --" He broke off, his hands fisting. When he continued, his words came out in a rush. "I can't live without you. I won't. I'm done waiting, done holding back. I'm claiming you. Here and now. Fuck asking the club for their vote! When we get home, I'm telling them how it is, and to hell with whether or not they like it. I know your dad is going to be pissed as hell, and that's fine. We'll work it out."

"I'd thought we would take things a little slower, but..." I stared at him, trying to process everything he'd said, and what I felt.

After years of longing, of thinking he barely noticed me... knowing I'd be his forever, filled me with a warmth I'd never experienced before.

"I've tried to make it as plain as possible. I

clearly keep fucking that up." Tempest's voice was urgent, demanding. "You're mine. I'll keep you safe, protect you with everything I've got. But I need you to understand what that means."

My heart pounded so hard I thought it might burst from my chest. I searched his face, seeing the raw emotion there, the vulnerability beneath his fierce exterior. This was Tempest laid bare, offering himself to me completely.

"I understand," I whispered, feeling a weight lift from my shoulders. "I've always been yours. I just didn't think you wanted me. Then when you showed interest, I was too afraid of complicating things."

"*Want* you? Christ, Kasen, I've wanted you for so long it's been tearing me apart. I wanted you even when I damn well shouldn't have. Do you have any idea how much guilt I had over that? You were still a kid, only sixteen when I first took notice, but you didn't fucking look like one."

The air between us shifted, charged with electricity. Tempest leaned closer, his eyes boring into mine. I could see the struggle within him, the way he fought to maintain control even as his desire threatened to overwhelm us both.

"I need to know. Is this what you want? Because once I start, I won't be able to stop. You ran before. If you run again, that's it. I'll let you go, and this time, I won't chase after you."

My breath caught in my throat. Years of longing, of stolen glances and secret dreams, had led to this moment. I searched his face, looking for any hint of doubt or hesitation. There was none. Only raw need and a fierce protectiveness that made my heart race.

"I --" My voice failed me. Words weren't enough.

Tempest's hand came up, fingers gentle as they

traced my cheek. The tenderness of the gesture contrasted sharply with the intensity in his eyes. "Tell me. I need to hear it. Need the words."

I swallowed hard, gathering my courage. This was Tempest -- the man I'd loved for so long. The one who'd just saved my life, who'd always been there, a steady presence even when I thought he didn't see me.

My chin lifted. I met his gaze squarely and gave a small, deliberate nod.

"Say it," he growled.

"Yes," I whispered. "God, yes, Tempest. I want this. I want you."

The world narrowed to a pinpoint as Tempest closed the distance between us. His lips brushed mine, featherlight at first, then with growing urgency. The kiss was a contradiction -- tender yet passionate, controlled yet wild. My hands fisted in his shirt, pulling him closer as the last barriers between us crumbled.

Tempest growled low in his throat, the sound vibrating through me. His fingers tangled in my hair, angling my head to deepen the kiss. I gasped, and he took advantage, his tongue sweeping into my mouth. The taste of him -- danger and something uniquely Tempest -- made my head spin.

"Kasen," he murmured against my lips. "You have no idea how long I've wanted this."

I couldn't speak, could barely breathe. The world outside ceased to exist. There was only Tempest, his solid warmth surrounding me, his scent filling my senses.

The kiss intensified, months -- years -- of pent-up desire finally finding release. Tempest's hands roamed my body, leaving trails of fire in their wake. I arched into him, desperate for more.

"Easy, sweetheart," he said, his voice rough. "We've got all the time in the world now."

I pulled back just enough to meet his gaze. The raw emotion I saw there stole my breath. "Promise?" I whispered.

"I swear it. You're mine now, and I protect what's mine."

His words sent a shiver down my spine. This was more than just a kiss -- it was a vow, a declaration of intent.

I nodded, unable to find my voice. Tempest's lips curved before he claimed my mouth once more, sealing our newfound bond with a kiss that left no doubt about our future.

As we parted, Tempest rested his forehead against mine. His breath came in ragged pants, matching my own. I could feel the tension in his body, coiled tight like a spring. His eyes, usually hard as flint, had softened to molten silver.

"Christ. You've no idea what you do to me."

I swallowed hard, my fingers tracing the lines of his face. "I think I'm starting to get it."

Tempest's arm snaked around my waist, pulling me flush against him. The solid warmth of his body grounded me, chasing away the last vestiges of fear from our ordeal.

We sat in silence, the weight of everything that had transpired settling over us. The beach house, once just a refuge, now felt charged with possibility. Each creak, each whisper of the ocean outside, seemed to echo with the promise of our future.

Tempest's fingers threaded through my hair. "This isn't going to be easy, but you know that. The club, your family --"

"I don't care," I interrupted, pulling back to meet

his gaze. "I've waited too long for this -- for you. Whatever comes, we'll face it together."

A smile tugged at the corner of his mouth. "That's my girl."

I felt a thrill at his words, a warmth blooming in my chest. The uncertainty of our future stretched before us, but for the first time, I welcomed it. Tempest's presence was a bulwark against my fears.

"What happens now?" I asked, my voice barely above a whisper.

That familiar intensity flickered in his eyes. "Now? We make this work. Whatever it takes. If you were anyone else, it wouldn't be an issue. Your dad isn't going to take this well. Some will take his side. Others will just want you to be happy."

His hand found mine, calloused fingers interlacing with my own. The gesture was tender, at odds with his fierce reputation.

"The club will deal," he said, his tone brooking no argument. "You're mine now. That's all that matters."

I nodded, a mix of excitement and apprehension coursing through me. "And my family? Dad could have died in that accident, and now we're dropping this huge bomb on him. Like you said, he won't take it well. I'm worried how he'll react, and what will happen after. And mostly, about his health. What if this causes a setback in his healing process?"

Tempest exhaled slowly, his thumb tracing circles on my palm. "I can't make him accept our relationship. I can only hope he'll come around."

"If we have Mom's support, she'll help."

"Either way," Tempest growled, pulling me closer, "I'm not letting you go. Not now. Not ever."

The possessiveness in his voice sent a shiver

down my spine. I leaned into him, savoring the solid warmth of his body against mine. Outside, the waves crashed against the shore, a steady rhythm that seemed to echo the beating of our hearts.

"Tempest," I murmured, clinging to him tightly. His body felt hard and warm against mine, sending desire coursing through me. The sound of the ocean couldn't compete with the thundering of my heartbeat as I leaned into his strong embrace.

Despite everything I'd just been through, he was right about one thing. We were done waiting. If he was claiming me, then I wanted all of him. I wanted no doubts I was his when we returned home.

"Fuck, you have no idea how much I want you." Tempest groaned, pressing his lips to my neck.

I could feel the pounding of his heart against me and it mirrored mine. My breathing became ragged as he trailed kisses across my shoulder.

He breathed in deeply. "I just... can't get enough of you." His hand slipped under my shirt to trace circles on my bare skin, sending tingles throughout my body. It was the first time a man had done such a thing to me, and my pulse pounded, my cheeks flushed, and I felt a rush of liquid heat between my thighs.

I arched into him, unable to control the hunger that consumed me at that moment. My palms rested on his chest, feeling every beat of his heart beneath them. "I'm yours. And I want there to be no doubts whatsoever."

Our eyes locked as he lowered his mouth to mine in a searing kiss that left me reeling. His hands held onto me possessively and I willingly melted into him -- lost in every deep groan and rough caress from this man who felt so familiar yet unknown at the same time. The taste of him filled my senses. An undeniable pull drew us closer together even as our hearts raced wildly out of control.

"Bedroom," he murmured then stood, lifting me into his arms. I let him carry me to the room he'd used, and he eased me onto the bed. I lifted a hand to stop him.

"Wait. I need a shower."

He grunted and went into the bathroom. I heard the water running a moment later. Getting off the bed, I went into the bathroom and stripped off my clothes. Tempest watched me with a hungry gaze filled with heat. I stepped under the spray and took a breath to steel my nerves. Then I beckoned for him to join me.

It took him no time to remove his boots and clothes, and he stepped into the small shower, pressing me against the tiled wall. His mouth claimed mine even as he soaped his hands and gently rubbed them over me. My nipples hardened as his palms slid over them. I couldn't hold back my moan.

"So beautiful," he said, staring down at me.

"I feel so hot… and achy."

His gaze intensified. "Is this your first time?"

I bit my lip and nodded slowly. "Did you really think there was a way for me to date anyone seriously, much less sleep with them? You know my dad watches me like a hawk. Apparently, you do too."

He grinned. "Damn right I do."

His touch gentled, and soon, he had me begging for more. The need inside me built until I thought I would lose my mind.

"I don't want slow." I cupped his cheek. "I won't break. Just… give me all of you, Tempest."

"Patrick." He smiled faintly. "My name is Patrick Brewer. You don't have to call me Tempest when it's just us."

"Can I call you Rick?" I asked, wanting to use a nickname. Something only I would ever call him.

"You can call me whatever you want." His hands gripped my hips and lifted me. I curled my legs around his waist, and whimpered as he reached between us, teasing my clit. His thighs braced my ass, and the wall behind me held me upright. As I arched into his touch, I could feel something building. Pleasure hit me like a tidal wave and I cried out, my body trembling.

"That's it. Come for me," he murmured.

"Rick, please. I need you! Don't make me wait."

"Fuck..." he grunted, his grip on my hips tightening as he eased his cock into me. I could feel his heat penetrating deep inside, a pinch of pain and discomfort that only lasted a few moments.

I moaned softly against his skin, feeling the roughness of his beard scrape against my cheek. It wasn't enough -- not nearly enough for what I craved right now. With a sudden surge of desperation, I wrapped my legs tighter around him and arched my back. "More. I can take it!"

He paused, eyes raking over my body before he bit down harshly on his lower lip and growled low in his throat. Then, with surprising gentleness, he withdrew his hips and pressed into me again. His strokes were slow, and deep. Heat radiated from his large frame, one hand groping possessively at my hip while the other fisted my hair.

"You're still so fucking tight." He closed his eyes briefly before focusing on me again.

I shivered at the sound of his voice. "Please... I need... need..." I wasn't sure what the hell I needed, but I had no doubt he could give it to me.

Without further hesitation, Tempest began

thrusting into me with rough determination, no longer holding back. His strength was overwhelming yet oddly comforting as he pounded into me. It felt like coming home after a long absence. Each groan that escaped him sent shivers down my spine while also fueling the fire within me even further. We moved together like this for what felt like hours -- lost in each other's passion and desire.

The bit of pain only seemed to make me want more from him. He reached down to tease my clit again, and I came within seconds, screaming out his name. He barely held on for another minute or two before I felt the heat of his release inside me.

Briefly, I realized we hadn't used protection, but we could talk about it later. Right now, I just wanted to bask in the moment, and bathe in the afterglow of finally becoming his.

Chapter Twelve

Tempest
Beach House

The crash of waves pulled me from sleep, Kasen's warm body still tangled with mine. Soft morning light filtered through the curtains, casting a golden glow across her skin. My fingers traced idle patterns on her hip as her eyes fluttered open.

"Morning," she murmured, a smile playing at her lips.

"Sleep well?" I asked.

She nodded, nestling closer. "Better than I have in years."

I'd spent so long keeping my distance, convinced I wasn't the right man for her. Now, holding her in my arms, I wondered how I'd resisted for so long. "Kasen," I breathed, cupping her face. "I --"

She silenced me with a kiss, slow and deep. Fire ignited in my veins. I rolled her beneath me, drinking in the sight of her. My hands roamed her body, relearning every curve and plane. I kissed her back, tasting the sweetness of her lips. My body reacted to hers, instinctively knowing how to satisfy her.

"Please," she whispered against my mouth.

I slid into her hot, tight pussy. Her body welcomed me, and I moaned as she arched into me. With each thrust, I became more lost, completely consumed by desire.

"Fuck," I growled, unable to contain myself any longer.

She gasped softly, her fingers digging into my shoulders as we moved together in a frenzy of passion. "Rick," she whispered my name like a prayer.

Our hearts raced, and every thrust brought us

closer to release.

"Fuck," I gasped, no longer able to hold back. The sound of skin slapping against skin filled the room like a primal symphony. Every time our hips met, I felt her all the way down to my soul.

We both moaned softly, lost in the heat of the moment. The tension coiled deep within me began to unravel as wave after wave of pleasure washed over me. My entire body tensed up before exploding into ecstasy under her unskilled touch.

"Shit... Yeah..." I groaned out as I filled her with load after load of cum.

Our sweaty bodies pressed tightly against each other in the aftermath of our passion. "Damn," I murmured tenderly against her neck, kissing softly before pulling back. "You feel so good."

"I... I love you, Rick," she said softly.

My heart hammered in my chest at her words, and my throat grew tight. I knew I cared about her, didn't want to live without her, but I wasn't sure I knew what love was.

"You're my world," I said, hoping it would be enough to convey how much she meant to me.

My gaze dropped to the evidence of our lovemaking on her thighs. A primal part of me growled in satisfaction, but concern nagged at me.

"Kasen," I said hesitantly. "I should have said something before, but I'm clean. Haven't been with anyone in a long time."

She gazed up at me, eyes soft. "I trust you. Completely."

Her words hit me like a punch to the gut. Trust. Such a simple thing, but so precious. I tugged her close, burying my face in her hair.

"I don't deserve you," I muttered.

She pulled back, fixing me with a fierce look. "Don't say that. You're a good man. Maybe your temper leaves a bit to be desired sometimes, but I've always seen the good in you."

I wanted to argue, to list all the reasons she was wrong. But the conviction in her eyes stopped me. Maybe I could be the man she believed me to be.

I helped her out of the bed and we quickly showered together. I yanked on my boxers and jeans, and Kasen picked up one of my shirts, pulling it over her head. It fell to her knees, and I thought she looked fucking adorable. We headed to the kitchen, both of us starving for something other than each other. I'd never cooked with anyone before, but I had to admit, I kind of liked it.

The sizzle of bacon filled the air as I maneuvered around Kasen in the tiny kitchen. She was at the stove, expertly flipping pancakes while I grabbed plates from the cabinet.

"Watch it, hot stuff," she teased as I brushed past her, my hand grazing her hip.

I smirked. "Can't help it if you're in my way, darlin'."

She swatted at me with the spatula, but I caught her wrist, pulling her close. Our lips met in a quick, heated kiss before she pushed me away, laughing.

"Food's going to burn if you don't behave," she warned, but her eyes sparkled.

I held up my hands in mock surrender. "Yes, ma'am."

We fell into an easy rhythm, moving around each other like we'd been doing this for years. It felt... right. Domestic. A pang of longing hit me, sharp and unexpected.

"Penny for your thoughts?" Kasen asked, sliding

a stack of pancakes onto a plate.

I shook my head, pushing the feeling aside. "Just thinking how good you look in my shirt."

She rolled her eyes, but I caught the flush on her cheeks. "Smooth talker."

After breakfast, we headed out, the rumble of my bike a familiar comfort between my legs. Kasen's arms wrapped tight around my waist as we tore down the coastal road.

The wind whipped through my hair, carrying away the last threads of tension. Out here, there was no club, no responsibilities. Just me, Kasen, and the open road.

I felt her press her cheek against my back, her grip tightening. My heart raced, and it had nothing to do with the speed. For the first time in years, I felt truly free.

I pulled the bike to a stop at a secluded stretch of beach, the roar of the engine fading to the gentle crash of waves. Kasen slid off first, her legs a little unsteady. I caught her elbow, steadying her.

"You good?" I asked, unable to keep the smirk from my face.

She swatted my arm. "Just getting my land legs back, smartass."

We found a spot in the sand, close enough to feel the spray of the ocean. Kasen settled beside me, our shoulders touching. The silence stretched, comfortable but charged with unspoken words.

"Tell me about your family," she said suddenly, her voice soft.

I tensed, old instincts flaring. But when I looked at her, all I saw was genuine curiosity. No pity, no judgment. I took a deep breath.

"Not much to tell," I said, my voice gruff. "Dad

was a mean drunk. Mom… she was sunshine. Until the cancer took her. Hodgkins. Unfortunately, she didn't get checked early enough. It had progressed so far the treatments were only able to give her a few extra months."

Kasen's hand found mine, her fingers intertwining with my own. "I'm sorry."

I shrugged, fighting the tightness in my throat. "Long time ago."

She hesitated, then asked, "Have you heard anything about Rin? Wraith's old lady?"

The change of subject was a relief. Even though, the topic of Rin's rather recent breast cancer diagnosis wasn't exactly a happy one. When Wraith had found out, I thought the man was going to explode.

"Yeah, actually. Wraith says the treatments are working. They're expecting a full recovery."

Kasen's face lit up. "That's amazing news! Usually Akira keeps me up to date, but now that she's pregnant and married to Logan, we don't get to meet as often. We met not too long before we came to the beach, but I'm afraid I didn't think to ask about Rin. I feel awful, looking back. How could I have been so selfish as to only think about my own problems when she's going through so much? I'm sure she's relieved she'll have her mom around a long time, but I was a shitty friend."

I nodded, a smile tugging at my lips. "Yeah, it is good news. The whole club's been pulling for her. But for the record, I doubt she thinks of you as a bad friend. You needed someone and she was there for you. I'm sure you've been there for her plenty of times."

"You're right. I have been. That's what family does," Kasen said softly.

The words hit me harder than I expected. Family. The club was my family now, had been for years. But sitting here with Kasen, I realized I wanted more.

She must have sensed the shift in my mood. Her grip on my hand tightened. "What happens when we go back?"

I turned to face her, seeing the worry in her eyes. "What do you mean?"

"My dad," she said, her voice barely above a whisper. "He's not going to be happy about… us."

I cupped her face in my hands, forcing her to meet my gaze. "Listen to me. I don't give a fuck what anyone thinks, including your old man. I've got you, you hear me? No matter what."

She nodded, but I could still see the doubt lingering. I leaned in, pressing my forehead to hers. "I mean it. Anyone tries to come between us, they'll have to go through me first. For what it's worth, I'm fully prepared to take whatever beating your dad gives me. I need you to not interfere when it happens."

The tension in her shoulders eased slightly. "You're insane. You know that right? He's called Tank for a reason."

"Yep, but I can handle it." I then gave her a kiss that left us both breathless.

I pulled back, my heart racing. "C'mon," I said, rising to my feet. "Let me show you something."

Kasen took my outstretched hand, her brow furrowed. "What?"

"Self-defense," I replied, leading her to a flat stretch of sand. "If you're gonna be with me, you need to know how to protect yourself."

"Dad already showed me. I just… froze when I needed to use the things he'd taught me."

"No arguments," I cut her off, my voice brooking

no opposition. "Now, stand here."

I positioned her, my hands lingering on her hips. The proximity sent a jolt through me, but I pushed it aside. *Focus, damnit.*

"First, we'll work on your stance," I explained, demonstrating. "Feet shoulder-width apart, knees slightly bent."

Kasen mirrored my position, determination etched on her face. "Like this?"

"Close," I murmured, stepping behind her. I pressed against her back, adjusting her posture with my hands. "There. Feel the difference?"

She nodded, her breath catching. "Y-yeah."

I guided her through basic moves -- blocks, strikes, escapes. Her skin was warm under my touch, her scent intoxicating. But beneath the distracting sensations, I saw her potential.

"Good," I growled as she executed a perfect palm strike. "Again."

We moved together, my body shadowing hers. With each repetition, her confidence grew. Pride swelled in my chest, mixed with a primal possessiveness I couldn't shake.

"Now," I said, circling to face her, "let's see how you do against a real opponent."

Kasen's eyes flashed with challenge. "Bring it on."

I lunged, telegraphing my moves. She dodged, countering with the techniques I'd shown her. We grappled, sand flying as we struggled for dominance.

Suddenly, she hooked her leg behind mine, sending us both crashing to the ground. I landed on my back, Kasen straddling me triumphantly.

"How's that for self-defense?" she panted, grinning down at me.

The sight of her -- flushed, breathless, victorious -- undid me. I surged up, capturing her lips in a searing kiss. Kasen melted into the kiss, her body molding against mine. The heat between us sparked, threatening to ignite into an inferno. I rolled us over, pinning her beneath me in the soft sand.

"You're a quick study," I growled against her neck.

She arched into me, her fingers tangling in my hair. "I have a good teacher."

My hands roamed her body, relearning every curve. The thin fabric of her clothes was maddening, a flimsy barrier between us. I tugged at her shirt, desperate to feel her skin.

"Wait," she gasped, pushing against my chest.

I froze, immediately pulling back. "What's wrong?"

Kasen glanced around, her cheeks flushed. "We're on a public beach."

Reality crashed back. I cursed under my breath, rolling off her. "Shit. You're right."

We lay side by side, catching our breath. The sound of waves filled the silence, a gentle reminder of where we were.

"Rain check?" Kasen asked, a hint of mischief in her voice.

I turned to her, drinking in the sight of her disheveled hair and swollen lips. "Count on it."

We gathered our things and headed back to the bike. The ride home was charged with unspoken tension, Kasen's body pressed tight against mine.

As we pulled up to the beach house, my phone buzzed. I fished it out of my pocket, my stomach dropping at the name on the screen. "Fuck," I muttered.

Kasen peered over my shoulder. "What is it?"

I showed her the message. Two words that shattered our peaceful bubble: *Come home. -- Tank*

"Last night," I said. "Time to go home tomorrow and face reality."

* * *

The porch glowed with candlelight, casting flickering shadows across our faces as we sat down to dinner. Waves crashed rhythmically in the background, a soothing counterpoint to the tension crackling between us.

I watched Kasen across the table, mesmerized by how the soft light played on her features. "This is… nice," I managed, my throat tight.

She smiled, a hint of shyness in her eyes. "It is. I didn't know you could cook like this."

"There's a lot you don't know about me," I said, my voice low.

Kasen's gaze locked with mine. "I want to learn."

The air between us seemed to thicken. I reached for my drink, desperate for something to do with my hands. "Careful what you wish for, darlin'. I'm not an easy man to know."

"I'm not looking for easy," she countered, leaning forward. "I'm looking for real."

My heart pounded. I stood abruptly, needing to move. "Let's go inside."

As we stepped through the door, the atmosphere shifted. Kasen's fingers brushed mine, sending electricity up my arm. I turned, catching her wrist and pulling her close.

"Kasen," I growled, "tell me to stop."

She shook her head, eyes wild. "I can't."

That was all it took. I crushed my mouth to hers, years of pent-up desire exploding between us again. I started to think I'd never get enough of her. We stumbled through the house, shedding clothes, hands roaming desperately.

I paused at the bedroom threshold, searching her face. "You sure about this? You have to be sore."

Kasen's answer was to pull me down onto the bed. We came together in a tangle of limbs and breathless moans, exploring each other with a mix of hunger and reverence. She was so eager and ready, I slid inside her with ease.

As I moved inside her, the world fell away. There was only Kasen -- her scent, her taste, the sound of my name on her lips. For the first time in years, I felt whole.

The moment she came, I knew I couldn't hold on. I took her harder, deeper, not stopping until my balls drew up and filled her with every drop of cum I had in me. Afterward, I cuddled her against my side.

I traced lazy circles on Kasen's bare shoulder, her head resting on my chest. The room was quiet except for the distant crash of waves and our slowing breaths.

"Tank's gonna kill me," I muttered, tension coiling in my gut. It was one thing to tell him I was claiming his daughter. It was another to have already slept with her before talking to him.

Kasen propped herself up, eyes flashing. "I'm not a child. This is my choice. It's not his decision."

I cupped her face, my thumb brushing her cheek. "I know, darlin'. But your dad... you're his little princess, and he has every right to be pissed about how I handled this."

"Do you regret it?" Her voice wavered slightly.

"Hell no," I growled, pulling her closer.

* * *

As dawn broke, reality intruded. We packed in

near silence, the weight of our impending return pressing down. I caught Kasen's hand trembling as she zipped her bag.

"Hey," I said softly, pulling her into my arms. "We've got this."

She nodded against my chest. "I know. It's just... I'm not ready to leave our bubble."

I understood completely. This beach house had become our sanctuary, a place where we could just be us without the complications of the outside world.

"Me neither," I admitted. "But we can't hide forever."

Kasen squared her shoulders, a determined glint in her eye. "Then let's face it head-on."

I grinned, pride swelling in my chest. This was the woman I'd fallen for -- fierce, unafraid.

As I stood by my bike, my eyes were drawn to the ocean, its endless expanse a stark contrast to the confined world we were about to re-enter.

"One last look?" Kasen's voice was soft behind me.

I nodded, feeling her hand slip into mine. "It's been one hell of a week."

We stood there, the salty breeze whipping around us.

"You okay?" Kasen squeezed my hand.

I turned to her, drinking in the sight of her windswept hair, her eyes bright with a mix of apprehension and hope. "Yeah. Just... processing."

She nodded, understanding in her gaze. "It's a lot."

"Understatement of the fucking year," I muttered, then sighed. "But I wouldn't change a thing. Well, except the part where you were kidnapped. That I could have done without."

Kasen leaned into me, and I wrapped my arm around her shoulders. "But I think it brought us together. It gave me the final push I needed."

"And here I thought by coming with me, you'd already agreed to be mine." Honestly, I knew what she meant. For her, things had been moving too fast. Then she'd been kidnapped, thought she'd never see me again, and it made her realize moving fast wasn't always a bad thing.

We stood there for a moment longer, the crash of waves a steady rhythm. Then, with a deep breath, I stepped back. "Time to go."

The ride was silent, the tension palpable. I could feel Kasen's anxiety radiating off her in waves. Hell, I was feeling it too. The club, Tank, the potential shitstorm we were driving into -- it all loomed large. I hadn't even told Savior yet that I'd claimed her.

The road stretched out before us, an uncertain path. But for the first time in a long time, I felt ready to face whatever came our way. With Kasen by my side, I could take on the whole fucking world if I had to.

Chapter Thirteen

Kasen

The rumble of the bike echoed off the clubhouse as Tempest and I rolled to a stop. My heart hammered against my ribs. This was it. No turning back now.

I swung my leg over the seat, boots hitting gravel. Curious eyes peered from shadowy corners of the lot. Wary glances darted our way. Yeah, I'd known we were screwed before we got here. This only proved it.

Tempest's hand found the small of my back as we approached the entrance. His touch steadied me, but my palms were slick with sweat. My dad would be furious. I just wasn't entirely sure which of us he'd be the most angry with.

The heavy door groaned as we stepped inside. Conversation died instantly. Dozens of eyes locked onto us.

"Shit," I muttered under my breath.

His body coiled tight, ready to spring into action if needed. Although, he'd promised he wouldn't hurt my dad.

A sea of leather-clad bodies parted. My father's imposing figure cut through the crowd like the prow of a ship. Tank. The ex-Sergeant-at-Arms. And despite his age, he hadn't lost much muscle mass. I knew he was still really damn strong. His presence filled the room, commanding and undeniable.

My throat went dry. "Dad, I --"

He raised a hand, silencing me. His eyes, hard as steel, bored into Tempest. Okay. So he was furious with the man beside me, and not his precious daughter. Part of me felt relieved, but I was suddenly much more worried about Tempest than I'd been before.

The room held its breath. You could hear a pin drop.

Tempest's fingers twitched at his side. I knew he was fighting the urge to reach for me, to shield me from whatever storm was brewing. Except my dad would never hurt me. Yell? You bet. But he'd never so much as spanked me or my sisters. Although, he'd probably been tempted a few times to throttle us in our younger years.

Dad's gaze swept over us both. His face was an unreadable mask, but I caught a flicker of... something. Pain? Disappointment? Whatever it was, it vanished in an instant, replaced by the stern countenance I knew all too well. "You two," he said, his voice little more than a growl, "have some explaining to do." His gaze locked onto Tempest, a storm of emotions swirling within them. "Where the hell have you been? Any why the fuck did you think it was okay to take my daughter with you and not say a Goddamn word to me?" he demanded.

My heart hammered against my ribs. I wanted to speak, to explain, but the words caught in my throat. Not to mention, it was clear he didn't want the explanation from me. No, he wanted to hear from the man who'd stolen his little girl and run off for almost a week.

Tempest stepped forward, his shoulders squared. He met my father's gaze with unwavering resolve. "We needed space to figure things out." The tension in the room was suffocating.

"Figure *what* out?" Dad pressed, his voice dangerously low.

Tempest's jaw tightened. I could see the struggle within him, the battle between respect for my father and his own fierce emotions. "My feelings for Kasen," Tempest finally said, his voice steady despite the intensity burning in his eyes. Except, I knew he was covering for me. He'd clearly already known how he felt. I was the one who couldn't make a decision. "They run deep, Tank. Deeper than I ever thought possible."

A collective intake of breath swept through the room. I felt dizzy, caught between pride in Tempest's boldness and terror at my father's reaction.

Dad's eyes narrowed, flicking between Tempest and me. "And you couldn't have talked to me first? You didn't think I should know you planned to make a move on my daughter?"

"Would you have listened?" I found myself asking, surprising even myself with my sudden courage. "Because anytime I've tried to talk to you about dating anyone, you shut me down. You always said you wanted us to be happy, but then your actions don't always match your words. I know you worry about us, Dad, but we're all grown up now. Besides, you didn't seem to have an issue with other guys I dated. I knew there was one difference... they were safe. Boring."

The following silence was deafening. I held my breath, waiting for the explosion. But instead, I saw something unexpected flicker across my father's face. Was it... understanding?

It vanished as quickly as it had appeared. Dad's face contorted with rage. Before I could react, he lunged forward, his fist connecting with Tempest's jaw in a sickening *thud*. I gasped, my heart leaping into my throat. But Tempest didn't move. He absorbed the blow, his feet planted firmly on the ground. His eyes never left my father's face, his stance unyielding.

Blood trickled from the corner of Tempest's

mouth, but he made no move to wipe it away. The room fell deadly silent.

I couldn't stand it anymore. My legs propelled me forward before my brain could catch up. I planted myself between them, my back to Tempest, facing my father's thunderous expression. "Dad, stop!" I pleaded, my voice steadier than I felt. "I love him."

Dad's eyes widened, shock momentarily replacing his anger. I pressed on, my words tumbling out in a rush. "I've loved Tempest for years. This isn't some fleeting crush or rebellion. He's everything to me. I just... never felt like I was the right woman to stand beside him. Until he made me see I was stronger than I thought." Although, my dad would likely disagree once he heard I'd been kidnapped and nearly taken to Cuba.

I felt Tempest's hand on my shoulder, a gentle squeeze of support. I reached up, intertwining my fingers with his.

"Please," I whispered, my eyes locked on my father's. "Try to understand. I didn't say anything before because I was worried how you'd react, and... I thought I might disappoint you. But I can't live at home forever. Neither can Westlyn or Harlow. We're all grown up now, Dad. It's time to let us be adults and stop trying to shelter us like we're still little girls."

Dad's face was a battlefield of emotions as he processed my words. His eyes darted between Tempest and me.

I felt Tempest shift behind me, his hand leaving my shoulder. He stepped forward, not quite beside me, but close enough that I could feel the heat radiating off his body.

"Sir," Tempest's voice was low, controlled. The tension in the room ratcheted up another notch. "I know this isn't how you wanted things to go down. I'm sure you wanted someone far better than me to be with her, but my feelings for Kasen are real. There's nothing I wouldn't do for her. Hell, I'd die for her if it came down to it."

Dad's gaze narrowed. I held my breath, ready to jump between them again if necessary. He wasn't going to swing again, right? He'd just healed from his accident. If he strained or broke something, my mother would be furious, and he'd likely feel like less of a man, especially if it happened in front of everyone.

Tempest continued, his tone unwavering. "I understand the challenges we face. The age difference, my position in the club, your concerns as her father. But I swear to you, on my patch and my life, that I'm committed to Kasen. She'll never want for anything. You know I'd never cheat on her, never cause her pain. Not knowingly."

My heart swelled at his words. I wanted to turn and look at him, but I didn't dare take my eyes off my father.

"I'll spend every day proving myself worthy of her," Tempest said, his voice taking on an edge of intensity. "If that means facing your disapproval, so be it. But I'm not walking away from her. In fact, I'm not asking the club to vote. I'm just laying it out there -- Kasen is mine. I've claimed her."

The silence stretched on, unbearable. I could almost see the gears turning in my father's head, his expression an unreadable mask.

I watched as the veins in Dad's forearms pulsed. His eyes darted around the room, taking in the faces of his brothers. Torch nodded almost imperceptibly. Venom's lips tightened into a thin line. Wire's gaze never wavered from Dad's face.

My breath caught in my throat. The club's silent support was palpable, a living thing in the room.

Dad's eyes snapped back to us, boring into Tempest. I tensed, ready for another explosion.

Instead, Dad's shoulders sagged. He exhaled heavily, the fight draining from his massive frame.

"Goddamnit," he growled, running a hand over his face. "You're really gonna do this, aren't you?"

Tempest's voice was steady. "Yes, sir. I am."

Dad's eyes met mine, a storm of emotions swirling in their depths. "And you, baby girl? This is what you want?"

I swallowed hard. "More than anything, Dad."

Probably not the time to tell him I could be pregnant, right? I mean, sure… It wasn't likely, but I knew a lot of the women around here got pregnant within the first few months of being with their men. At times, I'd heard the ladies joking there must be something in the water at the compound.

He let out another long breath. "Fuck." He turned back to Tempest, his voice gruff. "You hurt her, I'll end you. Slowly."

Tempest nodded once. "Understood."

I felt lightheaded, hardly daring to believe what I was hearing. Dad was… accepting this?

"Don't make me regret this," Dad added, his tone carrying a clear warning.

"Never," Tempest replied, his hand finding mine and squeezing gently.

The tension in the room evaporated. I released a breath I hadn't realized I'd been holding, my knees suddenly weak. Tempest's hand tightened around mine, steadying me.

Dad's eyes softened as he looked at me, a look of resignation passing over his weathered features. He reached over to a table and picked up a sack I hadn't noticed before. My heart skipped a beat. What was he giving me?

"Here," Dad grunted, holding out the sack. "Figured you'd be needing this."

My hand trembled as I reached for it, and when I saw the property cut inside, I felt tears gather in my eyes. The patch was everything to me -- it was acceptance, belonging, a symbol of my place in this world I'd grown up in but now had become an even more integral part.

"Thank you," I whispered, my voice thick with emotion. "But how did you know I'd need one?"

Dad's eyes flicked to the side, landing on Wire. The tech guru was leaning against the bar, a barely-there smirk on his face. Of course. Wire always knew everything. In fact, it was likely him who'd help locate me when the traffickers had snatched me off the beach. Although, it was clear no one had told my dad about that part of our trip. I wasn't looking forward to him finding out, but I had a feeling sooner or later, the truth would come out.

"He likes to talk. A lot." Dad's gaze swung back to Tempest, his eyes narrowing. "This isn't just for her. It's for you too. You're responsible for her now. In every way."

Tempest nodded, his jaw set. "I understand. I won't let either of you down."

I could feel the tension radiating off Tempest, knew how much was riding on this moment. Dad might have given his grudging approval, but one wrong move could shatter his acceptance. Then we'd be back to flying fists.

Dad held Tempest's gaze for a long moment, searching for something. Whatever he saw must have satisfied him, because he finally nodded.

"See that you don't," he said, his tone a mix of warning and something that might have been respect.

The room exploded with cheers and whistles. Hands clapped my back, voices congratulating us. Through the chaos, I caught Tempest's eye. His intensity hadn't dimmed, but there was something softer there now, just for me.

"You good?" he murmured, his breath hot against my ear.

I nodded, leaning into him. "Yeah. I'm good."

The celebration swirled around us, but in that moment, it was just us. His eyes searched mine, a whole conversation passing without a word. Promise. Desire. A hint of fear, quickly masked.

"Let's get you home," Tempest said, his voice rough.

Home. The word sent a thrill through me. Not my childhood bedroom. His place. Our place now.

As we made our way to the door, the reality of what was happening hit me. This was it. The moment I'd dreamed of for years. And it was nothing like I'd imagined. It was better. Scarier. More real than any fantasy.

Tempest's bike rumbled to life, and I climbed on behind him, my arms wrapping around his solid frame. As we peeled out of the lot, the clubhouse growing small in the rearview, I felt a chapter of my life closing, and a new one, full of promise and passion, was just beginning.

But first I had to go pack…

The ride to my parents' house was short but intense. Every curve of the road, every rev of the engine, reminded me that my life was changing forever. Tempest's body was a solid wall of warmth against me, grounding me in the present.

We pulled up to the familiar two-story house, its weathered siding a testament to years of family life. My chest tightened. This had been my sanctuary, my prison, my whole world for so long. Now, it was just... a house.

Tempest cut the engine, the sudden silence deafening. He turned to me, his eyes searching my face. "You okay?"

I nodded, not trusting my voice. He squeezed my hand, a gesture of silent support.

Inside, the house was quiet. Mom must be out. Good. I wasn't ready for another emotional confrontation just yet.

My room wasn't what you'd expect of a twenty-five-year-old woman. Posters of bands I'd outgrown years ago covered the walls. Stuffed animals I couldn't bear to part with were in a corner. A life frozen in time. It hadn't mattered to me before, but now I wondered what Tempest thought of this juvenile space.

He leaned against the doorframe, watching as I moved around the room. His presence filled the room, making everything else seem small and insignificant.

I grabbed a duffel bag from my closet and started throwing clothes in haphazardly. My hands were shaking. This was really happening.

"Kasen." Tempest's voice was low, intense. I turned to find him right behind me, his eyes dark with emotion. "We don't have to do this now. If you need more time --"

I silenced him with a kiss, fierce and desperate. When we broke apart, both breathing hard, I met his gaze steadily. "I've waited long enough. I'm ready."

A slow smile spread across his face, predatory and full of promise. "Then let's get you home, darlin'."

He helped me finish packing the necessities with a promise we'd come back for everything else. As we walked out, my bag slung over Tempest's shoulder, I paused in the hallway. Family photos lined the walls. Me and my sisters as kids, gap-toothed grins and skinned knees. Mom and Dad when they first got together, young and hopeful. Well, Dad was young-er.

I touched one frame gently. My high school graduation. Dad's arm around me, pride shining in his eyes. Even though my sisters had graduated the same day, my parents had insisted we take individual pictures as well as group ones.

The ride to Tempest's place -- our place now -- was a blur. The setting sun painted the sky in shades of orange and pink, a fitting backdrop for the end of one chapter and the beginning of another.

As we pulled up to the small house, my heart raced. This was it. My new life was beginning, whether I was ready or not.

Chapter Fourteen

Tempest

The phone buzzed on the nightstand, jolting me out of a dreamless sleep. I snatched it up, adrenaline already coursing through my veins. Wire's voice came through the speaker, tight with tension.

"Tempest, we've got trouble. Tiger from Twisted Tides just called. Their compound was hit. Hard. They think the cartel's coming for us next."

"Fuck. Get to the clubhouse. Now." I hung up, fingers flying over the keys as I fired off a text to Savior: *Need to call Church. ASAP.*

Kasen stirred beside me, her sleepy eyes filled with concern. "What's wrong?"

I swallowed hard, tamping down the urge to pull her close and never let go. "Club business. I need you to stay here. Don't leave for any reason, got it?"

She nodded, fear flickering across her face. I hated seeing it there, knowing I was the cause.

The night air hit me like a slap as I strode out to my bike. The engine roared to life, a familiar comfort as I tore out of the driveway. My mind raced faster than the speedometer. How the hell had the cartel found us? And more importantly, how were we going to stop them?

The clubhouse loomed ahead, a beacon in the darkness. I barely remembered to kick down the stand before I was off the bike and striding inside. The air in Church was thick with tension and cigarette smoke. Savior's eyes met mine, hard as flint. Viking leaned against the wall, arms crossed, while Saint paced like a caged animal.

Prophet and Royal burst in behind me, followed by the rest of our brothers. The door slammed shut with a finality that sent a chill down my spine.

Savior's voice cut through the silence. "All right, Tempest. What the fuck is going on?"

I took a deep breath, steeling myself for the shitstorm that was about to rain down. "We've got cartel trouble headed our way. And it's my fault."

Before I could elaborate, the door swung open again. Wire strode in, his face grim, a tablet clutched in his hand like a lifeline. The room fell silent, all eyes locked on him.

I stopped my restless pacing, every muscle in my body coiled tight. Wire's eyes met mine for a split second, and I saw the gravity of the situation reflected there.

"What've you got?" I asked, my voice low and tense.

Wire tapped the tablet, his fingers flying across the screen. "It's worse than we thought," he said, his usually calm voice tinged with urgency. "The cartel's not just running drugs anymore. They've diversified. The women on the ship were just the tip of the iceberg."

"We?" Savior asked.

"Um, yeah. I might have helped Tempest with something tied to the cartel." Wire cleared his throat, looking uncomfortable. I was an ass for putting him in this position.

"Spit it out," Savior snapped.

Wire's eyes darted around the room. "Human trafficking," he said. "They've got a sophisticated network spanning the entire Southeast. And now they're pissed because someone fucked with their operation. More specifically, Tempest and the Twisted Tides did."

My jaw clenched so hard I thought my teeth

might crack. The pieces were falling into place, and the picture they formed was ugly as hell. The trafficking had been a given, considering what happened to Kasen. But I hadn't realized it was on such a large scale. And of course, Wire had just thrown a grenade I couldn't dodge. I'd known I'd have to come clean. Thankfully, Savior hadn't picked up on what he'd said just yet. Or he was biding his time to ask what the hell Wire meant.

"How connected are we talking?" I asked, dreading the answer.

Wire's fingers danced across the tablet again. "They're using the drug routes to move people. Shell companies to launder money. Even got some dirty cops on the payroll. For clarification, none of the cops in our town." He looked up, his expression grim. "It's a full-scale operation, boys. And they've got resources we can only dream of spanning Arkansas, Missouri, Tennessee, Alabama, Georgia, and Florida."

The room erupted into a cacophony of curses and shouted questions. But I barely heard them. My mind was racing, replaying every moment of what happened in Florida. Every decision I'd made. Every mistake.

"Tempest?" Savior's voice cut through my thoughts. "You got something to add?"

I met his gaze, knowing I was about to light a powder keg. But there was no turning back now. We were all in this mess together, whether they knew it yet or not.

"Yeah," I said, my voice rough. "I think I know why they're coming for us. And it's not gonna be pretty. Just not sure how they found me."

Back in Florida, I'd had a feeling something would happen. I hadn't known how it would go down, or if it would even be the cartel. I just knew bad shit was going to head our way. And when I got those feelings, I always paid attention. It had kept me alive this long.

I took a deep breath, feeling the weight of every eye in the room. "When Kasen and I were in Florida, she got picked up by human traffickers. Turns out they're tied to the cartel. Didn't know that until Wire started tracking her for me."

The following silence was deafening. I could practically hear the gears turning in everyone's heads as they processed what I'd just said.

Savior leaned forward, his knuckles white as he gripped the edge of the table. "What the fuck happened, Tempest? Is that what Wire meant about you and the Twisted Tides?"

"I got her back," I said, the words tasting like ash in my mouth. "And yeah, that's what he meant. With help from the Twisted Tides MC out of Miami. We took down the operation, rescued Kasen and a bunch of other women."

Wire stared at the device in his hand. "I've been picking up a lot of chatter. They've been looking for whoever hit them. I hadn't heard specific names mentioned, but it's clear they know who was responsible."

"How?" Saint asked.

Wire shrugged. "I didn't detect cameras on board when I was searching for Kasen and found the ship's signal, but it doesn't mean they weren't there. Could have been hidden well enough Tempest wouldn't have seen them. And if they weren't accessible other than from the ship itself, I wouldn't have had access. It's quite possible they used older tech and not cloud-based. But I'm speculating."

I nodded, my stomach churning. That would

make sense. Of course, we'd also left those men alive on board. Even though it was dark and we'd crept up on them, someone could have noticed our colors or our names. We hadn't exactly gone incognito. But like Wire had said, it was just speculation. Only the cartel could say for sure how they'd found us. "The Twisted Tides compound was hit. They think the cartel's coming for us next."

The room exploded into chaos. Questions and accusations flew like bullets, but I kept my eyes on Savior. His face was a mask of barely contained fury. I knew I needed to say something, but I couldn't get the words out.

Tank's chair screeched against the floor as he shot to his feet, the force sending it flying backwards. His face contorted with rage, veins bulging in his neck as he let out a roar. The sound made my ears ring.

"You motherfucker!" he bellowed, advancing on me. "You hid this shit from me? That's my daughter, you asshole!"

I held my ground, even as Tank's massive form loomed over me, trembling with the effort of not swinging at me. "I trusted you with Kasen," he spat, his voice dropping to a dangerous growl. "And this is how you repay that trust? By keeping me in the dark when she was in danger?"

"Technically, I was entrusted with every person at the compound. You didn't exactly hand her over to me or anything." My excuse was weak at best. I knew what he meant. Regardless of my role in Kasen's life, first and foremost I was the Sergeant-at-Arms, which means I should have kept her safe. The guilt hit me like a sucker punch to the gut. I'd fucked up, and I knew it. But before I could respond, Savior's voice cut through the tension.

"Tempest," he said, his tone icy. His eyes bored into mine, disappointment and anger radiating from him in waves. "You should have fucking told me. I don't give a shit about the excuses you gave. I had a right to fucking know!"

He was right. I knew it. He knew it. Hell, everyone here did. I glanced over at the Pres. Savior's gaze never left mine. I could see the wheels turning in his head, weighing my actions against the potential consequences we now faced.

The silence stretched on, thick with tension. I stood there, my heart pounding, waiting for the axe to fall.

Savior's fist slammed onto the table, the sound like a gunshot in the tense room. "Enough," he growled, his eyes sweeping over the assembled men. "We can deal with this shit later. Right now, we've got bigger problems."

Wire nodded, his fingers flying over his tablet. "The cartel's moving fast. I've been tracking their transactions the last half hour, and they're definitely coming our way. We need to lock this place down tight."

I felt the familiar surge of adrenaline, my body shifting into battle mode. "We'll need to fortify the perimeter," I said, my mind racing through potential weak points. "Set up surveillance on all access roads."

Prophet leaned forward, his face grim. "I've got contacts who can get us extra firepower. We're gonna need it."

Savior's eyes narrowed, his expression hard. "Good. Wire, I want eyes on every inch of this compound. Tempest, you and Prophet coordinate our defenses. I'll text everyone their assignments. As of now, we're on full lockdown."

The room buzzed with tightly controlled energy as we hammered out the details. My blood hummed with a mixture of anticipation and dread. This was what I was built for, but the stakes had never been higher.

As the meeting broke up, I felt a heavy hand on my shoulder. I turned to find Tank's eyes boring into mine, his anger barely contained. "We're not done," he growled. "I want the full story. Now."

I nodded, my throat tight. This wasn't going to be pretty.

I took a deep breath, meeting Tank's steely gaze. The tension in the room was thick enough to cut with a knife.

"It happened fast," I began, my voice low and controlled. "Kasen left the beach house at night while I was asleep. I woke to a scream and found her gone."

Tank's massive frame vibrating with barely contained fury. I pressed on, the words spilling out. "I saw her on a small boat, men holding her. She was fighting, but --" I swallowed hard, the memory searing through me. "Wire tracked her location. Got me in touch with the Twisted Tides in Miami."

Tank's eyes narrowed. "And you didn't think to call me?"

"There wasn't time," I shot back, feeling my own anger rising. "Every second counted. I chartered a plane, flew to Miami, and met the Twisted Tides. Their President, VP, and SAA joined me on the rescue."

I could see Tank processing, his enforcer's mind piecing together the tactical details. "We boarded the cartel's boat," I continued. "Got Kasen and the other women out. I wanted to blow the whole thing, but --"

"But what?" Tank growled.

"For one, it wasn't our territory. The Twisted

Tides didn't seem interested in killing those men, so I followed their lead. It also could have caused more problems down the line. We got them out clean, no bodies left behind. I have no idea how or if the Coast Guard or anyone else patrols those waters. I didn't need the law breathing down our necks if they managed to piece things together. We left the men alive but knocked out and bound. I guess the cartel went looking when they didn't show up in Cuba with a shipment."

Tank's fist slammed down on the table, making me flinch. "You should've told me the second she was safe!"

I met his gaze, unflinching. "You're right. I fucked up. But she *is* safe, and now we've got a bigger fight on our hands."

Tank's eyes blazed with a fury I'd rarely seen, even during our most intense club fights. He leaned in close, his breath hot on my face. "Listen here, Tempest," he snarled, jabbing a meaty finger into my chest. "If you ever hide shit like that from me again, if my daughter is in danger and no one tells me, heads will fucking roll. Starting with yours."

I stood my ground, though every instinct screamed to back away. "Understood," I said, my voice low and tight.

Tank held my gaze for a long moment, then stepped back. The tension in the room was suffocating. Without another word, I turned and strode out of Church, my boots echoing on the hardwood.

The cool night air hit me as I stepped outside, and I sucked in a deep breath. My mind raced, replaying the events of the past week or so. I'd fucked up, no question. Should've told the club the second Kasen was safe. But what was done was done.

Now, we had bigger problems. Somehow the cartel knew the Dixie Reapers were involved and they were coming. I lit a cigarette, inhaling deeply as I scanned the compound. We needed to fortify, fast. But more importantly, we needed to figure out how the hell the cartel had connected the dots.

I crushed out my cigarette and headed for my bike. The compound was already buzzing with activity as brothers rushed to secure our defenses. I revved the engine, tearing out onto the dark road.

My mind raced. How had the cartel traced us? The Twisted Tides compound hit first meant they'd followed that lead. But how?

I pulled up to my house, killing the engine. The house was dark, silent. My heart rate spiked. I drew my gun, approaching cautiously.

The door was locked. Good sign. I used my key, easing inside. "Kasen?" I called softly.

No answer. Panic clawed at my throat as I cleared each room. Empty. What the fuck? Right when I was about to call in reinforcements, I saw a note on the fridge.

Went to see my mom.

Son of a bitch! I'd told her to stay put. I stalked my way through the house and back out to my bike. Time to bring my woman home, then spank her ass until she couldn't sit down. She was about to learn when I said to do something, she'd better damn well do it. Especially when it was to keep her safe.

* * *

Kasen

I sat at the kitchen table of my childhood home and stared at the cup of tea my mom had placed in front of me. I'd been sipping on it, but my stomach was churning so bad I worried I'd throw it up.

"Are you happy?" Mom asked. "I know you had a crush on Tempest for a long time."

I glanced up at her. "Yeah, but Dad is going to be so mad."

She sighed and leaned back in her chair. "Honey, I love your dad, but let's be honest. That man gets mad at the drop of a hat. He'll get over it. Eventually."

"That's the part that worries me," I mumbled. "Talk about awkward family dinners moving forward."

Mom laughed softly. "Did I ever tell you how I met your dad?"

"A little. Something about Aunt Lupita sending you to him."

She nodded. "That's right. She'd met him before, and when she knew I was in danger, she sent me to him for safekeeping. Although, when she showed up later, finding out Tank and I had fallen for each other pissed her off. And you know how she can be."

I tipped my head to the side. "Only from what you've told us. I still don't understand why none of us have gotten to meet her."

"My sister did some bad things. Your dad was so mad at her. Even though he was a protector, I almost expected him to take a swing at her. It took her some time to get herself straightened out."

"And now?" I asked.

"She calls sometimes. Not often. She fell in love. Got married." Mom sighed and stared at the table. "She had three miscarriages. Her husband left her for another woman, one he'd knocked up. From what she's told me over the years, she tried dating other men. Even got married one more time. None of the relationships worked out."

"So she's all alone?" That sounded so... sad. Even if she'd done something wrong, it was clear Mom had forgiven her for whatever it was.

"Yeah, she is. I've tried to talk her into moving closer to us so we could visit. I think she's too embarrassed to see the Dixie Reapers. They all know what happened back then. And your dad isn't the most forgiving man, not when it comes to me anyway. Your Aunt Lupita put me in harm's way. I could have died, and that's not something your dad will ever forgive. He still gets upset when she calls."

"Do you think she'll ever find love?" I asked.

"I don't know. She's closed herself off." Mom gave me a soft smile. "But I hope that she'll find happiness someday. Even if children aren't in her future, it doesn't mean she can't have a good life and find a decent man. Some who won't care about kids."

I nodded, knowing she was right, and also wishing Aunt Lupita could find someone. Now that I had Tempest, I understood what I'd been missing all this time. My heart broke for my aunt, even though I'd never met her or spoken to her before. I didn't think Dad would keep us from seeing her. Maybe one day she'd come visit.

A motorcycle pulled up out front and I stood to look out the kitchen window. "Shit."

"Tempest?" Mom asked, a smirk on her lips.

"Yeah. Think I'm in trouble."

"You said he told you to stay put. I wondered when he'd show up to drag you back home." Mom stood and put our cups in the sink. "I'll just make myself scarce. Time to face the music."

This was bad. If Mom was leaving, she knew Tempest was going to be furious with me, and it meant he had her blessing to punish me. Damnit.

He pounded on the door and I tried to calm my racing heart. I slowly went to answer it, pulling the door open and staring up at him.

"What exactly did I tell you?"

"Um… To wait for you? Or something like that."

He gave a humorless bark of laughter. "Yeah, or something like that. Get your ass on the bike, Kasen."

I meekly did as he said, wondering just how bad this was going to be. And I found out soon enough. We'd barely cleared the front door of our home before he hauled me over to the couch and dragged me down over his knees, ass in the air. The crack of his hand was not only loud but hurt like hell. But the humiliation I felt quickly turned to something else, and my face felt hot. Who'd have ever guessed I'd get turned on by something like a spanking?

I was in so much trouble…

Chapter Fifteen

Tempest

The clubhouse reeked of sweat and tension. Savior's steely gaze swept the room, "We need volunteers for a supply run. Stock up before we're cut off completely. I don't want anyone leaving the compound after this, not until we know the cartel has been dealt with."

I'd brought this trouble here, all because I hadn't thought to warn Kasen to be careful while we were at the beach. If I'd been more alert, had heard her leave the house, then maybe we could have avoided all of this.

"We don't know where the cartel is right now, so there's a chance those who volunteer could be in danger. Don't take this lightly," Savior said.

Bull stepped forward first, his massive frame casting a shadow. "I'm in."

Rocky was right behind him, military precision in every movement. "Count me in too, Pres."

Pride and fear warred in my chest. These were my brothers, ready to put their lives on the line. Again. They were also some of our older members, which meant they'd been to hell and back again for this club more times than I could count. Both had been members before I'd even been a Prospect.

"Good men." Savior nodded. "We'll need at least four more. Safety in numbers."

I opened my mouth to volunteer, but Savior's sharp look silenced me. Right. As Sergeant-at-Arms, I had to stay behind. Protect the clubhouse. My jaw clamped so hard it ached.

Bull's hand clapped Rocky's shoulder. "Just like old times, eh, Marine? If you wanted an adrenaline rush, this might be your chance."

Rocky's lips twitched. "As long as there's less sand in uncomfortable places."

Sam, one of our Prospects, and Thunder's father-in-law raised his hand. "I'll go."

A ripple of laughter broke the tension. For a moment.

"Whoever else plans to go, let Bull or Rocky know. Load up and roll out in twenty," Savior ordered. "The rest of you, lockdown procedures. No one in or out without my say-so."

As the room erupted into motion, I caught Bull's eye. A silent nod passed between us. *Stay safe, brother. Come back to us.*

I turned away, throat tight. Time to do my job. Keep everyone safe. Even if it killed me to watch my brothers ride into danger without me.

Exactly twenty minutes later, the roar of engines filled the air as our convoy thundered down the highway. Wire had decided to keep watch using a drone, so we'd know if trouble came their way. Rocky and Bull had taken two of the club SUVs for hauling back everything we'd need. The other two were on their bikes, leading the way.

Thanks to Wire's tech, I was able to keep in contact with Rocky and Bull.

"Eyes sharp," I said into the comms. "Anything looks off, you get the hell out of there."

Bull's gruff voice crackled back. "Roger that, Tempest."

I scanned the roadside, the overpasses, every potential ambush point. It all seemed a little too peaceful. Too... quiet. They hadn't passed another vehicle, which was beyond strange.

"Tempest," Rocky's tense voice came through.

"Three o'clock. Black SUV."

Wire found it easily and I could see it on the computer screen. The SUV was pacing them, tinted windows hiding its occupants.

"Hold steady," I ordered, mind racing. "Could be noth --"

The world exploded.

Gunfire erupted from all sides. The SUV swerved, men with assault rifles leaning out the windows. More appeared from behind the brush and trees lining the highway.

"Ambush!" I roared. "Evasive maneuvers!"

I caught glimpses of my brothers scrambling for cover, returning fire. My heart pounded, adrenaline surging. They were outnumbered, outgunned. But they wouldn't go down easy.

"Form up!" I shouted. "Don't let them flank you!"

There was no way they could get out of there right now. Not without fighting back. They'd set a trap, and my brothers had walked right into it.

Bull and Rocky moved like a well-oiled machine, Rocky's military training kicking in instantly. They dove behind an overturned truck, using it as cover.

"Rocky, lay down suppressing fire!" Bull bellowed, his voice cutting through the chaos. "I'll flank left!"

Rocky nodded, his face a mask of concentration. He popped up, firing in controlled bursts, forcing the cartel members to duck.

I watched in awe as Bull used the distraction to sprint to a better position, his bulk moving with surprising agility despite his age. He signaled to Rocky, who immediately shifted his fire.

"Tempest!" Bull's voice said in my earpiece. "We

need to regroup! Rally point at the abandoned gas station!"

I was about to respond when a heart-stopping scream pierced the air.

"Sam!" Rocky's voice was filled with panic. "Sam's down!"

My blood ran cold. Sam, the Prospect -- Hammer's son. Thunder's father-in-law. He was caught in the open, blood blossoming on his chest.

Bull's face hardened. "Cover me!" he roared, already moving.

Rocky laid down a blistering barrage of gunfire as Bull charged toward Sam, bullets kicking up dirt at his feet.

My heart was in my throat as Bull reached Sam, dragging him behind a concrete barrier.

"He's hit bad, Tempest!" Bull's voice was strained. "We need evac, now!"

Rocky was already moving, his movements precise despite the urgency. "Use his belt as a tourniquet," he called out. "I'll keep them off us!"

My brothers needed me, no matter what Savior had said about me remaining behind. I ran for my bike, knowing if I didn't get there soon, we could lose good men. I wasn't the only one who'd been listening. Hopefully, someone would coordinate a rescue. Right now, I needed to get there and do what I could.

I gunned the engine of my Harley, pushing it to its limits as I raced toward the ambush site. The wind whipped past my face, but it couldn't drown out the sound of my heart pounding in my ears. I was too late. Too fucking late.

As I skidded to a stop, the scene before me made my stomach churn. Bodies lay scattered across the asphalt, both cartel and Reapers. The acrid smell of gunpowder hung in the air, mixing with the metallic scent of blood.

"Tempest!" Bull's voice was strained as he waved me over. "We need you here, now!"

I sprinted toward him, my eyes scanning the carnage. Sam lay motionless on the ground, Rocky working furiously to stem the bleeding.

Guilt crashed over me like a wave. I should have been here. Should have seen this coming. Rage built in my chest. "How bad?" I asked, my voice barely above a whisper.

Bull's eyes met mine, grim determination etched on his face. "Bad. But we're not losing him. Not today. Where's everyone else? You brought help, right?"

I pushed down the anger threatening to consume me. There'd be time for vengeance later. Right now, my brothers needed me. "It's just me right now."

"Jesus," Bull muttered. "If we can't get the fuck out of here, we're all dead. What were you thinking?"

"That this was my fucking fault and I needed to get here as fast as I could. Now, what do you need?" I asked, already reaching for my phone to call for backup. If our brothers weren't already on their way here, they would be as soon as I made the call. Now that I was here, I could see just how bad the situation was.

As we worked to stabilize Sam and secure the area, I couldn't shake the weight settling on my shoulders. This was on me. As Sergeant-at-Arms, I should have anticipated this. The cartel would pay, I'd make damn sure of that. But first, we had to get our people home.

The ride back to the clubhouse was somber, our usual rowdy convoy replaced by a grim procession. Sam's limp form was cradled in the back of Bull's SUV,

Rocky keeping pressure on his wounds. We'd had to leave the other vehicle behind, but I'd get it later.

As we pulled into the lot, I saw the fear and anger on the faces of our waiting brothers. Savior stepped forward, his usual stoic expression cracking as he took in the scene.

"How many?" he asked, his voice low and dangerous.

"Three wounded, including Sam. He got hit the worst," I reported, the words tasting like ash in my mouth. "Two... two didn't make it. Gears and Bats."

A collective growl rose from the gathered Reapers. I felt it in my chest, matching the fury building inside me.

"Get the wounded to the infirmary," Savior ordered, his eyes meeting mine. "Tempest, my office. Now."

I nodded, knowing what was coming. As I followed him inside, I couldn't shake the image of Sam's blood-soaked body. This wasn't over. Not by a long shot. The cartel had just started a war they weren't prepared to finish.

I stomped into the clubhouse, my fists so tight my knuckles turned white. The rage inside me was a living thing, clawing to get out. I needed to hit something, to break something, to make someone pay.

I followed Savior to his office and took a seat. He glared at me over the top of the desk.

"This is a clusterfuck of epic proportions. You should have told us when Kasen was taken. We would have at least known something might be coming. Thanks to your negligence, we were blindsided, and now we've lost two brothers. Hell, Sam may very well die. Are you going to be the one to tell Amity you're responsible for taking her father away?"

I swallowed hard. "Look, I know I fucked up. I can't change the decisions I made, or how things played out. Want me to step down as Sergeant-at-Arms? Because I will."

Savior sighed. "No. Tank personally picked you for that position, and I'm letting it stand. But there will be repercussions. I'm docking your pay fifteen percent for the next six months, and you're footing the bill for any funerals."

"Thanks, Pres." I rubbed at my chest, trying to get rid of the ache settling in from the lives we'd lost today.

"Now, go figure out how to get us the hell out of his mess. For one, we need to know how they knew to come here. I doubt you left a calling card."

"I'm on it." I stood and left his office, heading for the main room. I spotted Prophet nursing a beer at the bar.

"Prophet! Wire! Church. Now."

Both nodded, Prophet's face grim as he fell in step beside me. We strode into the small, windowless room.

"We need intel," I growled, slamming my palms on the table. "Where are they holed up? Who's calling the shots? And how the fuck did they know to come here?"

Prophet's eyes narrowed, his mind already working. "I've got a contact in the sheriff's office. Might be able to tell me if they've noticed anything on their end."

"Do it," I snapped, then forced myself to take a breath. "Sorry, man. It's just --"

"I know," Prophet cut me off, his voice low and steady. "We're all feeling it, Tempest. But we need clear heads if we're gonna hit back effectively."

I nodded, grateful for his level-headedness. It was why we worked so well together -- my fire and his ice.

"I'm still doing all I can, but I think the cartel has their own hacker. Maybe several considering how well they're trying to cover shit up and hide like a bunch of damn rats," Wire said.

"All right, what else?" I asked, my mind racing. "We need to know their supply routes, their safe houses. Every Goddamn thing about these pricks. They set that up too neatly for this to be their first time in this area."

Prophet pulled out his phone, fingers flying over the screen. "I'll reach out to some friends. I don't agree with their life choices, but if anyone is hiding out in those areas, they'll know about it."

"Good thinking," I said, feeling a spark of hope amidst the anger. "I'll get Bull and Rocky to map out the ambush site, see if we can figure out how they knew we'd be there."

We locked eyes, a silent understanding passing between us. This wasn't just about revenge -- it was about protecting our family, our way of life.

"We're gonna make them regret ever setting foot in our territory," I growled.

Prophet's lips curved into a cold smile. "Amen to that, brother. Let's go hunting."

"I'll call in help from Surge and Wizard. Maybe they'll see something I'm missing. I've been staring at this shit for some long my eyes are crossing," Wire said. "But we'll figure it out."

* * *

Kasen

I watched Tempest from across the clubhouse,

my heart aching. His eyes blazing with that fiery intensity that both thrilled and terrified me. He was in full Sergeant-at-Arms mode, barking orders and radiating danger.

God, I wanted to go to him. To wrap my arms around his taut frame and tell him it would be okay. But I couldn't. That wouldn't be helpful to him right now.

I bit my lip, fighting the urge to fidget. Tempest's gaze swept the room, and for a split second, our eyes met. My breath caught.

"You okay, sweetie?" A gentle voice broke my trance.

I turned to see Ridley, concern etched on her face. Venom's wife. If anyone could understand, it'd be her. Although, I knew she had a lot on her plate right now. After being shot, Venom had been in a coma for months, only to wake up without over thirty years of memories. He still hadn't remembered Ridley, his kids, or grandkids. I knew it had to be hard on all of them. I felt awful for even wanting to ask her for help right now.

"I... I don't know," I admitted, my voice barely above a whisper. "Can we talk?"

Ridley nodded, leading me to a quiet corner. "What's on your mind?"

I took a shaky breath. "It's Tempest. I want to help, to be there for him, but..."

"But you're afraid he'll push you away," Ridley finished, her eyes knowing.

I nodded miserably. "How do I show him I can be of help to him?"

Ridley's hand found mine, squeezing gently. "Oh, honey, trust me, he knows you want to. But Tempest... he's got a job to do, and right now, that's where he's focused."

"So what do I do?" I asked, desperation creeping into my voice.

"Be steady," Ridley said firmly. "Show him you can handle the storm. Don't push, but don't back down either. Let him see your strength."

I straightened, resolve filling me. "I can do that."

Ridley smiled. "I know you can. Just remember, Kasen -- you're worth fighting for too. He's not just doing this for his brothers."

I glanced back at Tempest, my heart racing. This time, I'd be ready when he looked my way.

I squared my shoulders and took a step forward.

"Kasen." Ridley's voice was low. "Be careful. He's not his usual self right now."

I nodded, not looking back. My heart thundered, but my stride was steady as I crossed the clubhouse. Tempest's gaze snapped to me, dark and turbulent.

"What?" he growled.

"Need anything?" I kept my voice neutral, chin lifted.

His eyes narrowed. "What I need is for everyone to stop asking me that."

"Okay." I didn't flinch. "Then I won't ask. I'll just be here."

"I don't need a babysitter."

"Good. Because I'm not offering to be one."

For a moment, the anger in his eyes flickered, replaced by something I couldn't quite read. Then it was gone, his walls slamming back into place. "Whatever," he muttered, turning away.

I didn't move. The clubhouse buzzed with activity around us -- men cleaning weapons, voices low and urgent. The air crackled with anticipation and fear.

Tempest glanced back at me, irritation clear on

his face. "Still here?"

"Yep."

His gaze narrowed again, but this time, I caught a hint of… curiosity?

Before he could speak, Savior's voice cut through the room. "We know where these fuckers are hiding, and it's time to settle the score. We ride in an hour. Get ready."

The energy in the room shifted. This was it. We were going to war. Or rather, our men were. All the rest of us could do was sit back and pray, hoping they came home.

Tempest's gaze held mine. "Make that two. There's something I need to do first."

My heart nearly skipped a beat at his words.

"I'll give you longer," Savior said. "Hell, maybe we all need a night or two. Who knows how many of us will come back alive from this shit storm."

Chapter Sixteen

Tempest

I closed the clubhouse door behind us, the *click* echoing in the stillness. Kasen's eyes met mine, a flicker of something unreadable passing through them. The tension from the last few hours still coiled tight in my muscles. "Ready to go home?"

She nodded and followed me to my bike, getting on behind me. I rode slowly through the compound, needing those extra minutes to calm myself.

We pulled into the carport and I turned off the engine, then helped her off the bike. As we entered the house, I flicked on the lights and scanned the interior, making sure no one had slipped in while we were gone. I didn't think the cartel could breach the compound, but I wasn't taking chances.

"You think the plan'll work?" she asked, breaking the silence.

I grunted. "It has to."

She nodded, worrying her bottom lip. My eyes tracked the movement.

"Tempest, I --"

"Don't." The word came out harsher than I intended. I softened my tone. "We can't afford distractions. Not now."

Kasen's eyes flashed. "Is that what I am? A distraction?"

Fuck. I scrubbed a hand over my face. "You know that's not what I meant."

She took a step closer, determination written across her features. My breath caught as she reached for my hand. Her fingers were soft against my callused skin.

"I'm here," she said quietly. "Whatever comes

next. I'm not going anywhere."

Part of me was proud of her for standing beside me, giving support to me and the club; the other part wanted me to send her far away from here. I needed her safe.

"They got their hands on you once. If they manage to take you again..." I couldn't even finish the thought, but I knew she understood what I was trying to say.

"Getting kidnapped terrified me, but not enough I'd run away from you, or what it means to stand by your side. Even if I'm shaking inside, I will do my best to remain strong and face my fears."

I lightly touched her cheek. "I know, baby. And I love you for it, but the thought of you being caught in this mess again scares the shit out of me."

I pulled her to me and kissed her, my touch gentler than I'd ever allowed myself to be. My fingers brushed a strand of hair from her face, tucking it behind her ear. Our eyes locked, and in that moment, everything else fell away. The club, the danger, the years of restraint -- none of it mattered.

Kasen's gaze held mine, a universe of unspoken promises passing between us. My heart thundered in my chest, a stark contrast to the stillness of the room.

"Tempest," she breathed, her voice barely audible. "Rick."

I couldn't hold back any longer. Slowly, deliberately, I leaned in. Our lips met, and the world ignited.

The kiss started soft, exploratory. But like a match to gasoline, it quickly blazed into something more. My hands cradled her face, thumbs stroking her cheeks. I was used to violence, to anger, to the harsh realities of club life. But with Kasen, my touch turned tender, reverent.

She pressed closer, fingers curling into my cut. A low growl escaped me as the kiss deepened. My mind raced, torn between desire and the ever-present awareness of the dangers we faced.

"We shouldn't," I murmured against her lips, even as I pulled her tighter against me. With the threat hanging over our heads, I needed to be focused on the club right now.

Kasen pulled back just enough to meet my eyes. "We should," she countered, her voice steady. "Life's too short for maybes. Especially in our world. We lost Gears and Bats. What if that had been you? We have no idea what's coming next, or if we'll lose anyone else."

I guided us toward the bed, our movements fluid, almost choreographed. My heart pounded, a mix of desire and the ever-present edge of danger that never quite left me. As we moved, my cut slipped from my shoulders, falling to the floor with a soft *thud*.

Kasen broke our kiss, holding up a hand. "Wait," she whispered.

My body tensed, old instincts kicking in. "What's wrong?"

She smiled, a gentle curve of her lips that eased the sudden tension in my chest. Without a word, she bent down, carefully picking up my cut. Her fingers traced the patches, lingering on the Sergeant-at-Arms rocker.

"This is part of you," Kasen said softly, draping it over a nearby chair. "It deserves respect."

The simple act hit me harder than any punch. This woman understood me, understood the life I'd chosen. Of course, she damn well should, considering who her dad was. I pulled her close, burying my face in her hair.

"Kasen," I breathed, my voice rough with emotion.

She reached for the hem of my shirt, her touch light but purposeful. "Can I?"

I nodded, lifting my arms as she peeled the fabric away. Her eyes roamed over my chest, taking in the scars and tattoos that told the story of my life. The way she looked at me made it feel like this was our first time.

"Your turn," I said, reaching for her.

One by one, I undid the buttons on her shirt, revealing smooth skin beneath. Kasen shrugged out of the garment, letting it fall beside my discarded shirt.

"Beautiful," I murmured, tracing the curve of her collarbone. "No matter how many times I get to see this sight, I'll always be in awe."

Kasen's breath hitched. "Rick, I --"

"Shh," I cut her off gently, pressing a kiss to her shoulder. "No more words. Not now."

She nodded, her hands moving to my belt. The *clink* of metal seemed impossibly loud in the quiet room. I stepped out of my jeans, then helped Kasen with hers.

Standing there, vulnerable in more ways than one, I felt a rare moment of uncertainty. This wasn't just sex. This was Kasen -- my woman. The one I'd desired for far too long. Now she had my property patch, and she'd be by my side the rest of our lives.

"You okay?" Kasen asked, her voice barely above a whisper.

I met her gaze, seeing my own mix of desire mirrored there. "Yeah," I answered honestly. "You?"

She smiled, reaching for me. "Never better."

I laid Kasen down on the bed, my rough hands a

stark contrast to her soft skin. Every touch was deliberate, gentle in a way I'd rarely allowed myself to be. My fingers traced the curve of her hip, the dip of her waist, memorizing every freckle and scar. I wanted the moment to last forever.

I looked up, meeting her eyes. The vulnerability there matched my own, and for once, I didn't fight it. Her hand cupped my cheek. I leaned into her touch, savoring it.

I leaned down, capturing her lips in a kiss that spoke volumes. It was slow, deep, conveying everything I didn't say out loud. My hands continued their exploration, reverent and careful, as if she might disappear at any moment.

Kasen's fingers trailed down my back and my arms, tracing the ink on my skin. I shivered at her touch, marveling at how she could make me feel so exposed and vulnerable. Not two words I typically associated with myself.

As we came together, it was with an intensity that took my breath away. There was no need for words; every caress, every gasp, every shared look said more than enough. She met my thrusts, as eager as I was. I pressed my forehead to hers as we moved as one.

The world outside ceased to exist. There was only Kasen, only this moment, only us.

When she came, my name was on her lips. The feel of her pussy squeezing my cock was enough to trigger my own release. I thrust into her, not stopping until every drop of cum flooded her pussy. We hadn't discussed children, but at this rate, we'd probably have one or two soon enough.

I traced lazy patterns on Kasen's skin, savoring the warmth of her body against mine. But the afterglow couldn't keep reality at bay for long. My mind raced, calculating risks, mapping out strategies. As much as I wanted to stay here, in the moment, with her, I had other responsibilities. Not to mention the guilt over losing Gears and Bats. They'd died because I'd been careless.

Kasen stirred, her fingers ghosting over my chest. "I can hear you thinking," she murmured.

I exhaled sharply. "Can't shut it off. The cartel --"

"I know." Her voice was soft but firm.

"You could still be a target. They had you before and may intend to grab you again."

Kasen propped herself up on an elbow, eyes flashing. "I've always been a target, Rick. Comes with being Tank's daughter. It's not the first time I've been placed in harm's way. I may not have been in the hands of the bad guys before, but it could have happened."

"It's different now," I said, frustration bleeding through. "They'll use you to get to me. They have to be pissed I took down their men, freed you and those other women. I essentially took money from their pockets. The cartel isn't going to let that go."

"Let them try," Kasen challenged, chin lifting defiantly.

I sat up, running a hand through my hair. "This isn't a game, Kasen. These guys -- they're animals. They won't hesitate to --"

"To what? Hurt me? Kill me?" Her words were sharp, cutting. "I'm not some naive little girl. I know the risks. I still remember how scared I was in Florida. But you showed me more self-defense moves, and now that I've faced them before, I don't think I'll freeze up if it happens again."

"Knowing ain't the same as living it," I snapped,

old fears clawing at my gut. "Look. I've not made it a secret I don't trust women. You're an exception. I've been screwed over one too many times. But there's one that…"

Kasen's hand on my arm, gentle but insistent. "Hey. Look at me."

I turned, meeting her gaze. The fire there matched my own.

"I'm not running," she said, each word clear and deliberate. "Whatever's coming, we face it together. And if you want to talk about the past, I'm here to listen. We're a team now, aren't we?"

I nodded and ran a hand over my face. "Yeah. Just not something I like re-living. Trusted the wrong woman. I was only a teenager. She was a little older. I thought I was hot shit because she was into me. Except it was all a game to her."

"What do you mean?" Kasen asked.

"I had a sister once. About nine years younger than me. I've never told anyone about her. Far as the club is concerned, I'm an only child."

"What happened?" She reached over and took my hand.

"The woman used me to get close to my family. Then she lured my little sister." My hands fisted as the memories washed over me. The fear. The helplessness. Betrayal. "Mary was only seven. She'd been a surprise for my parents, who thought they'd never have more children. We never found her."

"Then how do you know for sure what happened?" she asked.

"The woman I'd been dating was caught and questioned. They ran her prints. Found out she'd been a missing child herself. The men who took her used her up, then trained her to bring in more girls. But when the police went to check the location she'd given them, the men were long gone... and so was Mary."

"I'm so sorry." She leaned into me. "I guess when I was taken it made you feel like you were living it all over again."

"Except this time, I saw it happen and was able to get you back. I have no idea if Mary is still alive, or how much she suffered. Part of me hopes she died shortly after she was taken. I think that would be far more merciful." I sighed. "She'd be in her mid-thirties now if she were still alive."

I gripped Kasen's hand, my fingers intertwining with hers. The tension in my jaw eased slightly, but my voice remained low, intense. "I swear to you, Kasen, I'll protect you with everything I've got. No matter what it takes."

Her eyes softened, but there was steel beneath. "And I'll be right there with you, Rick. Not as a burden, but as your partner."

"Kasen --"

She pressed a finger to my lips. "Listen. I'm not helpless, despite the fact I got kidnapped before. I've grown up in this life. I'm well aware there are monsters in the shadows, those who wear human faces. I can handle myself, and I can have your back."

I pulled her closer, my forehead resting against hers. "Are you sure you know what you're signing up for?"

"Maybe not," she whispered, her breath warm on my skin. "But I'm choosing it anyway. Choosing you."

My heart thundered in my chest. This woman, so fierce, so loyal -- she was offering everything. I cupped her face in my hands, my thumbs tracing her cheekbones. "I don't deserve you," I murmured.

Kasen's lips curved into a smile. "Tough. You're stuck with me."

I chuckled, the sound rough with emotion. Then, sobering, I locked eyes with her. "I promise you. Whatever comes our way, we face it together. No secrets, no holding back. You're my old lady now, in every sense of the word."

She nodded, her gaze never wavering. "And you're my man. Through hell or high water."

I pulled her down, wrapping her in my arms. As we settled into the bed, I whispered against her hair, "I love you, Kasen. More than I ever thought possible."

"I love you too, Rick," she murmured, her body relaxing against mine.

As sleep began to claim us, I held her tight, my mind finally quieting. Whatever storms were brewing, we'd weather them side by side. For the first time in years, I felt a sense of peace. With Kasen by my side, I was ready to face whatever came our way. At least, I hoped like hell I was.

A distant crash jolted me awake. A quick glance at the clock showed I'd only been asleep a few hours. My body tensed, instantly alert. Kasen stirred beside me, her breathing still deep and even. I held my breath, straining to hear.

Silence.

Then, a flicker of movement caught my eye. A shadow passing across the window.

My hand instinctively reached for the gun under my pillow. "Kasen," I whispered, gently shaking her. "Wake up, darlin'."

Her eyes fluttered open, confusion quickly replaced by understanding as she caught my expression. "What is it?" she mouthed.

"Not sure," I murmured, sliding out of bed.

"Stay here."

Kasen sat up, shaking her head. "Like hell I will."

I bit back a growl of frustration. This woman would be the death of me. "Fine. But stay behind me."

She grabbed my shirt off the floor and tugged it on. I pulled on my boxers, and we crept toward the window, the floorboards creaking beneath our feet. I peered out, scanning the darkness.

Nothing.

Then, a flash of metal in the moonlight. A car, idling near the fence line. Maybe I hadn't heard a crash but a car door? I'd been asleep after all. I may not have heard what I thought I did.

"Shit," I hissed.

Kasen's hand found mine, squeezing tight. "Think it's the cartel?"

I nodded grimly. "Most likely. We need to move. Now."

As we scrambled to finish dressing, my mind raced. The peace we'd found was shattered, reality crashing back in. How the hell had they gotten so close? It just proved that no matter how tight we thought we had this place locked down, the evil bastards coming for us would always find a way inside.

I shot off a text to Savior, Saint, and Wire, alerting them. Hopefully, Wire would be able to get a better look at the vehicle on one of his cameras. It looked like shit was about to hit the fan.

Chapter Seventeen

Tempest

I pushed open the heavy clubhouse door, a wall of noise hitting me like a physical force. The air crackled with tension and urgency.

Voices shouted over each other, boots stomped across creaking floorboards, and the metallic *clang* of weapons being checked and loaded punctuated it all. My eyes swept the room, taking in the sea of leather cuts and patches from our allied clubs.

Scratch from Devil's Boneyard caught my eye, giving a curt nod. Beside him, Jackal and Irish stood alert. Angel and Killer from Twisted Tides huddled in a corner, heads bent in intense discussion. I'd been surprised when they'd shown up on our doorstep early this morning, but they said Tiger wanted retribution for what the cartel had done to their club. It was their way of lending a hand while getting even.

The Hades Abyss crew -- Stone, Poison, and Bones -- were spread out, watchful gazes scanning constantly. I'd been especially glad to see Bones, since I knew he was a doctor. I had a feeling we'd need all the medical help we could get.

And there, by the bar, Scorpion, Colorado, and Silver from Devil's Fury nursed drinks, coiled tension evident in every line of their bodies. The Savage Raptors had wanted to send men, but Bull had asked them to stay put, since his daughter, Isy, and his son, Foster, both lived there now. It probably gave him peace of mind knowing they'd be safe, and if no one from their club was present, they wouldn't be on the cartel's radar.

So many here, ready to spill blood for us. The weight of responsibility pressed down, threatening to crush me.

"Wire set up yet?" I asked of no one in particular, my voice cutting through the din.

A Prospect jerked his thumb toward a side room. "In there, Tempest."

I stalked over, my body humming with barely contained energy. Wire was hunched over a table, surrounded by a mess of wires, screens, and blinking lights. His fingers flew across keyboards, face bathed in the blue glow of multiple monitors.

"How's it coming?" I asked, leaning in.

Wire didn't even look up. "Almost there. Give me five more minutes and we'll have eyes everywhere within a five-mile radius. All the cameras inside the compound, as well as those monitoring our property line, are already up and running."

I grunted, impressed despite myself. "Good. We can't afford any blind spots."

Should have done this shit a long time ago. Maybe things had been too peaceful. Or we were just getting too old for this shit. Not that it would really matter. Something could still go wrong. Power outage would kill any advantage we had.

"Won't have 'em," Wire muttered, his focus laser-sharp. "I've got thermal imaging, night vision, motion sensors... if a fucking squirrel farts near this place, we'll know about it."

A savage grin tugged at my lips. "Perfect."

I watched him work for a moment, marveling at how his usual energy was channeled into absolute concentration. My own restlessness itched beneath my skin, demanding action.

"You need anything?" I asked, already knowing the answer.

Wire shook his head, still not looking away from

his screens. "Nah. Just keep everyone out of here for a bit. Can't have some drunken asshole tripping over my setup."

"I'd ask who the fuck would be drinking at a time like this, but shit. I'd down a bottle of whiskey if I could." I turned to leave. "You got it. Holler when it's ready for a test run."

"Wait," he said. "I want Lavender and Atlas here. They can help with all this, and both can hack into systems as well as I can. In fact, Atlas may have surpassed me already."

"What about Livvy?" I asked, wondering where his daughter would be if the rest of her family was here.

"She's already with Ares, Junie, Judd, and Marnie. Prophet is watching them for now, but when he's needed, he has a plan in place," Wire said.

"Fine. Get Lavender and Atlas here. You can have whatever you need."

As I stepped back into the main room, the noise washed over me again. My fists clenched involuntarily. So much left to do, so many variables to account for. And somewhere out there, enemies circling, waiting to strike.

My blood sang for violence, for the simplicity of fists and fury. But I couldn't indulge. Not yet. I had a club to protect, a woman to keep safe.

I took a deep breath, forcing the rage down. Time to get to work.

I strode down the hallway, the muffled sounds of preparation fading behind me. The supply room door stood ajar, and I pushed it open, revealing our Prospect, Caden, hunched over a clipboard.

"How we looking?" I barked, causing him to jump.

Caden spun around, eyes wide. "Jesus, Tempest! Didn't hear you coming."

I raised an eyebrow. "You'd better work on that. A distracted biker's a dead biker."

He swallowed hard, nodding. "Yes, sir. Sorry, sir."

"Cut the 'sir' shit," I said. "Just give me the rundown."

Caden's eyes darted to his clipboard. "Right. We've got enough water to last a week, maybe two, canned goods for at least two weeks. Medical supplies are good -- bandages, antibiotics, pain meds. Even managed to score some suture kits."

I grunted, impressed despite myself. Even though the last run had ended in disaster, we'd had no choice but to try again. At least this time, we'd managed to bring back some stuff. "Not bad, Prospect. What about ammo?"

"Enough to start a small war," he said, a hint of pride creeping into his voice.

"Good," I said. "Because that might be exactly what we're facing."

"And um, I also got my hands on some grenades. Probably not something we want to use at the compound, but we'll have them if we ever need them."

I just shook my head but smiled. Kid had a good head on his shoulders. One day, he'd patch in and be a brother. I had no doubt about it.

Leaving Caden to his inventory, I made my way to the war room, which had been Church until this morning. Viking stood hunched over a map. His eyes, cold and calculating, traced invisible lines across the paper.

"Talk to me," I said, stepping up beside him.

Viking's finger jabbed at a spot on the map.

"We've got three primary safe houses secured, all outside of town. The Devil's Boneyard came through big time. In addition to the men here, each club sent a few to guard the safe houses. Reckless Kings even sent Copper, Wrangler, and Nitro."

I nodded. "And the buses?"

"Two of 'em," Viking confirmed. "Small, windows tinted dark as night. They'll get our people out clean if it comes to that. Stashed them behind the compound. As long as we keep the cartel focused on us here, they should be able to slip away."

My mind immediately went to Kasen, her face flashing before my eyes. I pushed the image away, forcing myself to focus.

"What about here?" I asked, pointing to a winding road leading out of town.

Viking shook his head. "Too exposed. We'd be sitting ducks if they caught wind of us."

I cursed under my breath. "All right, what's our best option for getting Kasen and her sisters out?"

Viking's eyebrow quirked up slightly, but he didn't comment on my specific concern. Smart man.

"This route," he said, tracing a line with his finger. "It's longer, but there are multiple turnoffs, good cover. We can have decoys ready if needed. As you requested, there's an armored vehicle waiting for them and Emmie."

I studied the map, picturing the terrain. "It'll work. But we need a fallback. If things go to shit, I want options."

Viking nodded, his face grim. "Always. I've got three alternate routes planned. We're not leaving anything to chance. You sure about the place you're sending them?"

I grunted. Not entirely, but it was better to get

them all far from the club, and any other clubs. Which meant I'd have to fall back on someone I'd known my entire life. Joel Drewry had made a name for himself as one of the top assassins in the world. In fact, his kill count was higher than Casper VanHorne's and Specter's. Possibly combined. If anyone could keep them safe, it would be him.

I clapped Viking on the shoulder, feeling the solid muscle beneath my hand. "Good work, brother. Now let's make sure everyone knows their part."

I strode across the clubhouse, my boots echoing on the hardwood. The weight of responsibility pressed down on me, but I stood tall, shoulders back. This was my job now. Sergeant-at-Arms. Protector.

"Wire! Sticks!" I barked, my voice cutting through the din. "Kitchen. Now."

They snapped to attention, following me without question. Good men. Loyal. I'd need that loyalty in the hours to come.

We crowded into the room. I spread the map on the table, my fingers tracing the routes Viking and I had discussed.

"Listen up," I growled, my eyes boring into each of them. "We've got a storm coming. And we need to be ready."

Wire leaned forward, his tech-savvy brain already whirring. "What's the plan, Tempest?"

I took a deep breath, steadying myself. "Two buses. Tinted windows. We're getting our families out if things go south. Wire, I need you on comms. Every vehicle needs to be synced and secure. They're stashed out behind the compound. Hopefully, the cartel hasn't noticed them, or connected them to us if they did see them."

He nodded, fingers already twitching as if typing

on an invisible keyboard. "I'm on it. I'll have a closed network up within the hour."

"Sticks." I turned to our drummer, his usual easygoing demeanor replaced with fierce determination. "You're on escort duty. Your bike's the quietest. You'll lead the convoy if we need to move."

"You got it, brother," Sticks replied, his voice low and serious.

I leaned in, my voice dropping to a near-whisper. "We've got enemies closing in, and I'll be damned if they touch our people. Understood?"

They nodded, the gravity of the situation evident in their tense postures.

"Good. Now let's move. We've got work to do."

As they filed out, my mind drifted to Kasen again. Her smile. Her laugh. If I had to send her away, I could only hope I'd still be alive when the dust settled so I could go get her. But if anything happened to me and Tank, Joel had his orders.

I pushed the thoughts aside. I had to focus. Had to keep her safe.

Keep them all safe.

* * *

The room crackled with tension as my brothers absorbed the plan. Hammer cracked his knuckles, a grim smile playing on his scarred face. "About damn time we took the fight to them. I owe those bastards for what they did to my son."

His words were a reminder that Sam was still out of commission. For now, he was holed up in his house. I could only hope he'd be safe there.

Saint, the voice of caution, spoke up. "It's risky, Tempest."

I fixed him with a hard stare. "You got a better idea?"

He held my gaze for a moment, then shook his head. "No. I'm with you."

Wire cleared his throat, drawing our attention. He'd been unusually quiet, his fingers dancing across his tablet. "I've got updates on our surveillance," he said, his voice steady despite the gravity of the situation.

I nodded, giving him the floor. Wire's tech skills had saved our asses more times than I could count. Hell, he'd saved men in other clubs as well. When their own tech people couldn't handle shit, they came to him.

He tapped his screen, and a map materialized on the wall above the table. "I've set up a network of cameras and motion sensors around the perimeter," he explained, zooming in on key points. "We'll have real-time intel on any movement within a two-mile radius."

Sticks leaned in, his eyes narrowing. "What about blind spots?"

Wire's lips quirked in a smile. "There aren't any. I've even got drones patrolling the air space. You can thank Livvy for that one. She insisted on helping, even if she couldn't be here with us. Nothing gets in or out without us knowing."

I felt a wave of relief wash over me. This was exactly what we needed. "Good work, Wire," I said, clapping him on the shoulder. "How long before it's fully operational?"

"It already is," he replied, a hint of pride in his voice. "I've synced it with our comms. Everyone will have access to the feed through their phones and we'll all be connected through earpieces."

The tension in the room eased slightly. Having eyes everywhere gave us an edge we desperately needed.

"All right," I said, straightening up. "We've got our plan. We've got our tech. Now let's make sure we're ready for whatever comes our way."

As the others nodded and began to disperse, I caught Wire's eye. "Keep monitoring those feeds," I ordered. "Anything looks off, I want to know immediately."

He gave a curt nod. "You got it."

I turned away, my mind already racing to the next steps. We were as prepared as we could be. Now, we just had to wait for the storm to hit.

The door burst open, and Caden strode in, clipboard clutched tight in his hand. His eyes were bright with nervous energy. Had he gone over the inventory again?

"Found some additional medical supplies. Everything's accounted for," he said.

I nodded, feeling a mix of pride and unease. The kid was stepping up, but the fact we needed all this... it didn't sit well.

"What about sleeping arrangements?" I asked, trying to keep the edge out of my voice. We had too many people here and needed beds. The rest of us could sleep in our homes, but not our guests. I knew a few had already claimed the townhomes near the clubhouse.

Caden straightened, puffing out his chest. "Each bedroom can sleep four now. I've set up bunk beds. It's tight, but we can house everyone who came to help."

"Good work." I turned to find Viking bent over the map, casting a shadow across the table. His finger traced a line, brow furrowed in concentration.

"Viking," I called, moving to join him. "Problem?"

"No, just making sure I didn't miss anything. I

think we're good, or as good as it's going to get."

Now that I'd done what I could, I couldn't help but search for Kasen. I needed to see her. My eyes scanned the crowded clubhouse until I spotted her across the room. She was with Dessa, Savior's old lady, herding kids and organizing the women. My chest tightened.

I made my way over, dodging Prospects and patched members alike. Kasen looked up as I approached, her eyes widening slightly.

"Tempest," she said, voice soft but steady. "Everything okay?"

"Just checking in." I grunted, fighting the urge to reach out and touch her. "You good here?"

Kasen nodded, a determined set to her jaw. "We've got it under control. The kids are scared, but we're keeping them calm. Most are already grouped together in various houses toward the back of the compound."

Dessa chimed in, "We're packing go-bags for everyone, just in case."

"Smart," I said, my gaze locked on Kasen. There was so much I wanted to say, but the words jammed in my throat. Instead, I growled, "You stay close to the exit, you hear me? First sign of trouble, you get these people out."

I'd need to go over the specifics with her, and make sure she knew about the separate vehicle taking her, her mom, and her sisters to safety. There was still too much shit to do.

Kasen's eyes flashed. "I know my job, Tempest. We've got this."

I felt a surge of pride mixed with fear. She was strong, capable. But the thought of her in danger made me want to tear the world apart.

"I know you do," I said, softer this time. Our eyes met, and for a moment, everything else faded away. I saw the worry she was trying to hide, the strength she was determined to show. Without thinking, I reached out and squeezed her hand. "Be safe."

She squeezed back, a small smile tugging at her lips. "You too."

Reluctantly, I turned and walked off. The air crackled with tension, every face set in grim determination. Savior stood at the center of the room, his presence commanding attention without a word.

I took my place beside him, surveying our assembled force. Dixie Reapers, Devil's Boneyard, Twisted Tides, Hades Abyss, Devil's Fury -- all united, ready to face whatever came our way.

"Brothers." Savior's voice cut through the noise. "The storm's coming. But we're ready for it, and this time, we're going to get ahead of it."

A chorus of agreement rumbled through the room. I felt it in my bones, this collective resolve. I only hoped we weren't lying to ourselves and we really were ready for anything. We were more than a club. We were family. And God help anyone who tried to fuck with us.

Chapter Eighteen

Kasen

A deafening roar shattered the quiet evening, the thunderous rumble of motorcycles growing louder as they approached. I stood outside the clubhouse, my heart racing with a mix of excitement and trepidation. The air filled with the acrid scent of gasoline and burning rubber as the Dixie Reapers and their allies rolled in, a sea of leather and chrome.

Tempest's bike led the pack, and I couldn't tear my eyes away from him. He dismounted with fluid grace, his muscled frame commanding attention. My breath caught in my throat as he exchanged nods with the other riders, their silent acknowledgment heavy with the weight of the impending battle.

I hung back, watching as leather-clad men clasped hands and embraced, their gruff voices a low rumble beneath the dying engines. My father, Tank, caught my eye and gave me a subtle nod. I returned it, swallowing hard.

"Quite a sight, isn't it?" Emmie, my mom, appeared beside me.

"Yeah," I murmured, my gaze drifting back to Tempest. He was deep in conversation with Preacher, their expressions grim.

The clubhouse doors swung open, and the bikers began to file inside. I followed, the sudden quiet almost deafening after the roar of engines.

Inside, the atmosphere crackled with energy. Laughter erupted from a corner where Wraith was regaling a group with some outrageous tale. The clinking of glasses and the sharp *crack* of pool balls punctuated the air.

I made my way to the bar, snagging a soda. My

sisters were already there, huddled together and whispering. They waved me over, but I shook my head. My eyes were drawn, as always, to Tempest.

He stood with a group of senior members, his presence magnetic. I wondered, not for the first time, how I'd been so lucky to snag a man like him.

"Earth to Kasen." Owen's voice broke through my thoughts. He nudged me with his elbow. "You're staring again."

I felt heat rush to my cheeks. "Shut up," I muttered, taking a long sip of my drink.

Owen chuckled. "I'm glad the two of you finally figured things out."

I tuned him out, but I had to admit he had a point. If Tempest hadn't kissed me that day, hadn't been watching me, would we be together right now? Probably not. I'd been too chicken to make the first move. Okay, so I'd sort of made a move. At least, to me I had. I wasn't sure how Tempest saw it. I knew he'd had women throw themselves at him over the years. Before the club tossed out all the whores and locked the compound down, except for people Wire and Lavender vetted. Compared to those women, I'd probably been like an awkward teen.

The laughter and chatter around us seemed to swell, a defiant roar against the danger that loomed on the horizon. I let the noise wash over me, trying to lose myself in the moment, but my eyes kept finding their way back to Tempest.

As if sensing my gaze, Tempest's eyes locked with mine. My breath caught in my throat. He moved toward me with purpose, his stride eating up the distance between us. Before I could process what was happening, his arm was around my shoulders, pulling me close.

"Let's give them something to talk about," he murmured, his breath hot against my ear.

My heart hammered as we walked into the center of the room together. Conversations stuttered to a halt, all eyes turning to us. Tempest's arm, heavy and warm across my shoulders, felt like a brand. A declaration.

"I think we can all agree it's amazing our Sergeant-at-Arms got his head out of his ass," Preacher's voice boomed.

Laughter rippled through the crowd. I felt my cheeks burn, but Tempest's grip only tightened.

"I'd started to think they were a lost cause," someone called out.

That familiar tension radiated off Tempest, but when he spoke, his voice was controlled. "All of you think it's so funny. Exactly how many of you were aware of how we felt about each other?"

Silence fell. I held my breath, acutely aware of every pair of eyes on us.

"Everyone but her parents," Saint said.

Then Wraith raised his glass. "To Tempest and Kasen!"

The room erupted in cheers. Glasses clinked, liquor sloshed. The celebration took on a new energy.

"To fallen brothers," Preacher's voice cut through the noise. The mood shifted instantly, smiles fading. "And to the fight ahead."

"To fallen brothers," the crowd echoed, voices thick with emotion.

I glanced up at Tempest. His eyes were dark, filled with a mix of grief and determination that made my heart ache. I knew he blamed himself for what happened to Bats and Gears.

"We'll make it through this," I whispered.

He looked down at me, his expression softening for a moment. "Yeah," he said gruffly. "We will."

I tugged gently on Tempest's hand, leading him away from the crowd. We found a quiet corner, the thumping bass muffled by the old wood paneling. My heart raced as I turned to face him.

"Tempest." I knew my voice was barely audible over the distant roar of the party. "I... I'm scared. I don't want to be, but I am. I'm supposed to be strong, and a support for you and the club, but..."

His calloused fingers brushed my cheek. "Me too, darlin'. Everyone here is worried about tomorrow, but we're all dealing with it in our own ways."

"Promise me you'll be safe," I demanded, gripping his cut. "Promise me."

Tempest's eyes, usually shining with barely contained fury, were uncharacteristically gentle. "I'll always come back to you. Always."

I pressed my forehead against his chest, inhaling the scent of leather and gasoline. I had a feeling he was lying to me, but I'd take it right now. "I've waited so long for this. For us. I can't lose you now."

His arms encircled me, strong and protective. "I know. I'm sorry it took me so long to see what was right in front of me."

Across the room, I caught sight of my father. He stood motionless, his expression unreadable as he watched us. My stomach knotted. He'd begrudgingly given his approval when we'd returned from Florida, but I knew he hadn't liked the thought of me and Tempest together.

I saw Dad's massive frame shift, his boots scuffing against the wooden floor as he began to move in our direction. Each step seemed to echo, despite the noise around us.

Tempest tensed, his grip on me tightening fractionally. I held my breath, waiting for the confrontation I'd feared since I was sixteen.

Dad's imposing figure loomed over us, his eyes flicking between Tempest and me. The air crackled with tension. I felt Tempest's muscles coil, ready to defend us if necessary. He knew as well as I did that my dad didn't like us being together.

But then, something unexpected happened. Dad's stern expression softened, just slightly. He gave a single, curt nod to Tempest. "Take care of her. You get through this and don't leave her alone."

My heart leapt. Was this... acceptance? A true one this time.

Tempest's grip on me loosened, but he didn't let go. "I will defy the devil himself to stay with her."

I opened my mouth, overwhelmed, but before I could speak, Preacher's voice boomed across the room. "Brothers and friends! I need your attention!"

The cacophony of the party died down as all eyes turned to Preacher. He stood on a chair, his presence commanding even without the added height. "Our family has a surprise for Tempest and Kasen," Preacher announced, a smile playing at his lips.

My pulse quickened. What was going on?

Preacher's eyes found ours in the crowd. "We're gonna make it official. Right here, right now. I'm gonna marry you two."

Gasps and cheers erupted around us. I turned to Tempest, shocked. His eyes were wide, mirroring my surprise. It seemed he hadn't known anything about this either.

Preacher held up his hands for silence. "Now, technically, Lavender already did the deed. You know how and she and Wire are about this sort of thing. So if anyone goes digging, they'll find a marriage certificate on file. But I wanted to give you a proper ceremony, surrounded by your family."

Tempest's hand found mine, squeezing tight. "What do you say, darlin'? Ready to be Mrs. Tempest in front of everyone?"

I snorted then giggled. "That's not what my name will be. I'll be Mrs. Brewer."

"You know what I mean. You ready for this?"

My heart soared. This was everything I'd ever dreamed of, and more. "God, yes."

Preacher's voice cut through the excited murmurs, steady and solemn. "Brothers, family, and friends, we gather here to witness the union of two souls forged in fire."

I stood before him, Tempest's hand a lifeline in mine. My heart hammered against my ribs as Preacher's words washed over us.

"Love in our world isn't soft," he intoned. "It's as hard as the road beneath our wheels, as fierce as the wind in our faces. Tempest, Kasen -- you've chosen a path that demands loyalty above all else."

Tempest's grip tightened. I glanced up, catching the intensity burning in his eyes.

Preacher continued, "In this family, in this life, we stand together against all storms. Your love must be a shield, your bond unbreakable."

I swallowed hard, feeling the weight of every word. This wasn't just a ceremony. It was a vow to the club, to our way of life. He'd never done a ceremony like this one before. Was it because I was the daughter of the ex-Sergeant-at-Arms and was now marrying the new one?

"Tempest." Preacher's gaze locked onto him. "Do you swear to protect Kasen, to cherish her, to stand by her side come hell or high water?"

Tempest's voice was raw with emotion. "I swear it. On my life, on my patch."

"Kasen." Preacher turned to me. "Do you swear to support Tempest, to be his anchor, his home no matter how dark the road ahead?"

I looked up at Tempest, seeing our future in his eyes. "I do," I said, my voice stronger than I expected. "Always."

Tempest's hand trembled in mine as we exchanged rings -- simple bands that felt heavier than the world. I didn't know how they had gotten them, or how they'd known our sizes, but they fit perfectly.

"By the power vested in me," Preacher's voice rang out, "I now pronounce you husband and wife. May your love be as eternal as the brotherhood that binds us all."

The room exploded. A deafening roar of cheers and whistles engulfed us as Tempest pulled me into a searing kiss. I melted against him, the world fading away for a heartbeat.

"Get it, brother!" someone hollered, followed by raucous laughter.

We broke apart, grinning like fools. Hands reached for us from all sides -- palms slapping Tempest's back, gentler touches squeezing my shoulders. The air was thick with cigar smoke and the scent of leather.

"Welcome to the family, asshole," Dad said, holding his hand out to Tempest. My husband shook it, just grinning like a fool. Then Dad gave me a bear hug, lifting me off my feet, before he walked off to join Mom and my sisters.

Tempest leaned in close, his breath hot on my ear. "You okay?"

I nodded, overwhelmed. "Never better."

Someone cranked up the music, and Lynyrd Skynyrd's "Free Bird" blasted through the speakers. Bodies moved, a sea of leather and denim.

"Drinks!" Preacher bellowed. "Let's give these two a proper send-off!"

I caught a glimpse of his face -- the stern officiant replaced by a grinning brother, already reaching for a bottle of whiskey.

Tempest's arm snaked around my waist, anchoring me. "Ready to face the madness, Mrs. Brewer?"

A thrill shot through me at the name. I grinned up at him. "Bring it on."

The music shifted, a slower melody threading through the air. Tempest's grip on my waist tightened, his eyes shining as he pulled me close.

"Dance with me," he said, more command than request.

We swayed together, an island of calm in the swirling chaos. Tempest's body was a solid wall of heat against mine, his hands splayed possessively across my lower back. I breathed in his scent -- leather, motor oil, and something uniquely him.

"Never thought I'd have this," he murmured, his voice rough with emotion.

I looked up, meeting his intense gaze. "Have what?"

"You. This." His fingers flexed against my skin. "A Goddamn future worth fighting for."

"We're going to make it through this, Tempest. Together."

He nodded, jaw tight. I could feel the tension radiating off him, the barely contained rage that always simmered beneath the surface. But when he looked at me, his eyes softened.

"I love you, Kasen," he said, the words fierce and low. "Whatever happens tomorrow --"

I silenced him with a kiss. "Don't. We have tonight."

As we danced, I noticed the mood in the room shifting. Laughter died down, replaced by hushed conversations. Couples clung to each other a little tighter. Children, yawning, were ushered toward the exit.

Dad caught my eye from across the room. He jerked his chin toward the door, a silent command. It was time. Somehow, he knew exactly what I needed right now, and he was making sure I had it.

Tempest noticed too. His arm tightened around me possessively. "Ready to go home, wife?"

The word sent a shiver down my spine. "Lead the way, husband."

I slipped my hand into Tempest's, our fingers intertwining as we stepped outside. The cool night air hit my flushed skin, a stark contrast to the stuffy warmth of the clubhouse.

The parking lot was nearly empty now, most of our family and friends having already left. The roar of engines had faded to an eerie silence, broken only by the chirp of crickets and our soft footsteps on gravel.

We walked a short distance, coming to a stop at the edge of the lot. I tilted my head back, taking in the vast expanse of stars above us. They seemed impossibly bright tonight, as if the universe itself was bearing witness to our union.

Tempest's grip on my hand tightened. I glanced up at him, struck by the play of moonlight across his features. He scanned the dark outside the compound as if searching for unseen enemies.

"What are you thinking?" I asked softly.

He exhaled sharply. "That I should be focusing on strategy, on keeping everyone safe tomorrow." His gaze dropped to mine, intense and conflicted. "Instead, all I can think about is you."

My heart raced. "Is that such a bad thing?"

"It's fucking terrifying." He pulled me closer. "I've never had so much to lose."

I pressed my palm against his chest, feeling the rapid thud of his heartbeat. "You're not going to lose me, Tempest. We're in this together, remember?"

He cupped my face in his large hands. "Promise me something, Kasen."

"Anything," I whispered.

"If things go sideways tomorrow… you follow instructions and get your ass to the back of the compound. I have a vehicle waiting to get you, your sisters, and your mom the hell out of here. No matter what happens, you get to that vehicle. Understand?"

I opened my mouth to argue, but the raw fear in his eyes stopped me. Instead, I nodded, knowing it was a lie even as I spoke. There was no way in hell I'd leave him behind. "I promise."

Chapter Nineteen

Tempest

The roar of motorcycles faded as we approached the cartel's hideout, slowing our pace. Once we stopped, the silence that followed was thick with tension. I raised my fist, signaling my team to wait. My heart pounded, a steady drumbeat of anticipation.

"Eyes sharp," I said, my voice barely above a whisper. "One wrong move, and we're fucked."

The rough side of town stretched before us, a maze of dilapidated buildings and shadowy alleys. Perfect for an ambush. I scanned our surroundings, every muscle coiled tight, ready to spring into action. Once we'd informed Chief Daniels the cartel was lurking here and out for blood, he'd guaranteed we'd have the time we needed to clean this up. Without worrying about the involvement of the local law. Sometimes it was good to have a police chief who had family in a club.

The cul-de-sac loomed ahead, a hive of criminal activity. From what we'd discovered, they'd taken over all four houses. I just hoped like fuck our intel was correct. I didn't need any damn surprises. My jaw tightened as I spotted the first line of cartel guards, their weapons glinting in the dim streetlights.

Bastards won't know what hit them.

I gestured to my team, watching with grim satisfaction as they fanned out, taking their positions with practiced precision. Pride swelled in my chest, tempered by the weight of responsibility. As Sergeant-at-Arms, their lives were in my hands.

"Remember," I murmured, locking eyes with each of my brothers. "No hesitation. No mercy."

They nodded, faces set with determination. I

took a deep breath, steadying the rage that always simmered just beneath the surface. Tonight, I'd unleash it.

With a sharp nod, I gave the signal. The air erupted with gunfire, shattering the night's silence. I surged forward, my weapon an extension of my arm, my anger fueling each shot.

"For our fallen!" I roared, my battle cry echoing through the streets.

Chaos engulfed us, bullets whizzing past as we pushed deeper into enemy territory. The acrid smell of gunpowder filled my nostrils, mixing with the metallic tang of blood.

This is what I was made for.

A cartel guard appeared in my sights. I pulled the trigger without hesitation, watching him crumple to the ground. No time for remorse. Only survival.

"Tempest!" one of my brothers shouted. "On your six!"

I spun, narrowly avoiding a bullet that grazed my cheek. The sting of it only fueled my rage. I returned fire, my aim true and deadly.

As we advanced, the weight of my role pressed down on me. Every decision, every life lost or saved, rested on my shoulders. But I'd be damned if I let the cartel win.

Not today. Not ever.

Savior's voice crackled through my earpiece, sharp and authoritative. "Tempest, watch your left flank. Wire's picking up movement."

I pivoted, scanning the shadows. Sure enough, two cartel thugs emerged, guns blazing. I ducked behind a rusted-out car, bullets pinging off the metal.

"Copy that," I said, my heart pounding. "Saint, we need cover fire on the east side."

"On it," Saint's voice came back, calm despite the chaos. "Wire, got eyes on any snipers?"

A burst of static, then Wire's analytical tone cut through. "Thermal's showing two heat signatures on the roof, northwest corner. Could be spotters or shooters."

I processed the info, my mind racing. "Boneyard, take those roof rats out. Prophet, Tank, Venom, and Stone, with me. We're pushing forward."

Gritting my teeth against the pain in my cheek, I signaled and we moved as one, a well-oiled machine of violence and vengeance. Even though Venom didn't remember a lot of things, he was still a Reaper down to his soul, and I knew I could rely on him. But his woman would lose her shit if he got hurt again.

The air was thick with gun smoke and screams. I fired, reloaded, fired again. Each shot was for our club, for our family.

"Tempest." Savior's voice filled my ear again, urgent this time. "Wire's picked up chatter. They're calling in reinforcements from the south."

"Shit," I muttered, ducking as a bullet whizzed past my ear. "Saint, can you send someone to intercept?"

"Negative," Saint replied, frustration evident. "Everyone's actively fighting or pinned down."

My mind raced, anger threatening to cloud my judgment. I took a deep breath, forcing myself to focus. "Wire, how long till they arrive?"

"They're coming in from the surrounding homes. They're already there."

We were outnumbered, outgunned, and running out of time. But giving up wasn't an option. Not for me, not for the Dixie Reapers, or the other clubs fighting with us.

"Listen up," I said into the comm. "We've got to end this. Hit 'em hard, hit 'em fast. No prisoners, no mercy."

With renewed fury, we surged forward into the fray, the fate of our families hanging in the balance.

As we pressed forward, my eyes caught a flash of movement. Through the chaos, I spotted him -- a cartel bigwig barking orders, orchestrating the reinforcements. His crisp suit and air of authority stood out amidst the bloodshed.

"Cover me," I said to Viking.

Without waiting for a response, I broke from our formation, weaving through the melee. Bullets zinged past, but I was focused, driven. This bastard was the key.

I vaulted over a smoldering car, landing in a crouch just yards from my target. Our eyes locked. In that moment, everything else faded away. It was just us -- predator and prey, though who was which remained to be seen.

He sneered, reaching for his weapon. "You're out of your league, biker trash."

"We'll see about that," I said, lunging forward.

Our bodies collided with brutal force. I felt the air rush from his lungs as we hit the ground. But he was no pushover. A vicious elbow caught me in the ribs, sending shockwaves of pain through my body.

I retaliated with a headbutt, feeling cartilage crunch beneath my forehead. Blood sprayed, but neither of us relented. We rolled, trading blows, each strike fueled by desperation and hate. I needed to make this fucker hurt! A quick death was too fucking good for him.

He managed to get a hand on his gun. Instinct took over. I grabbed his wrist, twisting savagely. The crack of bone was barely audible over the din of battle, but the agonized howl that followed was music to my ears.

"Not so tough now, are ya?" I taunted, my own voice rough with exertion.

He spat blood in my face. "Fuck you and your whole club. We'll bury every last one of you."

Rage surged through me, white-hot and all-consuming. I wanted to end him, to feel his life drain away beneath my hands. But we needed information. I needed to know how they'd found us and the Twisted Tides. Where had I fucked up?

Instead, I leaned in close, my voice a deadly whisper. "You first, asshole."

The chaos around us intensified. Gunfire erupted in deafening bursts, punctuated by the sharp crack of explosions. Through the comms, I heard Saint's voice, tight with tension.

"You've got incoming! At least a dozen more from the east!"

I risked a glance away from my captive. The street had transformed into a war zone. Smoke billowed from burning vehicles, obscuring visibility. My brothers fought with ruthless efficiency, but we were outnumbered.

"Hold the line!" I roared, hoping my voice carried over the din.

Beneath me, the cartel leader bucked, nearly dislodging my grip. I slammed him back down, pinning him with my full weight.

"You're finished," I growled. "Tell me where --"

A flash of movement caught my eye. Pure instinct took over.

I rolled, narrowly avoiding the spray of bullets that tore into the pavement where I'd been kneeling.

My captive wasn't so lucky. He jerked and went still, caught in the crossfire.

"Shit!" I scrambled for cover behind a burnt-out car, my heart pounding. Where the hell had that come from? Had they killed one of their own on purpose?

Another burst of gunfire answered my question. A sniper, hidden in one of the upper windows. I was pinned down, exposed, with no clear shot.

"Wire!" I barked into my comm. "I need eyes on that shooter, now!"

The bullet sliced across my bicep, a line of fire that ignited every nerve. I hissed through clenched teeth, adrenaline dulling the worst of it. No time for pain. Not now.

"Second floor, northwest corner!" Wire said.

I took a steadying breath, letting the familiar rage fuel me. In one fluid motion, I pivoted from behind the car, my gun already raised. The world narrowed to my sights and the shadowy figure in the window.

Two shots. Clean. Precise.

The sniper's rifle clattered to the street below. A beat of silence, then the thud of a body following.

"Target neutralized." I scanned for any other immediate threats.

A low chuckle drew my attention. The cartel leader had dragged himself to his feet, blood seeping from a wound in his side. I'd thought for sure the fucker was dead, but no such luck. The fact he was standing wasn't the issue. It was the gun in his hand making my blood run cold.

"Impressive, Tempest," he sneered, leveling the weapon at my chest. "But this ends now."

I didn't flinch, meeting his gaze with barely contained fury. He knew who I was. Sure, my name was on my cut, but I didn't know if he'd read it while we fought, or if he'd looked into me beforehand.

We circled each other slowly, predators sizing up their prey. The sounds of battle faded to a dull roar in my ears. There was only us, locked in this deadly dance.

"Your little crusade ends here," the leader taunted. "You have no idea what forces you're messing with."

I spat blood, never taking my eyes off him. "I know exactly what I'm dealing with. Scum like you, thinking you can come into our town and run things. You took my fucking wife! Your fucking men started this shit."

His finger tightened on the trigger. "Unfortunate choice of target. I can admit as much. But you should have just let her go. Plenty of women out there. You're in over your head. Last chance to walk away."

A humorless laugh escaped me. "That's not how the Dixie Reapers operate. We finish what we start."

The tension crackled between us, a powder keg waiting for a spark.

The cartel leader's eyes narrowed. He fired.

I twisted the moment I saw him squeeze the trigger, the bullet searing across my side. Pain exploded, but I channeled it into action. In one fluid motion, I closed the distance between us.

"Fuck!" I snarled, driving my fist into his solar plexus.

He doubled over, gasping. I wrenched the gun from his grasp, tossing it aside. My next blow caught him square in the jaw.

"That's for thinking you could take our town," I growled, following up with a vicious uppercut. "For taking my woman."

The leader staggered, blood streaming from his

split lip. He swung wildly, but his movements were sluggish. I easily dodged, retaliating with a swift kick to his knee.

As he crumpled, I seized the front of his shirt. "And this," I hissed, "is for the Dixie Reapers. The men you've killed or injured."

My final punch connected with a sickening crunch. The cartel leader slumped to the ground, unconscious.

Breathing heavily, I surveyed the chaos around me. Gunfire still echoed, but it was sporadic now. Through the haze of smoke, I saw my brothers advancing, cartel members retreating or surrendering.

"Status report," I barked into my comm.

"We've got the upper hand, Tempest," Wire's voice crackled. "They're falling back on all fronts."

A grim smile tugged at my lips. "Good. Let's finish this."

I took a step toward my team, ready to regroup and push our advantage. That's when the world exploded.

The blast hit like a freight train, hurling me off my feet. My back slammed into something hard, knocking the wind from my lungs. Debris rained down, pelting my skin with stinging shrapnel.

"Fuck!" I gasped, struggling to breathe through the thick cloud of dust.

My ears rang, muffling the chaos around me. Blinking furiously, I tried to clear my vision, but everything swam in a hazy blur. The coppery taste of blood filled my mouth.

"Tempest!" Someone was shouting, their voice distant and distorted. "Tempest, report!"

I attempted to respond but only managed a ragged cough. My body felt like one massive bruise, every movement sending jolts of pain through my nerves.

Gritting my teeth, I forced myself to move. *Get up. Get the fuck up*!

Slowly, agonizingly, I pushed myself to my knees. The world tilted dangerously, and I had to fight the urge to vomit. As the dust began to settle, I could make out shadowy figures moving through the wreckage.

"Wire," I croaked into my comm. "What the hell was that?"

Static crackled, then Wire's voice came through, tense and urgent. "IED, looks like. Bastards had a failsafe. Tempest, you need to move. Now!"

I staggered to my feet, swaying. That's when I saw him -- a cartel member emerging from the smoke, pistol aimed squarely at my chest.

Our eyes locked. Time seemed to freeze.

"Well, shit," I muttered, staring down the barrel of his gun.

Chapter Twenty

Tempest

My eyes fluttered open, the world a blur of muted colors and hazy shapes. Where the hell was I? The sterile smell hit me first -- antiseptic and bleach. Hospital. Fuck.

I blinked hard, trying to clear my vision. A warm pressure on my hand. Soft fingers intertwined with mine.

"Tempest?" A familiar voice, barely above a whisper. "Can you hear me?"

I turned my head, wincing at the sharp pain that lanced through my skull. Kasen's face swam into focus, her blue eyes wide with concern.

"Hey," I croaked, my throat raw. "What happened?"

Kasen leaned in closer, her breath warm on my cheek. "You're okay. You're safe now."

Safe? What the fuck did that mean? My mind raced, grasping for memories that slipped away like smoke.

"The club..." I started, but Kasen squeezed my hand, cutting me off.

"Shh, don't try to talk too much. You need to rest."

I growled in frustration, struggling to piece together the fragments in my head. Gunshots. Screaming. The metallic tang of blood.

Kasen's thumb traced soothing circles on my palm. "I was so worried," she murmured, her voice cracking slightly. "When they brought you in..."

I stared at her, really seeing her for the first time. Dark circles under her eyes, hair pulled back in a messy ponytail. How long had she been here?

"You stayed," I said, the words coming out rougher than I intended.

A faint blush colored her cheeks. "Of course, I did. I couldn't leave you."

"What if they'd had two groups? The compound could have been hit. The club would have been blindsided, and you'd have…"

She pressed her finger over my lips. "I'm fine. Nothing happened at the compound."

Something shifted in my chest, an unfamiliar warmth spreading through me. "The others. Are they…"

Kasen's expression tightened. "Later," she said firmly. "Right now, you need to focus on getting better."

I opened my mouth to argue, but exhaustion hit me like a freight train. My eyelids grew heavy, the room starting to fade around the edges.

"Rest," Kasen whispered, her lips brushing my forehead. "I'll be here when you wake up."

As I drifted off, one thought echoed in my mind: Thank God I'd made it out of there alive.

* * *

I gritted my teeth, determined to push through the fog of pain and medication. With a grunt, I tried to lever myself up on my elbows. A searing bolt of agony ripped through my side and chest, stealing my breath.

"Tempest, no!" Kasen's voice was sharp, her hand pressing firmly against my shoulder. "You're not ready to move yet."

I glared at her, frustration boiling in my veins. "I'm fine," I said, but even I could hear the weakness in my voice.

Kasen's eyes flashed, a hint of steel beneath her concern. "You're not fine. You're hurt, and you need to rest." Her tone softened, "Please, just... lie back down. Do you have any idea how close I was to losing you? Please. Do this for me?"

Something in her voice, a mix of worry and determination, made me relent. I sank back into the pillow, hating how vulnerable I felt.

"What happened?" I demanded, my words clipped. "Tell me everything."

Kasen sighed, her fingers intertwining with mine. "We hit them hard. The cartel's operations are in shambles. But you didn't manage to take them all out, and there are apparently a lot more scattered all over the world." A ghost of a smile crossed her face. "For now it's over."

"But?" I interrupted, sensing the weight behind her words.

Her smile faded. "But it came at a cost. We lost... we lost good men. Not just the Dixie Reapers."

A familiar rage building inside me. "Who?"

Kasen's gaze met mine, filled with a mix of sorrow and resolve. "Stone and Smoke from the Hades Abyss. Scorpion from the Devil's Fury. And... Slayer. We lost Slayer."

The names hit me like physical blows. Gone. All of them. "Fuck," I whispered, squeezing my eyes shut against the onslaught of emotions threatening to overwhelm me.

My knuckles went white against the hospital sheets. Slayer's face flashed in my mind -- that cocky grin, the way he'd strut despite his prosthetic. Gone. All of them, gone.

"There's more," Kasen said softly, her hand tightening on mine. "Sticks, Hammer, Scratch, and Poison... they're alive, but badly hurt. Bones arranged for Poison and Scratch to return to their hometowns, but they're in the hospital like you."

A roar built in my chest, my body tensing to spring into action. But pain lanced through me, a brutal reminder of my own injuries.

"I should've been there," I snarled, more to myself than Kasen. "I could've --"

"You'd be dead too," Kasen cut in, her voice sharp. "You almost were. Do you remember anything?"

I turned to her, noting the look in her eyes stopped me. Fierce determination mixed with something deeper, something that made my chest tighten. "No. What happened to me?"

"Gunshot to the chest, another to your abdomen, and the man kicked you in the temple while you were down. Viking killed the man responsible. You were in surgery for so damn long. Flatlined twice. I've never been so terrified in my life!"

She took a breath and I saw tears mist her eyes. I squeezed her hand, letting her know I was still alive, still with her.

"You've been out for three weeks. They induced a coma so you could properly heal. They said you had cerebral edema, most likely from the kick or even the explosion."

I tried to process everything she'd said. Fuck. I really had nearly died, hadn't I? No, according to her, I had died -- twice. Which meant I'd almost made her a widow less than twenty-four hours after we'd been married.

"We need you alive, Tempest," she said softly. "The club needs you. I..."

She trailed off, busying herself with adjusting my pillows. Her hands were gentle, a stark contrast to the turmoil I felt inside.

"We're not beaten," Kasen continued, her voice low and steady. "The brothers are rallying. Plans are being made to rebuild, to come back stronger."

I watched her, noting the subtle tremor in her hands, the tightness around her eyes. She was holding it together, for me.

"Tell me," I said, my voice rough. "Tell me everything."

I gripped the hospital bed rails, my knuckles turning white. "I need to know more, Kasen. What's happening with the club?"

Kasen hesitated, her eyes flicking to the monitors beside me. "You need rest, Tempest. Your body --"

"Fuck rest," I said, the words clipped and sharp. "I'm Sergeant-at-Arms. I need to know."

She sighed, relenting. "The club is in utter chaos, but we're not broken. Funerals..." Her voice caught. "We've arranged services for Gears, Bats, and Slayer. Savior said he'd told you that you'd be responsible for paying for them, but the club disagreed. Everyone split the cost."

Gears, with his magic touch for engines. *Bats*, whose ears could pick up a whisper from across the room. *Slayer*, tough as nails even with his prosthetic. Their lives all snuffed out far too soon. "The other MCs?" I pressed.

"They took their dead and wounded home," Kasen replied. "But they're with us, Tempest. This attack... it's united us like never before. None of them blame you for what happened, so please don't feel guilty. They've all said to call if we need anything, and I'm supposed to update everyone on your recovery."

I nodded, my mind already racing. Alliances to solidify, revenge to plan, a club to rebuild. The pain in my body faded to background noise as determination surged through me. "We'll hit back," I said, my voice low and deadly. "Harder than they could ever imagine."

Kasen's eyes met mine, worry and admiration warring in her gaze. "I know you want to, but this is far bigger than anything we can all handle. Savior and the other club presidents all agree we need to stand down and see if the cartel makes a move. Wire is watching them like a hawk. One sign they're going to retaliate, and we'll start strategizing again. Until then, we're all supposed to just recover."

I didn't answer. I couldn't. The rage was building, a familiar inferno that threatened to consume everything. But as I looked at Kasen, I felt an anchor. A reason to hold on to some piece of myself in the coming storm. "What about the neighborhood we were in?" I asked.

"Chief Daniels had already made sure no citizens were present. The homes there might be nothing but rubble, but no innocents were hurt."

I swallowed hard, the inferno in my chest dimming to embers. "Kasen, I..." The words stuck in my throat. Vulnerability wasn't my strong suit.

She leaned closer, her eyes searching mine. "What is it, Tempest?"

"I'm scared," I admitted, the confession tasting like ash. "Not of dying. Of failing them. The club, the dead, you. If I'd just done something different, would they all be alive?"

Kasen's hand tightened on mine. "You haven't failed us. We're in this together. All of us."

I looked away, shame burning hot. "You don't know the darkness in me, Kasen. The things I'm capable of... What I wanted to do to those men. What I *still* want to do."

"I've seen your darkness," she interrupted. "And I'm still here."

My eyes snapped back to hers, surprised. She reached out, her fingers brushing a stray lock of hair from my forehead. The gentleness of her touch sent a shiver through me.

"You're not alone in this fight," Kasen murmured. "I promise you that."

I squeezed her hand, words failing me. In that moment, the connection between us deepened, and it felt as if we had a silent understanding.

I took a deep breath, wincing at the pain. "What happens now, Kasen? The club's in shambles, so many of our brothers are dead or wounded."

Her eyes flashed with determination. "We may be down, but we aren't out! I told you we could rebuild. Stronger than before."

"Just like that?" I couldn't keep the bitterness from my voice.

"No, not 'just like that,'" Kasen shot back. "It'll be hell. But we've got each other. The remaining brothers. My family. Your strength."

I snorted. "My strength? I'm laid up in a hospital bed."

"Your strength isn't just physical, Tempest." She leaned in, her face inches from mine. "It's here." She gently placed her hand right over my heart.

The warmth of her touch spread through me, battling the cold fury I'd had as a constant companion. "I don't know how to do this without violence," I admitted.

"Then we figure it out together," Kasen said. "Build something new. Something lasting. Maybe start small. Like in our own home."

"Our home?" I asked.

She smiled softly and placed my hand over her belly. "Found out this morning we're going to be parents. So see, you have so much to live for."

I closed my eyes, overwhelmed by the emotions crashing through me. Kasen's presence was a balm to my battered soul, a lighthouse in the storm of my thoughts. She believed in me, in us, with a ferocity that both terrified and exhilarated me.

When I opened my eyes again, I saw my future reflected in hers. And all I felt right then was hope.

Kasen's hand found mine, her fingers intertwining with my own. I met her gaze, the intensity in her eyes mirroring my own. No words were needed. The air between us hung heavy with unspoken promises.

I tugged her closer, ignoring the pain from my injuries. Kasen came willingly, perching on the edge of the bed. Her free hand cupped my cheek, her touch gentle yet firm.

We stayed like that, frozen in time, drinking in each other's presence. The hospital sounds faded away, leaving only the steady rhythm of our breathing.

In that moment, I knew. Nothing else mattered as long as I had her.

Epilogue

Tempest

I stood at the center of the clubhouse, my fingers entwined with Kasen's. The air was thick with tension, a hundred eyes boring into us. And it wasn't just because it was my first time back here since getting shot. I'd been laid up for weeks and still felt a twinge of pain now and then. But for the most part, I was fine.

My throat tightened as I cleared it.

"Listen up." My voice carried over the low murmur of conversation.

The room fell silent. I could feel Kasen trembling beside me, her palm sweaty against mine. My heart thundered in my chest, threatening to burst through my ribcage. We'd decided this was the best time to share our news. But we were both nervous as fuck about it.

"Kasen and I have an announcement," I said, struggling to keep my voice steady. "We're expecting a baby."

The words hung in the air for a heartbeat. Two. Then the room exploded.

Cheers erupted from every corner. Bodies surged forward. Hands clapped my back, voices shouting congratulations.

"Way to go, Tempest!" Viking yelled.

"About damn time!" Wire shouted.

I blinked, overwhelmed by the sudden onslaught. Kasen's grip on my hand tightened, anchoring me.

"You okay?" I murmured, leaning close to her ear.

She nodded, her eyes shining. "Perfect."

Relief flooded through me. We'd done it. Told

everyone. No more secrets.

Bull's booming laugh cut through the chaos. "Looks like our Sergeant-at-Arms is gonna be changing diapers!"

A ripple of laughter spread through the crowd. Kasen's thumb traced soothing circles on my wrist. This was a celebration. Our celebration.

Suddenly, a blur of motion caught my eye. Akira, her own baby bump visible beneath her flowing top, pushed through the crowd. She made a beeline for Kasen, her face alight with joy.

"Oh my God, Kasen!" Akira squealed, throwing her arms around my girl. "I can't believe it! We're going to be moms together!"

Kasen laughed, returning the embrace. "I know! It's crazy, right?"

I took a step back, giving them space. My chest tightened at the sight of Kasen's radiant smile. She deserved this moment.

Akira pulled away, her hands flying as she spoke. "We have to start planning your baby shower right away! Oh, the themes we could do…"

"Motorcycle onesies?" Kasen suggested, grinning.

"Yes! And tiny leather jackets!" Akira gasped. "Maybe a 'Born to Ride' cake?"

Before I could blink, Kasen's sisters materialized, surrounding the pair. Their voices overlapped in a cacophony of excitement.

"Did someone say baby shower?" Harlow asked.

"We call dibs on decorations!" Westlyn grinned from ear to ear, clearly thrilled over the idea of being an aunt.

"Forget that, I'm in charge of games. No boring stuff allowed." Akira nudged her good-naturedly.

I watched as Kasen was enveloped in a whirlwind of sisterly affection, their chatter rising above the general din of the clubhouse. My throat tightened. This was family. Our family. And soon, we'd be adding to it.

A hand clapped my shoulder, startling me from my thoughts.

I turned to find Viking's towering form beside me, his blue eyes twinkling with mischief. "Congrats, brother. Hope you're ready for sleepless nights and diaper duty."

I chuckled, the tension in my chest easing slightly. "Bring it on. Can't be worse than patching up your sorry ass after a bar fight. Seem to remember doing that a time or two."

Sticks materialized on my other side, his trademark grin in place. "Oh, just you wait. Babies are like tiny drunk people. Loud, messy, and always demanding more booze -- or in their case, milk."

The guys around us roared with laughter. I felt my face heat up, a mix of embarrassment and pride swelling in my chest.

"Real helpful, assholes," I muttered, but there was no heat in it. These men were my brothers, and their teasing was born of genuine affection.

Viking leaned in, his voice low. "Seriously though, Tempest. You'll be a great dad. Just remember, we've got your back. Lots of babysitters around here when you need a break."

I nodded, swallowing hard against the sudden lump in my throat. "Thanks, man."

The crowd shifted, and I caught sight of a familiar bulk moving through the crowd. Tank approached, his face an unreadable mask. The celebratory noise around us seemed to dim as he stopped in front of me, towering and intimidating as ever.

For a moment, we just stared at each other. I fought the urge to clench my fists, acutely aware of the tension radiating from the man who'd once been ready to put me in the ground for even looking at his daughter.

Then, slowly, Tank extended his hand, engulfed mine as I grasped it firmly. The clubhouse noise faded to a dull roar as I searched his face for any hint of his thoughts.

"Congratulations," Tank rumbled, his grip tightening a fraction.

"Thanks," I managed, my voice rougher than I'd intended.

As our hands dropped, Tank leaned in close, his breath hot on my ear. "Hope you're ready for the ride of your life, boy," he murmured, a hint of dark amusement coloring his words. "Sleepless nights, endless diapers, and a woman who'll make pregnancy look like a cakewalk compared to what comes after."

I stiffened, my pulse quickening. Tank pulled back, a ghost of a smirk playing on his weathered features. "Welcome to fatherhood, Tempest. It's a whole new kind of chaos. Just wait until it's *your* baby girl running off with some guy you don't feel is worthy of her."

His words hung in the air between us, a challenge and a warning rolled into one. I opened my mouth to respond, but Tank had already turned, melting back into the crowd of well-wishers.

My smile faltered, the weight of Tank's words crashing over me like a tidal wave. Chaos. That's what my life was about to become. My mind raced, images of a screaming infant and an exhausted Kasen flashing before my eyes. Then her all grown up and riding off on the back of someone's bike. A flicker of dread crawled up my spine, settling in my chest like a cold, hard stone.

"Shit," I muttered under my breath, running a hand through my hair. The clubhouse suddenly felt too small, too crowded. I needed air, needed --

A gentle pressure on my hand snapped me back to reality. Kasen's fingers intertwined with mine, her touch warm and grounding. I turned to find her blue eyes searching my face, concern etched in the slight furrow of her brow.

"You okay?" she asked, her voice barely audible over the din of the celebration.

I swallowed hard, forcing a weak smile. "Yeah, just... processing. Don't think it really hit me until just now."

Kasen squeezed my hand, her thumb tracing soothing circles on my skin. "We're in this together. Besides, how hard can a baby be compared to everything we just faced?"

I took a deep breath, feeling my shoulders relax slightly. "You better hope you didn't just jinx us. Now our kid might turn out like Lanie over at the Devil's Boneyard."

She paled a little, then the moment was shattered by the sharp *clink* of glass on metal. I turned to see Viking standing on a nearby table, beer bottle raised high.

"Listen up, you sorry bastards!" he bellowed, his voice cutting through the chatter. "Time to raise a glass to our Sergeant-at-Arms and his wife!"

A chorus of whoops and hollers erupted. Bottles and glasses lifted in unison, a sea of raised arms surrounding us. The air crackled with electricity, a palpable excitement I hadn't felt in a while.

"To Tempest and Kasen!" Sticks shouted from across the room. "And to the littlest Reaper on the way!"

"To family!" someone else chimed in.

"To sleepless nights and dirty diapers!" another voice added, eliciting a round of laughter.

I felt a grin tugging at the corners of my mouth, despite the lingering unease from Tank's words. The camaraderie, the genuine joy radiating from my brothers -- it was infectious. These were the men I'd ride into battle with, the ones I'd trust with my life. And now, they were rallying around me, ready to support this new chapter.

Kasen's grip on my hand tightened, and I glanced down to see her beaming up at me. The sight of her, radiant and strong, sent a surge of warmth through my chest. Tank's warning echoed in the back of my mind, but it felt distant now, overshadowed by the love surrounding us.

"You know," I murmured, leaning close to Kasen's ear, "I think we might actually pull this off."

She laughed, a sound that never failed to set my heart racing. "Damn straight we will. After all, we've got the toughest family in the state backing us up."

I nodded, feeling my resolve solidify. Whatever challenges lay ahead we'd face them head-on. Because that's what Reapers do. We protect our own, no matter what.

Sticks fired up the sound system, and the raw chords of Southern rock filled the air. I watched as Viking dragged a reluctant Akira onto our makeshift dance floor, her protests dissolving into laughter as he twirled her with surprising grace.

"Never thought I'd see the day," I muttered,

shaking my head at the sight.

Kasen followed my gaze and grinned. "Love changes people. He sees her as a little sister. No greater type of love, except possibly that of a parent for their child. Speaking of love…"

She nodded toward the far corner where her sisters huddled, deep in animated conversation. Their eyes kept darting our way, poorly concealing their excitement.

"I think they're plotting something," I said.

Kasen chuckled. "Knowing them, it's probably the baby shower to end all baby showers. God help us."

I groaned. "Can't we just, I don't know, skip that part?"

"Not a chance, tough guy," she teased, poking me in the ribs. "Besides, look how happy everyone is."

"Fine," I conceded. "But I draw the line at diaper-themed games."

Kasen's laughter rang out, drawing the attention of those nearby. Her sisters waved her over, and she gave my hand a squeeze before joining them. I watched as they enveloped her in a group hug, their excited chatter rising above the music.

The sight of Kasen, radiant and surrounded by love, hit me like a punch to the gut. This was real. We were really doing this. And despite all the unknowns, I couldn't wait to face them with her by my side.

Reclaiming Venom (Dixie Reapers MC 22)
A Dixie Reapers/Swift Angels Crossover Novella
Harley Wylde

What happens when the memories of a lifetime fade away, leaving only a faint echo of love?

Ridley -- Life can change in an instant. For me, it was the day I got that devastating call -- my world crumbled when I found out my husband, Venom, had been shot. He woke up, but the man I loved was a stranger. Then someone gave me a great idea. Make him fall for me all over again! Venom might not remember our past, but deep down, I know our connection is still there.

Venom -- I woke up in a hospital, no idea how I got there or what the hell happened. The angel by my bed seems familiar and yet not. Then she tells me she's my wife. What the hell? But as I spend time with Ridley, every story she shares awakens something deep within me. Her laughter, her warmth... the taste of her lips ignites a spark that feels so right. I may not remember our years together, but I know one thing for sure: she's mine.

Fall in love with the thrill of the ride, the heartache of forgotten memories, and the fierce determination of a love that refuses to die.

Prologue

Venom

I moved quickly, coming up behind Tinker. I couldn't believe this asshole was still alive. Pressing the barrel of my gun to his head, I made sure I had his fucking attention. "Drop it. Now!"

Tinker froze, a string of curses spilling from his lips. Slowly, he turned to face me, realization dawning in his eyes.

"You sneaky bastards," he snarled.

Torch and Bull emerged from the shadows, their own weapons trained on Tinker. The old man's face contorted with rage. "This is all your fault," he spat at us. "You and your damned club!"

Torch stepped forward. "Until you decided to stir up shit, we all thought you were dead. Why now, Tinker? Why didn't you just stay gone?"

Tinker's laugh was bitter. "You want to know why?"

His gaze darted to Justin, the President of the Swift Angels MC. "I only found out about him a year ago. My own flesh and blood, a cop. I watched. I waited. Hoped maybe he'd at least be dirty, something I could work with."

I got it. Sort of. I hadn't been too pleased to find out my son, Dawson, was not only a fireman, but also the VP of another club. I'd hoped he'd follow in my footsteps. But now, I had to admit I was proud of the man he'd become.

"Then I realized," Tinker continued, a cruel smile twisting his features, "that the Swift Angels had ties to you Dixie Reaper scum. That's when I knew it was time to make my move. All these decades, waiting for a chance to get revenge, and it fell right into my lap."

"It's over, Tinker. You've lost. Do you really think you'll get out of this alive? We may not have made sure you were dead last time, but things are different now," I said.

Tinker's grin widened. "You sure about that, Venom?"

Without warning, chaos erupted. Two men materialized from the shadows behind Justin. Shit! Wire had said Tinker would be alone. Where the hell had these men come from?

"Justin, down!" Logan yelled, but it was too late.

A deafening crack split the air. Justin's body jerked, his blue eyes wide with shock. Blood bloomed across his chest, a crimson stain spreading rapidly. "Shit," he muttered, his voice barely audible before his knees buckled.

Logan appeared shocked at first, then the paramedic sprang into action. He snatched the med bag he'd brought as a precaution and sprinted toward Justin's fallen form.

Two more shots went off, and pain hit me like a fucking freight train. I stared at Tinker in confusion as I sank to the ground, everything going dark around the edges of my vision. I could hear everything around me, even though it felt like I was down a long tunnel, voices echoing.

"Logan! Hurry the fuck up!" Dawson's frantic voice cut through the chaos.

I felt something pooling beneath me and realized it was my own fucking blood. The world got darker and darker, and I knew I was going under. Jesus fucking Christ! I'd lived this damn long, and a snake like Tinker got the drop on me?

Ridley... What the hell would she do without me? I didn't want to leave her. There was still so much

I wanted to see and do with her. Regret slammed into me, as I tried to recall if I'd told her I loved her before we left.

"Diego!" Logan barked. "Keep pressure on Justin's wound. I need to check on Venom."

I felt someone drop beside me, but I couldn't make out any shapes anymore.

"We need ambulances," Logan shouted. "Two of them. Now!"

I felt someone rip open my shirt and try to staunch the flow of blood, but I knew it was too late. Nothing could save me now.

"Dad." Dawson's voice broke as someone knelt beside me. Was it Dawson? "Dad, can you hear me?"

I heard Logan's voice on the other side of me. "He's lost a lot of blood. We need to get him to the hospital immediately."

Logan worked on packing my wounds. I wanted to tell him to save someone else, that I'd finally come to the end of my journey, but I couldn't form the words. My body felt cold, and soon even the noises around me faded to nothing.

Ridley... I'm so fucking sorry for leaving you. I'll always love you.

* * *

Ridley

I stared at my son in horror, seeing my husband's blood all over him. I wordlessly handed him a change of clothes and watched as he rushed off to a bathroom. Jesus. He'd told me it was bad, but... there was so much blood.

I looked over at Torch, and he came closer.

"What happened?" I asked. "There were so many of you. Was Tinker really that hard to take down?"

Torch sighed and ran a hand over his beard. "He wasn't alone. Not Wire's fault. Somewhere he picked up two helpers. While Venom had his gun to Tinker's head, the other two came out of nowhere. They shot Justin first, and while our focus was on him, the other one shot Venom."

I pressed a hand to my chest, my knees feeling weak. "How bad? And don't fucking lie to me, Torch."

"It's bad, Ridley," he murmured. "He nearly coded in the ambulance. By some miracle, the paramedics were able to get him back. They rushed him to surgery the minute we arrived. If it hadn't been for Logan, he'd have died before they even got there."

Right when my knees gave out, someone caught me. I glanced up to see Viking behind me. He hugged me tight before picking me up and carrying me over to a chair. He gently eased me down, and I leaned forward, pressing my head to my knees.

"This can't be happening," I whispered. "All these years, and this happens now? He was supposed to be safer. He stepped down as VP, and I thought, for sure, most of the danger was behind us."

Torch took the spot beside me, and Savior sat on the other. We remained silent, praying and hoping for good news. It felt like an eternity before two doctors came out. One talked to the Swift Angels first about Justin, and the other came to me. He faced me, his expression grim, and my heart dropped.

"Venom has a long road to travel before he's back on his feet. He made it through surgery, but… we lost him. We were about to call time of death, when his heart started beating again. He's been moved to recovery, but it's been decided it would be best to place him in a coma to help with the healing process."

"What…" I licked my lips. "What does that

mean?"

"He's going to sleep until his body is mostly repaired. Then we'll see if we can get him awake again."

"What do you mean you'll see?" Panic welled inside me. "He has to wake up!"

The doctor nodded. "I understand how you feel, but his situation... it's not the best. For a man his age, well. There's a lot of trauma to his body. There's no way of telling when he'll wake up."

"Or if, right?" I asked, giving a bitter laugh. "You're telling me he's alive, but I may never get the chance to talk to him again? To see his eyes open, or hear him laugh? What the hell am I supposed to do with that?"

I heard my voice rising but couldn't stop it. Tears streaked my cheeks, and I felt the hysteria welling inside me. Then my son was there. Dawson wrapped me in his arms, and I sobbed against his chest while he spoke with the doctor.

Venom. You better come back to me! I can't live without you.

Chapter One

Venom

The antiseptic scent of bleach and stale air assaulted my nostrils as I clawed my way back to consciousness. My eyelids felt like lead weights, refusing to cooperate as I struggled to open them. When I finally managed to pry them apart, harsh fluorescent lights seared my retinas, sending sharp daggers of pain through my skull.

I blinked rapidly, trying to bring the blurry room into focus. Sterile white walls. Beeping monitors. The rhythmic hiss of oxygen. Hospital. But why? My mind felt foggy, memories just out of reach.

I attempted to shift positions, but my body refused to obey. Every muscle ached, protesting even the slightest movement. This couldn't be my body -- it felt alien, unfamiliar. Panic started to bubble up in my chest.

The soft *click* of the door opening caught my attention. A petite blonde woman entered, her blue eyes widening as they landed on me. Relief flooded her delicate features, quickly followed by apprehension. She hesitated at the threshold, one hand still on the doorknob as if debating whether to flee.

"You're awake," she said, her voice barely above a whisper. "I'll get the doctor."

She raced out and soon a team of doctors and nurses came in. They immediately checked the machines, someone checked my pulse, and the doctor stared at a device in his hand.

"We're going to remove the tube from your throat in just a moment," the doctor said. "I'll let the nurses help you get comfortable, then I'll go over a few things with you. It's good to see you awake."

He stepped out of the room and someone else entered. The process of removing the tube was far from fun, but I was glad to have it out. A nurse offered an ice chip.

"I know your mouth and throat are dry, but drinking water right off could make you sick. I need you to suck on these for the moment," she said, placing the cup within reach.

I opened my mouth to ask a question but couldn't get words out. Instead, I ended up coughing. The nurses helped me calm down, fluffed my pillows, and helped me sit up a bit more. By the time they'd finished, the doctor returned.

"First, do you know the date?" the doctor asked.

I stared at him, trying to figure out why he was asking me that. I rattled off what I thought was the correct answer, and he made a note but didn't comment.

"And your name?"

"Venom," I said. He stared at me over the top of his glasses but fuck if I was telling him my legal name. I hadn't used it in forever. "I'm the VP for the Dixie Reapers MC. Venom is the only name you're getting out of me."

I saw his lips slightly twitch, but he just made another note on the device in his hand.

"What do you remember?" he asked.

My brow furrowed. "Look, I don't know why I'm here, but I want to go home."

The doctor set the device aside and folded his arms. "Mr. Venom, you're in the ICU. You were shot twice in an altercation, died twice and came back, and you've been in a coma for months. My questions may seem tedious, but I assure you there's a reason for them."

"Months?" I asked. What the fuck? And shot? I didn't remember doing anything that would have gotten me into that situation. At least, not recently. It wasn't like I was an angel. The club had good days and bad days. Had a job gone wrong? I doubted the doctor knew the particulars, but I did know things had to have been really fucking bad for the club to send me to the damn hospital.

"It seems you're suffering from amnesia. It could be temporary, or... Well, there's always the chance it's permanent."

"But I remember things just fine."

The doctor stared at me, as if trying to decide what he wanted to say. When he did speak, it didn't give me a lot of confidence.

"Mr. Venom, the situation is more serious than you realize, but I don't think we should push. It could end up having disastrous results. It's best to let your memory return on its own. The brain is complex. What we may think wouldn't be a big deal could have lasting consequences."

Clearly I wasn't going to get anywhere with this asshat. "Where's the woman who was here before?"

"Ridley?" one of the nurses asked.

"Pretty blonde with blue eyes," I said.

Her lips parted and then she snapped them shut. She quickly pasted a smile on her face. "We'll send her back in when we step out."

Her reaction said I'd forgotten more than just how I'd ended up in this damn hospital bed. Who was that woman to me? Why did these people seem to think I should know her? I had to admit, she'd seemed a bit familiar, even though I couldn't place where I'd seen her before.

"You have a catheter in," the doctor said. "We'll

take it out today and you'll be able to get up to use the restroom. Please don't try to get out of bed on your own. Press the call button and a nurse will help you."

"Why the fuck would I do that?" I asked.

"Because you're a fall risk, Mr. Venom. You've been lying prone in that bed for months. Your legs aren't going to be as strong as you're expecting them to be."

Fine. I'd do as he said. Once. After that, all bets were off. I wasn't a fucking child who needed someone to take them to the damn bathroom.

It took a while longer before everyone finally left the room. I closed my eyes and breathed a sigh of relief. And after what felt like forever, the woman they'd called Ridley came back into the room, giving me a cautious smile. She looked like she'd been crying, and for some reason, I wanted to pull her into my arms and comfort her.

"How are you feeling?" she asked, her tone gentle.

I cleared my throat. "Like I've been hit by a damn semi," I said, my voice sounding more like a growl. "What the hell happened? The doctors wouldn't tell me much. Something about being shot and being in a coma."

A flicker of pain crossed her face before she schooled her expression. "Did they tell you that you were unconscious for months?"

I nodded. Yeah, they'd mentioned that, the shooting, and not a hell of a lot else. Something felt incredibly wrong about this situation, but I didn't know why. Nor did I understand my reactions to this woman. Even now, I wanted to take her into my arms. What the fuck was wrong with me?

She reached out as if to touch my arm, then

thought better of it. Her hand hovered uncertainly in the air between us before dropping back to her lap. The gesture struck me as oddly intimate.

"Venom," she said softly, "do you know who I am?"

The use of my road name sent a jolt through me. The way that nurse had acted, I'd assumed I knew this woman somehow. I studied her face more closely, searching for any hint of recognition. There was something achingly familiar about her blue eyes, the curve of her lips. But try as I might, I couldn't place her.

"Should I?" I asked, my voice gruff with confusion and a hint of suspicion.

The hope in her eyes dimmed, her shoulders sagging almost imperceptibly. She took a deep breath, squaring those delicate shoulders as if steeling herself for battle.

"It's all right," she said, though the slight quaver in her voice betrayed her. "The doctor warned us this might happen. We'll figure it out together, okay?"

I nodded warily, unsure what to make of this woman and the complex emotions swirling just beneath her calm exterior. As she talked about mundane things like the weather, a festival I'd missed, and apparently any random thought that popped into her mind, I couldn't shake the feeling that I was missing something vitally important. The air between us crackled with unspoken tension, heavy with secrets I couldn't begin to fathom.

The woman's fingers traced abstract patterns on the edge of my hospital bed as she spoke, her gaze fixed on some distant point. "My name is Ridley. As to the rest, the doctor cautioned against telling you too much."

What the fuck? "Are you serious right now?"

She winced. "I know you don't like people telling you what to do. But he said if I told you about the time you've missed, it could actually hurt you."

I snorted. "Look, I was apparently shot twice, died and was brought back. I don't think you talking to me is going to make me keel over."

She smiled faintly. "I know you're tough. If anyone knows it, it's me."

"So, talk to me, pretty girl."

Tears welled in her eyes and she pressed her lips together. "Like I said, my name is Ridley... and we've been married for nearly thirty years."

Holy. Fucking. Shit. I didn't stop her. Just listened. But was she telling the truth? They'd said I had amnesia. I'd assumed that meant I was missing a few months of my life. Not decades!

"We have three beautiful children together -- Dawson, Mariah, and Farrah. Dawson is actually our youngest, and the only one who still lives in town. We also have several grandchildren."

The words hit me like a physical blow. Married? Children? *Grand*children? There was no fucking way! I wasn't old enough for that shit. Hell, I was only in my thirties. I searched my fragmented memories, desperately seeking any shred of truth to her claims. But there was nothing -- just a vast, echoing emptiness where those memories should have been.

"I'm sorry," I said, frustration seeping into my tone. "But I don't... I can't remember any of that. And no offense, but your claims are a bit unrealistic. How could I be a grandpa when I'm only in my thirties?"

Ridley's eyes snapped back to mine, a storm of emotions swirling in their blue depths. "Did you say thirties?"

I nodded, then winced at the pain and dizziness that hit me.

"Are you sure you want to know the entire truth?" she asked. "Even if it could end up making things worse?"

"Yeah. Hit me with it. I don't like that lying-ass fucking doctor. I'm an adult and can handle whatever you throw at me. Haven't run away so far, right?"

"I think there's something you need to see." She took a small compact out of her purse and handed it to me.

Apprehension filled me even though I wasn't sure why. I held the mirror up and immediately dropped it when I saw my reflection. "What the fuck? What the actual fuck?"

"Venom, you're in your sixties now." She paused. "As for who I am, other than your wife... I'm Bull's daughter."

My gaze snapped to hers. "You're... No fucking way."

She nodded. "Yeah. I came back to the Dixie Reapers about thirty years ago, in trouble and needing my dad. A Prospect detained me at the gate, and you let me through. We've been together ever since."

I held up a hand. "Just... wait. You're little Ridley? The girl who used to play at the clubhouse before moving to Florida with your mom? That Ridley?"

"Yes. I know this is a lot..."

Pain spiked through my head, and I gripped it, trying to make sense of everything. The alarms went nuts on the machines. A nurse came in to check on me, but I waved her off. Whatever this woman, Ridley, had to say, I knew I needed to hear it. And something told me the staff here would chase her out if they thought she might be stressing me out.

"It's okay," she said, reaching out as if to touch my hand before thinking better of it. "We'll take it slow. One day at a time."

I watched as she pulled a small photo from her wallet. "This is us," she explained, holding it out for me to see. "Back when you first claimed me. Or rather, I claimed you."

The image showed a younger version of myself, the version of me I remembered, with my arms wrapped around a radiant blonde. We both looked... happy. Content. It was like looking at strangers.

"You really don't remember?" Ridley asked, her voice cracking slightly.

I shook my head, my throat tight. "No. I'm sorry, but... you're a stranger to me. At least, this adult version of you."

The pain that flashed across her face was visceral, but she quickly masked it with a determined smile. "I'm not giving up on us, Venom. Not now, not ever."

I stared at Ridley, my mind a maelstrom of disbelief and frustration. The woman before me was undeniably beautiful, her blonde hair cascading over her shoulders, eyes filled with a mixture of hope and worry. But all I could see was the ghost of a teenage girl, Bull's daughter, superimposed over this stranger who claimed to be my wife. Even though she hadn't been back to the clubhouse since she was a small child, he'd shown me pictures, ones he'd received over the years. I might not remember much about my past, but I did recall how proud he was every time he got one of those pictures. He'd show them to everyone, bragging on his daughter.

"You were just a kid," I muttered, more to myself

than to her. "How the hell did we…"

Ridley's lips quirked into a sad smile. "We didn't exactly plan it. And trust me, my dad was far from pleased about it. It just… happened. You fought it at first, you know. Thought you were too old, too rough around the edges. Then Torch called me into Church, and I claimed you in front of all your brothers. You were amused by it."

As she spoke, I found myself hanging on her every word, desperate for any shred of connection to the life she described.

"You saved me, you know? My stepdad was trying to sell me off to some man called Montoya. You made sure he could never get his hands on me or hurt anyone else ever again."

Something stirred in the depths of my mind -- not a memory, exactly, but a feeling. In my gut, I knew she was right. I'd killed the man she spoke of. Then again, I'd killed quite a few men over the years -- the years I remembered. I doubted getting married had changed me that much.

"Sounds like something I'd do," I admitted grudgingly, my fingers twitching with the urge to reach out and touch her, to see if it would spark any recognition.

Ridley's face lit up at my words, and for a moment, I caught a glimpse of the vibrant, outgoing woman she must be when not weighed down by this impossible situation.

"Our lives weren't a fairy tale exactly, but we were happy. I loved you, and I knew you loved me. Even when the club was in chaos, even when things got tough, you were my rock."

I listened, torn between the evidence of a life well-lived and the vast emptiness where those memories should have been. Part of me wanted to believe her, to accept this reality where I'd found love and built a family. But the skeptical, hardened part of my nature -- the part that had kept me alive through decades in an MC -- couldn't quite let go.

"I want to believe you," I said finally, my voice rough. "But it's like you're talking about someone else. I can't... I can't feel any of it."

Ridley nodded, her eyes shimmering with unshed tears once more. I seemed to be doing a great job at making her cry. "I know. But I'm here, and I'm not going anywhere. We'll figure this out together, okay?"

As I looked at her, really looked at her, I felt a flicker of something. Not memory, not recognition, but... intrigue. A spark of curiosity about the life we'd supposedly built, the love we'd shared. And despite my reservations, I found myself wanting to know more.

The silence that fell between us was thick enough to cut with a knife. Ridley's words hung in the air, heavy with the weight of years I couldn't remember. I watched her, this woman who claimed to be my wife, as she fidgeted with the edge of her leather cut. And that's when it hit me.

"Turn around," I said.

Her eyes widened a moment, and she stood, then turned so I could see her back. There, for all the world to see, *Property of Venom.*

My throat tightened as I struggled to find words, any words, to bridge the chasm between us. The beeping of the heart monitor seemed to grow louder in the stillness, a stark reminder of how close I'd come to oblivion.

Ridley's gaze met mine, a storm of emotions

swirling in their depths. She lifted her hand, then froze, as if she were going to reach for me. I wondered how hard it was for her to hold herself back like that. The distance between us felt both insurmountable and paper-thin.

"I know this is a lot to take in," Ridley finally said, her voice barely above a whisper. She took a deep breath, squaring her shoulders. "Why don't I help you piece together the missing years? And it doesn't have to be today. We have all the time in the world."

I looked around the room. "Clearly not if I was injured bad enough to end up here."

She swallowed hard. "Um, about the shooting... It was someone you knew."

"Excuse me?"

She licked her lips. "Someone from the Dixie Reapers' past called Tinker showed up. Apparently, everyone had thought the man died. You were shot and nearly died during a confrontation with him."

Holy shit. Tinker hadn't been dead? Now I really felt like I was missing huge chunks of my memory. What else had happened over all the missing years?

I studied her face, noting the determination etched in the lines around her eyes, the vulnerability in the slight tremble of her lower lip. This vibrant woman, so different from the playful girl I remembered, was offering to be my guide through the fog of my own mind.

"And if I never remember?" The question slipped out before I could stop it, harsh and abrupt.

Ridley flinched, but her gaze remained steady. "Then, maybe we can start over," she said softly.

The resolve in her voice stirred something within me -- respect, perhaps, or the faintest glimmer of hope. I found myself nodding, despite the doubts still swirling in my mind.

"All right. One step at a time." It wasn't like I could deny anything she'd said. Not after seeing that picture and my name across her back.

Ridley's face lit up, a tentative smile curving her lips. The sight tugged at something deep within me, a feeling I couldn't quite name.

"Thank you," she said, her voice thick with emotion. She settled into the chair beside my bed, leaning forward slightly. "Where should we start?"

I shifted uncomfortably, the starched hospital sheets rustling beneath me. "The club," I muttered, latching onto the one constant I could remember.

"Right. When we first met, you were the VP."

"Why is that in past tense?" I asked.

"You stepped down several years ago. Now Saint is the VP. Um, you may remember a Prospect called Johnny? I'm not sure how far back your memories go."

Jesus Christ. I'd clearly gotten older, but why the fuck had I stepped down? Or had it even been my choice?

"Torch is no longer President either. In fact, all the old officers turned the club over to younger guys at the same time. Savior, who was the Prospect Gabriel, is now the President. Tempest... Um, I doubt you'd remember him. He was a Prospect after we got together. He's the Sergeant-at-Arms. There's more, but I don't want to overwhelm you more than I already have."

"Tell me more," I said gruffly, surprising myself with the request. "About... us."

Ridley's eyes softened, a mixture of hope and tenderness flickering across her features. Her perfume - - a delicate blend of lavender and vanilla -- wafting toward me. The scent stirred something deep within, a fleeting sense of comfort and desire that I couldn't fully grasp.

"Well," she began, her voice dropping to a lower, more intimate tone, "we've always had a bit of a wild streak together. I got pregnant with our first child, Farrah, almost immediately. She's with a guy named Demon at the Devil's Fury. In fact, he's their Sergeant-at-Arms. Our middle child, Mariah, is also with them. Her man is called Savage. There's a bit of story behind the two of them getting together. Let's just say, you arranged it."

"You said we had three children."

She nodded. "Dawson is our youngest. He's in his twenties, is a fireman, and is also the VP of a local club called the Swift Angels."

I held up a hand. "My son is a *what*?"

Her lips twitched. "You didn't handle it well the first time you found out either. He's really good at his job. He's married to a sweet woman named Nora. They have a little girl and just had a baby boy. In fact, our granddaughter likes you more than me."

I shook my head, frustrated by the void where that memory should have been. But as Ridley continued talking about our years together, painting a picture of stolen moments and passionate encounters, I found myself captivated. The way she described our connection -- the fire, the understanding, the unwavering support -- it resonated with a part of me I thought long buried.

"You've always been my rock, Jackson," she murmured. "Even when the world's gone to hell, you're there, steady as ever."

I jolted at the use of my real name, then swallowed hard, my throat suddenly dry. "Sounds like a fairy tale. You said it wasn't, but it sounds like one to me."

Ridley's laugh was rich and throaty. "Oh, trust me, it hasn't all been smooth sailing. We've had our share of fights. You're as stubborn as they come. And when I'm angry, I'm not exactly easy to deal with."

As she recounted one of our apparent disagreements, I found myself torn. Part of me still rebelled against the idea of this life she described -- husband, father, settled down. But another part, growing stronger with each passing moment, yearned for the connection she spoke of.

"I wish I could remember," I admitted gruffly, my fists clenching in frustration. "It's all there, just out of reach. Like trying to grab smoke."

Ridley's expression softened, and for a moment, I saw the weight of our situation reflected in her eyes. The silence that fell between us was heavy, laden with unspoken promises and shared uncertainty. I studied Ridley's face, searching for any hint of deception, but found only open vulnerability and a fierce determination that stirred something deep within me.

"I can't promise I'll ever be the man you remember, but…" I trailed off, struggling to find the right words.

Ridley leaned forward, her gaze intense. "But?"

I inhaled deeply, the sterile hospital scent mingling with the faint, enticing whisper of her perfume. "But I'm willing to try."

A small smile tugged at the corners of Ridley's lips, a spark of hope igniting in her gaze. "That's all I ask."

The air between us crackled with a tension I couldn't quite name. My body seemed to lean toward her of its own accord, drawn by some inexplicable magnetism. I clenched my jaw, fighting the urge to reach out and touch her.

"So, where do we start?" I asked, desperate to break the charged silence.

Ridley's smile widened, a mischievous glint in her eye. "How about with your favorite meal? I make a mean chili that always gets you talking. Of course, that can't happen until you're able to go home."

For the first time since waking up in this strange new reality, I felt the ghost of a smile tug at my lips. "All right, darlin'," I drawled, the endearment slipping out naturally.

A nurse came in and let us know visiting hours were over. I wanted to argue, and beg for Ridley to stay, but she'd given me a lot to think about.

As Ridley stood, gathering her things, I couldn't help but feel a flicker of anticipation. The road ahead was uncertain, fraught with obstacles, but something told me this fiery woman would make the journey worthwhile.

Chapter Two

Venom

The scent slammed into me like a runaway train, a heady mix of lavender and leather. The combination was unfamiliar, yet strangely comforting, making my nostrils flare involuntarily. I paused, one hand still gripping the doorknob, as my eyes struggled to adjust to the dimness within.

Shadows danced across the walls, twisting the familiar into something alien. For a fleeting moment, I felt like an intruder in my own home.

With measured steps, I moved forward, the floorboards creaking softly beneath my heavy boots. Family photos adorned the walls, their smiling faces staring back at me with an accusing intimacy. Ridley was in most of them. Children with my eyes. My throat tightened, a lump forming that I swallowed with difficulty.

"Who are you people?" I murmured, reaching out to touch a gilt frame. My calloused fingertips left smudges on the glass, marring the smiles.

In some photos, I recognized myself -- younger, less gray in the beard, but undeniably me. My arm around Ridley's waist, a little girl perched precariously on my shoulders. But try as I might, I couldn't summon a single memory to match the images. The past remained stubbornly locked away, a treasure chest buried beneath layers of amnesia.

My fists clenched at my sides, a surge of frustration bubbling up inside me. I was a man who thrived on control, who always knew where he stood. This helplessness was maddening, a betrayal of my very identity.

My gaze landed on a photo of myself, my cut

emblazoned with patches, arms crossed over my chest, radiating the kind of "don't-fuck-with-me" energy that had served me well as VP. At least that felt familiar, a tangible reminder of who I used to be.

But as I stared at my younger self, a different kind of ache bloomed in my chest. Who was I now, stripped of those memories? Without the stories behind each smile, each embrace frozen in time?

The lavender scent intensified as I moved deeper into the house, clinging to the air like a cloying perfume. It should have been soothing, but instead it only heightened my disorientation. This place that should have felt like a sanctuary was as foreign as a distant land, the echoes of my past haunting me like ghosts.

And yet... and yet there was something. A flicker of recognition, a whisper in the dusty corners of my mind. Or maybe it was just wishful thinking. I couldn't be sure.

I paused before the large family portrait, the colors faded and the edges softened by time. I studied the faces of the children, my children, trying to etch them into my memory. "I'm sorry," I whispered, the words catching in my throat like unwanted guests. "I'm trying. I swear I'm trying to remember."

But the smiling faces were a cruel reminder of a life I couldn't recall. Just glimpses, tantalizing fragments that slipped through my fingers like smoke. The frustration was a physical ache, a knot in my stomach that wouldn't loosen.

The sudden creak of floorboards ripped through the silence, making me jump. I whirled around, my body instinctively tensing, and found myself face-to-face with a whirlwind of blonde hair and boundless energy.

Ridley.

She strode toward me with a confidence that seemed to light up the room, her eyes sparkling with a mixture of hope and fierce determination. The contrast between her vivacity and my somber mood was stark, yet somehow comforting.

"There you are, handsome," she said, her voice rich and warm. "Thought I might find you brooding in here."

My breath caught in my throat. This woman -- my wife -- exuded a strength that both intrigued and intimidated me. "I wasn't brooding," I muttered, though the lie felt weak even to my own ears.

Ridley's laugh was like summer thunder, bold and unapologetic. "Sure you weren't, tough guy. But let me tell you a story that might put a smile on that ruggedly handsome face of yours."

She perched on the arm of a nearby chair, her petite frame somehow commanding the entire room. "Like I told you before, I'm the one who claimed you."

"Tell me more about it. I need the details. Maybe then…"

She started in on the story, and painted such a vivid picture, I could see the scene in my mind. Almost like a movie was playing.

"Ridley, do you remember me?" Torch asked.

She hesitantly nodded. "You're the president of the Dixie Reapers."

"That's right. And the man beside me is my VP."

Her glaze clashed with mine.

"I understand that Bull sent you home with Venom when you arrived. Did you go with him willingly?" Torch asked.

"Yes," Ridley said.

"And anything that happened while you were there

was consensual? He didn't force himself on you in any way?"

"Venom would never hurt me," she said.

"If you had your choice, would you want to remain with Venom? Or would you prefer to move to another house? I could even arrange for your dad to stay with you," Torch said.

Her gaze met mine again and held. It was like she was looking to me for answers, but I couldn't say anything.

"Ridley, I'm asking you, not Venom," Torch said.

"I want to stay with Venom," she said softly. "If that's okay with him."

"Ridley, I know you came to us because your father is here," Torch said. "But I need to know if you plan to stay even after the danger has passed. There's not a lot of room in our club for women. You're either a club slut or an old lady, and right now, you aren't either."

"If staying is an option, I think I'd like to," she said. "But I could never be a club slut."

"You don't have a problem wearing someone's brand?" Flicker asked.

"What's a brand? Like you literally burn a brand into my skin?" she asked, her face paling.

"This is ridiculous," Bull said. "My daughter isn't going to be a slut or an old lady. There's a reason I didn't fight for sole custody. I didn't want her around all this shit."

"Not your decision," Torch said.

"A brand means you're tattooed," I said.

"Tattooed with what?" she asked.

"You're marked as property," Flicker said. "You can wear it on your arm or on your back. You'll also be given a cut that says you're property of the biker who claims you."

Ridley's brow furrowed. "I don't remember my mom having that."

Bull snorted. "Because I would have never made your mom my old lady. We were only together for a few days, then she came and found me when she discovered she was pregnant with you. But no matter what I think of your mother, I have always loved you. You're my sweet girl, and I hate to think of you living this life."

Ridley focused on him. "You taught me about bikes and introduced me to different MCs whenever you would visit. You never kept this way of life a secret from me, even if I don't know all the details. I don't need to know them. You're a good man, Daddy, and I'm sure you're not the only one in this room." Her gaze met mine. "I know you aren't. I've known Venom all my life, even if I wasn't around the last fourteen years. He would never hurt me."

Torch chuckled. "Are you laying claim to my VP?"

Her chin jutted up. "Maybe I am. Does that mean he has to get tattooed with Property of Ridley?"

As quickly as the memory hit me, it slipped away again. But it had come to me, and that was enough for now. I hadn't just seen it through her story. I'd *been* there. For a brief moment, I'd recalled that day.

Despite myself, I felt a smile tugging at the corners of my mouth. This woman was utterly fearless, a force of nature. And she was mine.

"I can picture it," I said, my voice gruff. "You, all fire and sass, claiming me like a prize."

Ridley's eyes lit up, a connection sparking between us that transcended my fractured memories. I didn't want to tell her I'd remembered for a moment. It might give her hope when there shouldn't be any. There was no way of knowing when or even if my memories would return.

"Oh, you were the best prize, darlin'. Still are."

She reached for my hand, her touch both familiar and electrifying. "Come on, let me show you the rest of our kingdom."

Ridley led me through the house, and I drank in

every detail. The kitchen wrapped around us, the lingering scent of cinnamon and coffee tickling my senses. My fingers trailed over a dent in the countertop.

"Your attempt at homemade bread," she teased, a playful lilt in her voice. "Let's just say your talents lay elsewhere."

I couldn't picture myself trying to make fucking bread. I had a feeling there was a story behind it. One I didn't recall.

In the living room, I spotted a weathered leather jacket hanging on a hook. My fingers had itched to touch it. The worn material whispered of countless rides and shared adventures.

"Your favorite," Ridley murmured. "You always said it was lucky."

The bedroom unfolded like a sanctuary, soft light filtering through gauzy curtains. A quilt draped across the bed, its patchwork telling stories I couldn't quite grasp.

"A Christmas gift from our daughter, Mariah, about five years ago," she explained. "Some of the patches are from clothes we've worn over the years, all of us, and a few are from the kids' favorite blankets when they were little."

My throat tightened as I turned to Ridley, overwhelmed by the evidence of a life so rich and full of love. "I wish I could remember."

Her hand found my cheek, her touch infinitely tender. "We'll make new memories, tough guy. And who knows? Maybe the old ones will find their way back home, just like you did."

My chest tightened as I stood in the hallway, surrounded by the remnants of a life I couldn't recall. Each photograph, each trinket on the shelves whispered of shared moments, laughter and tears that slipped through my fingers like sand. The weight of it all pressed down on me, a bittersweet ache that left me breathless.

"It's all here," I murmured, more to myself than to Ridley. "A whole life, right in front of me, and I can't..." My voice trailed off, frustration coloring my words.

Ridley stood beside me, her presence a steady anchor. Her vibrant energy cut through the turmoil swirling in my mind. "What did you feel when you looked at these things, Venom?" she asked, her voice gentle yet probing.

I closed my eyes, focusing on the emotions swirling within me. "Like I'm on the edge of something important," I admitted. "Like I should know more, feel more. It's... maddening."

As we moved farther down the hall, a large portrait caught my eye. I stopped, transfixed by the image of myself surrounded by three young faces -- two girls and a boy. My children. My family.

Without thinking, I reached out, tracing the outline of each face with my calloused fingers. The eldest girl's mischievous grin mirrored Ridley's. And the boy's serious expression reflected my own, his wide eyes full of wonder.

"Farrah, Dawson, and Mariah," Ridley named each child again.

My voice thickened with emotion when I finally spoke. "They're beautiful. Our kids..." The words felt foreign on my tongue yet undeniably right. "Tell me about them."

Ridley's eyes were full of pride and love as she responded. "Farrah's our firecracker. Takes after me, I'm afraid -- she was always up to something. Still is, but now she gives Demon a headache and not us. Dawson's the thinker, quiet but sharp as a tack. He's always been a little different from the other kids around here. And Mariah? Well, she's got you wrapped around her little finger. The day you sent her off was the hardest on you. I could tell it gutted you, but we both knew it was for the best."

A lump formed in my throat. "I can't remember them," I whispered, the admission tearing at my heart. "But I feel... God, Ridley, I feel so much. Do they know? I mean, that I can't remember them?"

Ridley's warm hand slipped into mine, her fingers intertwining with my own. The simple touch sent a jolt through me, grounding me in the moment. I turned to face her, struck by the depth of emotion in her eyes.

"It's okay," she murmured, her voice a soothing balm. "And yes, they're aware. Which is why Dawson won't be bringing our granddaughter around for a bit. He thought it might be confusing for her."

The air between us crackled with unspoken tension, a familiar yet foreign electricity. I was drawn to her, noticing the faint scent of lavender that clung to her skin. Now I knew where the smell in the house had come from.

"Come on," Ridley said, gently tugging my hand. "I want to show you something."

She led me through the house, past the kitchen where the aroma of fresh coffee still lingered, and out into the backyard. My breath caught as I stepped onto the patio, taking in the sight before me.

A riot of color greeted my eyes -- vibrant purple irises swayed alongside delicate pink roses and fiery orange marigolds. The garden sprawled across the yard, a patchwork of life and beauty. In the center stood a massive oak tree, its branches spreading wide to provide dappled shade.

"You did all this?" I asked, awe tinging my voice.

Ridley nodded, a proud smile lighting up her face. "It's been a labor of love. Started small, just a few flowers here and there. But it grew, just like our family. And it wasn't easy. I had a lot of help."

I walked along the winding stone path, drinking in every detail. A small vegetable patch nestled in one corner; tomatoes ripened on the vine. Near the fence, sunflowers stretched toward the sky, their golden faces following the sun's path.

"It's incredible," I said, turning back to Ridley. The late afternoon light caught her hair, setting it ablaze with golden highlights. "You're incredible."

A faint blush colored her cheeks, and I felt a surge of affection for this vibrant woman who had built a life with me -- a life I was determined to rediscover.

"Tell me about that," I said, gesturing to a weathered wooden bench beneath the oak tree.

Ridley's eyes lit up with memory. "That's where we'd sit in the evenings, watching the kids play. Where you taught Dawson to whittle and where I read bedtime stories to the girls on warm summer nights."

I closed my eyes, trying to picture it all. Though specific memories eluded me, I could feel echoes of contentment and belonging wash over me. When I opened my eyes again, Ridley watched me intently.

"What is it?" I asked, suddenly self-conscious under her gaze.

She shook her head, a soft smile playing on her lips. "Just... seeing you here, in our space. It feels right, doesn't it?"

I nodded, surprised that it did. Despite gaps in

my memory and lingering uncertainty, this felt like home.

I could see the mischief in her eyes as she led me to the bench, her fingers intertwined with mine. The wood creaked softly beneath us as we sat, a familiar sound that stirred something deep within me.

"You want to hear about the time you nearly set the clubhouse on fire?" Ridley asked, her voice laced with humor.

I raised an eyebrow. "I did what now?"

She laughed, the sound rich and inviting. "Oh yeah, it was during a Christmas party. You were trying to impress me by making flaming shots."

The way her eyes sparkled as she spoke, the way the sun gilded her hair, I couldn't help but lean in, entranced by her every word.

"And there you were" -- Ridley chuckled, gesturing wildly -- "surrounded by your brothers, playing bartender." A sly grin spread across her face. "Had a bit too much liquid courage yourself."

My stomach lurched. I already knew where this story was heading. I didn't know how I knew, but I did. "So I spilled the damn alcohol."

She nodded, barely containing her laughter. "All over the bar. And then, in your infinite wisdom, you decided to light a match."

"Jesus," I groaned, burying my face in my hands. "How bad was it?"

"Let's just say the Christmas tree went up faster than a rocket." She snickered. "Torch nearly choked you, but the look on your face..." A wave of uncontrollable laughter erupted from her, the sound infectious. "The entire bar caught on fire. Had to be replaced shortly after."

Against my better judgment, I found myself

joining in. The mental image was so vivid, I could practically smell the singed wood and hear the shouts of alarm. It all felt so real, so tangible, yet the actual memory remained elusive.

"Then what?" I urged, wanting to hear more about this absurd incident from my past.

Her eyes softened, a gentle smile gracing her lips. "Right in the middle of all that chaos, you looked at me and said, 'Darlin', I'd burn down the entire world just to see you smile like that.'"

Those words, hanging heavy in the air, sent a tremor through me. My breath hitched as I looked at Ridley, really looked at her. The fading sun caught the golden flecks in her eyes, their depths pulling me in like a whirlpool.

Without even thinking, I reached out, brushing a stray strand of hair from her face. My touch sent a shiver through her, her eyes flickering with a mix of hope and something more.

"I might not remember saying that," I admitted, my voice low and husky, "but I can see why I would have."

The space between us was filled with unspoken desire and feelings coming to the surface. Ridley leaned in, her lips just a whisper away from mine.

"Venom," she breathed, her voice barely a murmur against the frantic beat of my heart. "I've missed you so much."

I closed the gap, claiming her lips in a kiss that was both familiar and thrilling. Her body melted against mine, arms snaking around my neck as I pulled her closer. My hands found her waist, marveling at how perfectly she fit against me.

The years seemed to melt away as we kissed, leaving nothing but the raw emotions simmering between us. It felt like coming home after a long, arduous journey, finding solace and belonging in this one perfect moment.

As I pulled away, her eyes, filled with laughter and something more profound, locked with mine.

With a soft smile, she rested her forehead against mine. "Let's not waste even a second."

In her eyes, in the soft curve of her lips, I saw a future brimming with possibilities, a second chance. And as I held her close, the past fading into a hazy dream, I knew I wouldn't let it slip away.

"I think I should stay in the guest room," I said. "There's definitely something between us, even if I can't remember it. But..."

"You still feel like we're strangers," she said softly.

"Something like that. I just need a night or so. Get my bearings a bit more," I said. I could see the hurt in her eyes and it gutted me. It was clear we'd had a good life together, and that we'd loved each other. But right now, I wasn't *her* Venom. I knew there was a chance I may never be that man again. It felt like she was latching on, needing the husband she remembered. I worried if we took things too fast, she'd end up getting hurt.

She nodded. "All right. Whatever you think is best."

I kissed her cheek, wishing I could take all her pain away. If only I knew how...

Chapter Three

Venom

The door burst open, flooding the dimly lit room with sunlight. Ridley strode in, her blonde hair a halo around her face. Her every movement shouted her determination. I squinted, caught off guard by her sudden appearance and the intensity radiating from her petite frame.

"Rise and shine, big guy!" she exclaimed, her voice carrying a note of excitement that seemed at odds with the unfamiliar surroundings. "We've got plans today."

I hesitated, my mind still foggy with sleep and confusion. The room, with its generic furnishings and gray walls, felt alien. Even though we were apparently married, I hadn't felt right staying in the master bedroom. Instead, I'd decided to sleep in the guest room.

Ridley's infectious enthusiasm tugged at something deep within me, a half-remembered sensation of warmth and belonging.

"Plans?" I grunted, my voice rough from disuse.

Ridley's smile widened, a mischievous glint in her eyes. "Oh yes, Mr. Grumpy Pants. We're going on an adventure."

I raised an eyebrow, torn between skepticism and an inexplicable urge to follow her lead. "I don't know if that's a good idea. I'm not exactly…"

"Not exactly what?" she challenged, hands on her hips. "Are you thinking you're too old? Too forgetful? Too stubborn?"

Her words stung, but there was no malice behind them. Instead, I sensed a fierce protectiveness, a determination to drag me back into the world -- her world -- whether I was ready or not.

"Fine," I conceded, pushing myself up from the bed. "Let me get dressed."

Ridley's triumphant grin was almost worth the discomfort of agreeing to this unknown excursion. As I changed, I caught her watching me, a mixture of longing and sadness in her eyes that made my chest tighten with an emotion I couldn't name.

We stepped outside, the bright sunlight momentarily blinding me. As my vision cleared, I saw it -- my motorcycle, gleaming in the morning light. The sight of it stirred something primal within me, a surge of recognition that cut through the fog of uncertainty.

"Ready to ride?" Ridley asked, her voice soft and hopeful.

I nodded, unable to speak past the lump in my throat. My hands found the handlebars, the grips familiar against my calloused palms. I swung my leg over the seat, the weight and balance of the machine as natural as breathing.

When I'd first woken in the hospital, I hadn't realized how weak I'd become. Before I'd gotten to come home, I'd had to go through physical therapy. If I hadn't done that, I had a feeling I wouldn't be able to ride right now. As much as I'd hated every second of being there, it had been the right call.

The engine roared to life beneath me, a deep, throaty rumble that resonated in my bones. It was a sound I knew, a part of me I hadn't realized was missing until this moment. Ridley climbed on behind me, her arms wrapping around my waist with practiced ease.

As we pulled away from the house, I felt a glimmer of something long forgotten -- freedom, possibility, and the intoxicating promise of the open road.

We exited the compound and she pointed to the right, taking us away from town. I didn't know what she had up her sleeve, but I was willing to find out.

The wind whipped against my face as we tore down the highway, the rhythmic thrum of the engine pulsing through my body. Ridley's arms tightened around my waist, her warmth seeping into my back.

My mind raced with questions, each turn of the wheels bringing a new uncertainty to the forefront. Who was I really? What life had I forgotten? But with each mile that passed, the anxiety began to ebb, replaced by the soothing cadence of the ride.

"You okay?" Ridley's voice carried over the roar of the wind, concern lacing her words.

I nodded, not trusting my voice. Her presence behind me anchored me to the moment, a tether to a life I was struggling to remember.

After what felt like both an eternity and mere minutes, we pulled into the parking lot of a quaint roadside diner. The neon *OPEN* sign flickered in the window, casting a warm glow on the weathered exterior.

As I cut the engine, Ridley slid off the bike with grace. She turned to me, her eyes bright with an emotion I couldn't quite decipher. Without a word, she reached out and took my hand, her fingers intertwining with mine as if they'd done so a thousand times before.

The ease of the gesture caught me off guard, a jolt of electricity shooting up my arm at her touch. I followed her lead, allowing her to guide me toward the entrance.

As we stepped inside, a wave of nostalgia washed over me. The scent of freshly brewed coffee mingled with the sizzle of bacon on the grill, creating an aroma that tugged at the edges of my memory.

"Two for breakfast?" a cheery waitress called out, already reaching for menus.

Ridley squeezed my hand, a silent reassurance. "Yes, please," she answered, her voice carrying a warmth that seemed to light up the room.

I found myself studying her profile, wondering at the familiarity of her features and the comfort of her presence. Who was this vibrant woman who claimed to be my wife? And why did every fiber of my being want to believe her?

As we slid into a worn leather booth, Ridley's infectious laughter filled the air. Her eyes sparkled with mischief as she leaned across the table, her voice dropping to a conspiratorial whisper.

"Remember that time you tried to make bread?" she asked, her lips curving into a teasing smile. "I had this insane craving for homemade bread, and you, being the tough biker you are, decided to tackle it head-on."

I raised an eyebrow, trying to conjure the memory she spoke of. "I don't..." I began, but she waved away my protest.

"Oh, Venom." She chuckled. "You should have seen yourself. Flour everywhere, you cursing up a storm... You looked like a ghost had exploded in our kitchen. That's when the kitchen counter got ruined."

As she spoke, I found myself hanging on every word, desperately trying to piece together the fragments of a life I couldn't recall. The warmth in her voice, the way her eyes crinkled at the corners when she laughed -- it all felt achingly familiar.

"Did I actually manage to make the bread?" I asked, surprising myself with my curiosity.

Ridley's laughter bubbled up again. "Oh, honey, you tried. But let's just say we ended up ordering pizza that night."

I couldn't help but smirk at the image she painted. It was so at odds with the tough, no-nonsense biker I knew myself to be, and yet... there was something about it that rang true.

As we ordered our food, the conversation flowed effortlessly. Ridley's vibrant personality filled the space between us, her words weaving a tapestry of shared experiences I longed to remember.

"You know," she said, her voice softening as she reached across the table to touch my hand, "you may not remember it all right now, but we've had a good life, Venom. You, me, and our kids -- we've built something special."

Her fingers traced patterns on my skin, sending a shiver down my spine. I found myself captivated by the way the diner's lights reflected in her eyes, creating depths I wanted to lose myself in.

"Tell me more," I said, my voice gruffer than I intended. "About us. About... our family."

Ridley's smile widened, and as she launched into another story, I realized I could listen to her talk forever. I was desperate to reclaim the life she described -- a life that, despite my foggy memory, felt undeniably right.

* * *

As we stepped out of the diner, the late morning sun bathed everything in a warm glow. Ridley's blonde hair caught the light, shimmering like spun gold.

"How about a walk?" she suggested, gesturing toward a nearby path that wound its way along the riverbank. "It's a beautiful day, and there's a spot down there that's always been special to us."

I nodded, intrigued by the prospect of exploring more of this world we shared. "Lead the way," I said, my voice a low rumble.

As we strolled side by side, the gentle lapping of the river against its banks filled the air. The scent of wildflowers and sun-warmed earth surrounded us, stirring something deep within me.

Ridley's hand brushed against mine, and without thinking, I intertwined our fingers. Her small hand fit perfectly in my larger one, as if they were made for each other.

"You know," Ridley began, her voice light but tinged with nostalgia, "if you want stories about the kids, I should tell you about the time you taught Farrah to ride a bicycle."

She squeezed my hand reassuringly. "You were so patient with her. Spent hours running alongside that little pink bike, holding her steady. And not two hours after she finally got the hang of it, she rode straight through my newly planted flower beds."

I chuckled, picturing the scene. "I bet that went over well."

Ridley laughed, the sound as clear and refreshing as the river beside us. "Oh, I was furious for about five seconds. But then I saw how proud she was, and how proud you were of her... I couldn't stay mad."

As we continued our walk, Ridley regaled me with more stories of our life together. With each tale, I felt a growing warmth in my chest, a sense of belonging I couldn't quite explain.

"Oh! And then there was the time we caught Mariah with a wine cooler," Ridley said, her eyes twinkling with mischief. "Poor thing panicked when we walked in. She threw it, and that fruity alcohol went everywhere. All over you, down your shirt, in your beard. You looked like a grizzly bear who'd raided a liquor store."

I ran my hand through my beard, now shot through with silver, imagining the sticky mess. "Bet that was a bitch to clean up."

Ridley nodded, still grinning. "Your cut smelled like artificial strawberries for days. But you know what? You didn't lose your temper. You just looked at her and said, 'Next time, pick a better hiding spot.'"

As I listened to Ridley's stories, I felt a burning curiosity, a desperate need to know more about this life -- our life -- that I couldn't remember.

The riverbank path narrowed, forcing us closer together. Ridley's arm brushed against mine, sending an electric current through my body. I inhaled sharply, caught off guard by the intensity of my reaction. Her scent -- a mix of lavender and something uniquely her -- filled my senses, stirring something deep within me.

"You okay?" Ridley asked, her gaze searching my face.

I nodded, not trusting my voice. My hand flexed at my side, an inexplicable urge to reach out and touch her overwhelming me. As if reading my thoughts, Ridley's fingers grazed mine, a featherlight touch that set my nerves on fire.

"I used to love walking here with you," she murmured, her voice low and husky. "We'd come down here when the kids were driving us crazy, just to get a moment of peace. My dad would come over to watch them, and we'd take a ride. Always ended up walking this same path."

The sun dipped lower on the horizon, casting long shadows across the water. We paused at the river's edge, the gentle lapping of waves against the shore filling the silence between us. Ridley turned to face me, her blonde hair glowing like a halo in the fading light.

"Venom," she said softly, her eyes searching mine. "Do you... do you feel anything? Anything at all?"

I hesitated, caught in her gaze. The logical part of my brain screamed that this was all wrong, that I couldn't possibly have forgotten an entire life. But my body, my heart -- they told a different story. Every fiber of my being ached to remember, to reclaim the life she described.

"I..." I started, my voice gruff with emotion. "I don't know what I feel, Ridley. It's all a jumble. But there's something... something I can't explain."

Ridley's eyes flickered with a mix of hope and determination. In one fluid motion, she closed the distance between us, her hand sliding up my chest to rest over my thundering heart. The scent of her perfume enveloped me, stirring a memory just out of reach.

"Then let me help you remember," she whispered, her breath warm against my lips.

Before I could respond, her mouth captured mine in a searing kiss. The world around us faded, the sound of the river and rustling leaves giving way to the roar of blood in my ears. My body reacted instinctively, arms wrapping around her petite frame, pulling her flush against me.

The kiss deepened, Ridley's tongue teasing the seam of my lips. I groaned, opening to her, lost in the taste and feel of her. It was familiar and new all at once, like coming home to a place I'd never been. My fingers tangled in her silky hair, angling her head to deepen the kiss further.

The slow burn of desire ignited into a raging inferno. Ridley's hands roamed my back, up under my cut, nails scraping lightly through my shirt, sending shivers down my spine. I couldn't think, couldn't breathe -- all I knew was the woman in my arms and the growing need to never let her go.

When we finally parted, both gasping for air, I rested my forehead against hers. My heart raced, and I struggled to form coherent thoughts.

"Darlin'," I rasped, my voice rough with want. "That was…"

Ridley's smile was radiant, a mixture of joy and mischief in her eyes. She pressed a softer kiss to the corner of my mouth. "We've got a lot of lost time to make up for, tough guy."

Ridley's hand found mine, her fingers intertwining with my own as if they'd always belonged there. The warmth of her touch sent a jolt through me, awakening something long dormant.

"So," I rumbled, my voice still husky from our kiss, "where do we go from here?"

Ridley's eyes met mine, a spark of determination igniting within their depths. "Wherever you want, Venom. This is your journey."

I glanced down at our joined hands, marveling at how natural it felt. "I don't know where I want to go," I admitted, the words tasting foreign on my tongue. "But I know I want to keep going… with you."

A gentle squeeze of her hand accompanied her soft smile. "Then let's keep walking. One step at a time."

We began to move along the riverbank. The scent of wildflowers mingled with the earthy aroma of the river, creating an intoxicating blend that seemed to clear my foggy mind.

"Tell me more." I still had so much I couldn't recall, and stories she hadn't shared yet. Maybe something would finally make me remember the family I'd forgotten.

Ridley's laugh was like music, light and airy. "Oh, where to begin? There's so much, Venom. So many years, so many memories."

As we walked, she regaled me with tales of our life together -- motorcycle rides across state lines, quiet nights spent stargazing from our back porch, the chaos and joy of raising our children. With each story, I felt a tug of recognition, like a faint echo of a life I once knew.

The uncertainty of my future still loomed, a shadow at the edges of my consciousness. But with Ridley's hand in mine and the promise of rediscovery before us, I found myself looking forward to what lay ahead, one step at a time.

Chapter Four

Venom

I stepped into the dimly lit room, the floorboards creaking softly under my heavy boots. The air hung thick with tension, scented with a hint of leather and lavender. Ridley stood by the window, her back to me, her petite silhouette outlined in the fading light of sunset. My breath caught in my throat at the sight of her.

As I approached, my gaze fell on her cut draped over a nearby chair. The worn leather called to me, and I found myself drawn to it. My fingers traced the words etched across the back: "Property of Venom." An unexpected surge of possessive pride coursed through me, primal and fierce.

"Ridley..."

She turned, gaze meeting mine. A small smile played at the corners of her mouth. "I was wondering when you'd show up."

She moved closer. The fading light caught the shimmering strands of her hair. "I still remember the day you gave me that."

My brow furrowed as I struggled to recall the memory. "Wish I could remember."

Ridley's hand came to rest on my arm, her touch electric even through the fabric of my shirt. "Everything all right? You seem... distracted."

I swallowed hard, fighting the urge to pull her against me. "Just thinking about how right it looks. You, wearing my mark."

Mischief danced in her eyes. "Oh? And here I thought you should be the one wearing my mark."

A chuckle rumbled in my chest, surprising me with its ease. "That so? You planning on staking your claim, little girl?"

Ridley's fingers trailed up my arm, leaving goose bumps in their wake. "Maybe I already have."

I reached out, my fingers grazing the worn leather of the cut. The texture was familiar, yet foreign. Each groove and imperfection told a story I couldn't quite remember. A war raged within me -- the urge to claim, to possess, battling against the uncertainty of my fractured memories.

"It feels... right," I admitted, my voice barely above a whisper. "But I can't shake this feeling that I don't deserve it. Don't deserve you."

Ridley turned to face me fully, her eyes meeting mine with a mixture of vulnerability and unwavering strength. The charged silence between us was palpable, heavy with unspoken emotions and the weight of our shared history.

"You've always deserved me. Even when you didn't think so."

I searched her face, drinking in every detail. The slight crinkle at the corners of her eyes, the determined set of her jaw. This woman knew me, inside and out. And despite everything, she was still here.

"How can you be so sure?" I asked, my fingers still lingering on the cut.

Ridley took a step closer, eliminating the space between us. The warmth of her body called to me.

"Because I know you," she whispered, her breath hot against my skin. "The good, the bad, and everything in between. And I chose you, just as you chose me."

The air crackled with tension, years of shared history and desire threatening to ignite. I cupped her face in my hands, torn between the urge to claim her lips and the need to unravel the mystery of our past.

"Tell me," I growled, my thumb tracing the curve of her cheek. "Tell me everything."

I searched Ridley's face for answers. The warmth of her presence enveloped me. It was familiar, comforting, grounding me in the reality of our connection.

Ridley broke the charged silence with a soft, teasing smile. "You know," she said, her voice lilting with amusement, "I still think you should have gotten one that said 'Property of Ridley' instead."

I raised an eyebrow, feeling a smile tugging at the corners of my mouth despite myself. "Oh yeah? And why's that?"

She reached out, her small hand resting on my chest. The touch sent a jolt through me. "Because like I told you, I was the one who claimed you, tough guy. Not the other way around."

I chuckled, the sound rumbling deep in my chest. "Is that so?" I wondered what I'd thought of her sass when she'd first done that. The idea of this vibrant, outgoing woman staking her claim on me -- a hardened biker -- was both amusing and oddly appealing.

"You bet your ass it is," Ridley shot back, her eyes dancing with challenge and affection. "Of all things for you not to remember. Forgetting how I swept you off your feet? You're missing out on some great memories."

I leaned in closer, drawn by her magnetic presence. "Why don't you remind me, darlin'?" I growled, my voice low and husky.

I wrapped my arms around Ridley, my calloused hands encircling her waist as I pulled her into a tight embrace. Her petite frame fit perfectly against my muscular body, like two pieces of a long-lost puzzle finally reuniting. The heat of her skin seeped through the thin fabric of her shirt, igniting a spark, one I wasn't sure I could ignore this time. I'd managed to hold back, but now...

"Jesus," I muttered, my breath catching as Ridley pressed closer. Her curves molded to me, soft where I was hard, yielding where I was unyielding.

Ridley's fingers traced the lines of my face, her touch both familiar and thrillingly new. "You feel it too, don't you?" she whispered, her gaze searching mine. "This connection between us?"

Instead of answering, I leaned in and captured her lips in a kiss that was both tender and demanding. The taste of her -- sweet with a hint of the coffee she had drunk earlier -- exploded on my tongue. I groaned, deepening the kiss as Ridley tangled her fingers in my salt-and-pepper hair, tugging gently.

The world fell away, narrowing down to just the two of us. My hands roamed over Ridley's back, relearning every curve and dip of her body. She responded in kind, her touch setting my skin ablaze even through my leather cut.

"Ridley," I breathed against her lips, my voice rough with need. "I might not remember everything, but this... us... it feels right."

* * *

Ridley

I pulled back slightly, my chest heaving as I caught my breath. My eyes locked onto Venom's. A flush crept into my cheeks, and my lips were swollen from our kisses. I saw the way he stared at me, captivated, and the look of possessiveness in his gaze.

"It's right," I murmured, running my fingers through his beard. "It's always been right between us,

Venom."

He cupped my face in his calloused hands, his thumbs brushing over my cheekbones. The tenderness of his touch surprised me, but it felt natural, as if his body remembered what his mind couldn't.

"I can't remember anything," he admitted. "But kissing you... holding you like this... it feels like coming home. Some part of me knows you're mine, even if I can't recall the details."

My eyes shimmered with unshed tears, but I couldn't help the radiant smile that broke free. "And I'm yours," I whispered fiercely. "Always have been, always will be."

He leaned his forehead against mine, closing his eyes and breathing me in.

"Tell me," he murmured, his lips brushing against mine as he spoke. "Tell me more about us, about our life together. I need all the details. Every single thing I've forgotten."

My lips curved into a mischievous smile. "How about I show you instead? Maybe you'll remember if we keep going."

Venom's breath caught as I slowly began to undress, my movements deliberate and seductive. He couldn't tear his eyes away from me, drinking in every inch of exposed skin. The soft glow of the setting sun painted my body in warm hues, highlighting my curves.

"Christ, woman," he growled, his hands clenching at his sides. "You're a Goddamn vision."

My laughter was low and throaty. "And you're overdressed, big man," I teased, reaching for him.

As I pulled him down onto the bed, our bodies fit together perfectly, as if we'd been molded for each other. He buried his face in the crook of my neck, inhaling deeply.

"You smell like home," he murmured, his lips brushing against my skin.

I arched against him, my fingers tangling in his hair. "Then come home to me."

Venom groaned against my throat, his breath hot and ragged as his hands roamed over my body with a desperate sort of reverence. I felt the tremor in his fingers, the unspoken emotions weighing heavy between us. He might not remember every moment we'd shared, but his body did. His touch was instinctive, knowing exactly where to linger, where to press harder, where to make me gasp.

His name spilled from my lips as I arched beneath him, back bowing as he pressed kisses down the line of my neck, his beard scraping deliciously over sensitive skin. It wasn't just lust -- we had that in spades -- but it was deeper. It was familiarity, history, a love forged through battles and scars.

I pulled at his shirt, shoving it up until he finally helped me strip it away. The moment his bare skin met mine, he let out a guttural sound that sent a shiver down my spine. His hands splayed across my back, holding me tightly as if grounding himself in my warmth.

"Tell me," he rasped against the shell of my ear as he laid me back against the mattress. "Tell me how it was between us." His lips found mine again, slow and consuming.

I tangled my fingers in his hair, reveling in the way he responded to my touch. "It was intense," I whispered against his mouth. "Passionate. Like wildfire -- sometimes dangerous, but always unstoppable."

Venom exhaled sharply, as if recognizing

something familiar in my words. His gaze locked onto mine, dark and searching. "And now?"

I slid a hand down his chest, feeling the steady thrum of his heartbeat beneath my palm. "Now?" A slow smile played on my lips as I pulled him back down to me. "Now it's still burning."

* * *

Venom

My lips crashed against hers, the taste of her intoxicating, pulling me into a tide I didn't want to fight. She was right -- this wasn't a flicker or some fleeting heat. It was an inferno, roaring between us, consuming rational thought and leaving only the raw edges of who we were together.

The leather cut still draped over the chair caught my eye as I pulled back just enough to rest my forehead against hers, my chest rising and falling in tandem with hers. I grazed her swollen bottom lip with my thumb. "Burning's dangerous. Uncontrolled fire tears everything apart."

Ridley cupped my jaw, her fingers brushing through the silver streaks in my beard as if anchoring me to this moment. "Not all fire destroys," she said softly. "Some of it purifies. Some of it builds something stronger from the ashes."

Her words twisted something deep inside me -- both a comfort and a challenge I hadn't realized I needed. Her hands trailed down my arms, over skin and muscle that jumped under her touch, until she reached the tattoos marking my forearms: reminders of loyalty, brotherhood, and scars that would never fade.

"I used to think you'd burn me alive," she murmured against my throat, pressing a kiss there that had me clenching my fists to keep control. "But instead, you gave me warmth in a world that was so damn cold."

I sucked in a breath and tilted her chin up with one hand so I could see all of her -- the flushed cheeks, those captivating eyes glowing like embers under their own firelight. "You talk like I'm some kind of savior. I know myself well enough to realize I've fucked up more times than either of us could probably count."

Ridley arched into me slightly, pinning me with a look equal parts fierce and tender. "Yeah, you've screwed up," she said boldly, tracing a finger along the edges of one of my scars before dragging it up to rest on my chest over my hammering heart. "And so have I. It's not about perfection -- it's about fighting for what we are."

Something inside me cracked wide open at her words -- a floodgate releasing emotions I couldn't begin to name but wanted to drown in anyway. I crushed her against me again in a kiss that spoke more than my words ever could.

But even as desire coiled tighter between us -- a hot blur of hands and lips -- there was an ache beneath it all. The pieces of myself still missing gnawed at me like shadows whispering just out of reach.

I stood and quickly stripped off my clothes, not giving myself a chance to second-guess my decision. We were married, even if I didn't remember making her mine. If Ridley wanted me, then she'd have me. Maybe she was right and being together like this would jog my memory.

She held her hand out to me. "I won't break. You've never hurt me, and I know you won't start now."

I covered her body with mine, and she parted her thighs, welcoming me. My cock brushed against her pussy, and I felt how wet and ready she was. My heart thundered in my chest, and I held her gaze, as I slowly sank into her. The feel of her wrapped around my cock had me closing my eyes and fighting to hold back a groan. *Fuck me.*

"Yes! Don't stop," she said, clawing at my back. "It's been far too long. I've missed you so much."

"Then I'm all yours," I said, claiming her lips once more as I pounded into her. Every stroke felt like pure bliss as I sank into her heat. The soft sounds she made only spurred me on. I couldn't have held back if I wanted to.

It was going to end all too soon, but I felt her tighten around me, and she was coming. Her release coated my cock and I took her harder, deeper. I felt my balls draw up and then I was coming, filling her up. She cried out as she came again, and I realized that even if I didn't remember her, this felt incredibly familiar. Some part of me recognized her.

I collapsed beside Ridley, pulling her close as our heartbeats slowly returned to normal.

Ridley curled into me, her head resting on my chest. "I love you," she murmured, her voice thick with emotion. "I've always loved you, Venom. No matter what."

I tightened my arms around her, a lump forming in my throat. I might not remember anything, but in that moment, I knew with absolute certainty that this woman was my whole world.

I traced idle patterns on Ridley's skin as the afterglow settled over us. The fading light cast long shadows across the room, giving everything a dreamlike quality. I inhaled deeply, savoring the scent of her hair mingled with the lingering musk of our lovemaking. And I knew that's what it had been.

As we lay there, bodies entwined and hearts beating in sync, I felt a sense of peace wash over me. The future might be uncertain, but with Ridley by my side, I knew we could face anything. Together, we would rediscover our love, one memory at a time.

Chapter Five

Venom

The Dixie Reapers clubhouse, a place I once knew like the back of my hand, felt strangely alien. When I'd first walked through the door, the changes had been drastic enough to slap me in the face. And yet, a lot remained the same. I scanned the room, my eyes adjusting to the shadows. Faces I once knew intimately were now strangers, their expressions unreadable in the dim light. The low hum of conversation and clinking of bottles, a soundtrack that had been the backdrop of my life for decades, was now a foreign melody.

I ran a hand over the worn leather of my cut, the weight of it both comforting and unsettling. Like an old coat I hadn't worn in years, it felt both familiar and ill-fitting. My gaze landed on a group of officers gathered around the bar, their patches gleaming dully in the low light. Most of them I didn't recognize. A few seemed vaguely familiar.

"Torch," I muttered, my voice rough from disuse. I scanned the area and spotted him a little farther down the bar.

He looked up, a bottle of whiskey raised in a crooked salute. A ghost of a smile touched his lips. "Well, look what the cat dragged in. You got home from the hospital and then vanished on us. Glad to see you found your way here."

As I moved closer, I noticed the new faces among the officers. Younger, with fire in their eyes and a swagger in their step. Their youthful energy was a stark contrast to my own weathered presence.

Damn, when did I become the old man in the room? I ran a hand through my silver-streaked beard. That was hard to get used to seeing in the mirror.

One of the new officers straightened as I approached. "Glad to see you again, Venom. You had us all worried."

I grunted, unsure how to respond. I'd been in the hospital for months, but for me, more than thirty years had passed.

I felt a twinge of something -- nostalgia, perhaps, or regret -- as I looked around at the changed faces of my brothers. The clubhouse itself hadn't changed much, still reeking of spilled beer and decades of hard living, but the men within it... that was a different story. And I didn't see a damn club whore anywhere. Ridley had mentioned they were no longer allowed here, even though I hadn't gotten the full story behind why something like that had changed.

How much have I missed?

I approached the bar. If I'd ever needed a drink in my life it was now. Laughter and banter filled the air, a cacophony of voices both familiar and strange. I knew my wife was around somewhere. She'd stuck to me for the first little bit, then she'd wandered off. Probably thought if she wasn't glued to me, I'd go mingle. "Whiskey. Neat."

As the bartender, a Prospect I didn't recognize, poured my drink, my gaze swept across the room once more. The weight of memories pressed down on me, suffocating in their intensity. I took a long pull from my glass, savoring the burn. *I used to know every damn face in the room. Now I feel like a stranger.*

Ridley slid onto the stool next to me, her presence a balm to my frayed nerves. She flashed me a reassuring smile, her eyes twinkling with understanding.

I snorted. "I remember the days you wouldn't be

allowed in here. Now you're sitting next to me like it's nothing, and there's not a naked woman in sight. I can't figure out where I fit in the present."

Ridley's hand found mine, her fingers intertwining with mine. "You fit right here."

A towering figure approached, his leather cut adorned with patches I didn't recognize. He'd been among the group of officers I'd spotted earlier. His eyes held a mix of reverence and wariness as he extended his hand.

"Venom," he said, his voice deep and resonant. "I'm Royal. I figured you didn't remember me."

"He joined the club about seven or eight years after you and I got together," Ridley said, helping me figure out the timeline.

I clasped the offered hand, feeling the strength in Royal's grip. He was younger than me, confident, shoulders squared. I saw the officer patch on his cut: Secretary.

"Royal," I echoed, keeping my tone neutral.

"When all of you stepped down and handed your positions to new officers, you and Torch decided it was time the club had a secretary. I was honored to be offered the position."

"Good to meet you, kid," I said, my voice gruff. "Again. Sorry I don't remember you."

"It's okay. Ridley says they think your memories will come back in time. We're all here for you."

I nodded, unsure how to respond.

Ridley's hand on my arm broke the tension. "Come on, babe," she said, her voice light but brooking no argument. "Let's make the rounds."

We moved through the clubhouse, the scent of leather and old beer growing stronger. Old faces emerged from the crowd, weathered and worn but achingly familiar.

Torch approached. His silver hair gleamed in the dim light, his gray eyes full of mischief and melancholy. We'd spoken briefly, but it hadn't felt the same. At least, not the way I remembered things being between us.

"For me, I just fought beside you a few months ago. But for you... guess it's been a lot longer. You doing okay? I mean with all this." He waved a hand at the room in general. "You've lasted longer than I thought you would. Figured you'd have been overwhelmed by now and gone home."

My chest tightened. "Yeah. Just taking it one day at a time. Or in this case, one hour at a time. Ridley is helping a lot."

"She's always been good for you," Torch said.

We exchanged stories, Torch filling me in on club business and family news. I listened, nodding and grunting at appropriate intervals, but my mind whirled. I recognized some of the events Torch spoke of, but they felt distant, as if belonging to someone else's life. Fleeting memories – there, then gone again.

"Your boy's doing well," Torch said, clapping me on the shoulder. "Dawson's got your fire, that's for damn sure. That club of his isn't like ours, but they're good men."

Pride warred with a sense of loss in my gut. I'd missed so much of my son's life, of all my children's lives. The realization left a bitter taste in my mouth. I hadn't even had the chance to meet any of them yet.

We moved on, and Bull's massive form loomed before us. My father-in-law regarded me with a mix of affection and wariness.

"Welcome home," Bull rumbled, pulling me into a bone-crushing hug.

I returned the embrace, inhaling the familiar scent of motor oil and cigars that clung to Bull's cut. When we parted, I saw the questions in his eyes -- questions I wasn't sure I was ready to answer.

"Good to be back," I said, the words feeling hollow even as I spoke them.

As we continued our circuit of the clubhouse, I felt the weight of eyes upon me -- some curious, some wary, all assessing. I squared my shoulders, determined to project the strength and confidence that had once come so naturally.

But inside, doubts gnawed at me. What would happen if my memories never returned? Would I still have a place in this world?

Ridley's laughter, bright and clear, pierced through the fog of my thoughts, yanking me back to the present. Her eyes, sparkling with mischief, held me captive as she leaned in close, her breath like a warm summer breeze against my ear.

"You're looking like you're trying to solve world hunger, old man," she teased, her fingers trailing playfully down my arm. "Relax those eyebrows before you scare off all the Prospects."

A reluctant smile tugged at the corners of my mouth, the tension in my shoulders easing with each playful stroke of her fingers. "Old man, huh? I'll show you old later, darlin'."

Ridley's cheeks flushed, her grin widening. "Promises, promises," she purred, loud enough for the nearby members to hear.

The response was immediate -- a chorus of good-natured whistles and catcalls erupted around us. A surge of possessive pride filled me as I wrapped an arm around Ridley's waist, pulling her close. Her presence was a grounding force, a steady anchor in the sea of uncertainty that was my life.

"Venom! Get your ass over here!"

The gruff voice belonged to Tank, one of my oldest friends in the club. The biker sat at a corner table, a half-empty bottle of whiskey his only companion.

"Go on," Ridley urged, giving me a gentle push. "I'll mingle a bit. Come find me when you're done catching up."

I made my way to Tank's table, sinking into the chair opposite my old friend. His face was more lined than I remembered, his beard also going gray like mine.

"Christ, you look like shit." Tank grinned, pouring a generous measure of whiskey for me.

"Speak for yourself, you old bastard," I retorted, raising the glass in a mock toast before taking a sip.

"Since you're missing your memories, how about I catch you up on few things?" Tank asked.

I nodded and he launched into one tale after another. A conflicting mix of emotions washed over me. But as I glanced across the room, I saw Ridley chatting with the other old ladies. It still blew my mind so many of us had settled down. I caught Ridley's eye and I felt a different kind of pull. The life I'd left behind called to me, but so did the future I was building with Ridley.

I turned back to Tank, forcing a smile. I raised my glass. "To the Dixie Reapers."

After our toast, I got up and wandered through the crowd again, finding a spot at the bar.

The laughter and clink of bottles, once jarring, now washed over me like a comforting wave. Leaning against the bar, my hands clasped around a cold beer, I felt the tension in my shoulders ease.

Torch was only a few spots away, and he started regaling me with funny things I'd missed -- or rather, couldn't remember.

"So there I was, ass-deep in mud, bike sputtering like a dying cat," Torch exclaimed, gesticulating with his usual flair. A chuckle escaped my lips, rusty but genuine.

"Let me guess," I surprised myself by saying, "You tried that shortcut through Miller's Creek again?"

Torch's eyes widened with delight. "Hell yeah, brother! How'd you know?"

I shrugged, a half-smile tugging at my lips. "Some things never change. I learned that lesson the hard way back in '89."

The group erupted in laughter, and a warm glow of belonging spread through my chest. Across the room, I caught Ridley's eye, her smile igniting a different kind of heat within me.

As the night unfolded, old memories bubbled to the surface, flowing effortlessly in the rhythm of conversation. The camaraderie I'd once taken for granted now felt like a precious gift, one I was determined to savor. I'd nearly lost all this. Even though I might not remember the last thirty plus years, at least I was here. Alive. They'd said I'd died twice. If things had gone down differently, I could be six feet under right now.

Later, Ridley tugged on my arm, leading me to a quiet corner of the clubhouse. The party's muffled sounds faded as she leaned in.

"You're doing great, you know," she murmured "They've missed you. We all have."

I exhaled slowly, my fingers tracing the curve of her hip. "It's different," I admitted. "I feel like I'm trying to wear an old skin that doesn't quite fit anymore."

Ridley cupped my face, her touch soft yet firm. "You're still you, Venom. Fierce protector, loyal brother -- that hasn't changed. The rest? We'll figure it out together."

Her words were a balm, soothing the raw edges of my uncertainty. I pulled her close, burying my face in her hair, letting her unwavering faith anchor me.

"One last look," I murmured, letting my gaze linger on the weathered wood of the clubhouse walls, the worn leather of the bar stools, the faded photographs of past members that lined the walls. It was a scene etched into my memory, a haven I'd feared lost forever. Things had changed, yet a lot still remained the same.

The familiar sounds of the clubhouse -- the laughter, the clinking glasses, the murmurs of conversation -- washed over me, a comforting symphony that resonated deep within my bones. It was the music of belonging, a melody I'd worried would be gone forever.

"Ready to head out?" Ridley's voice, soft and warm, interrupted my reverie. Her hand rested on the small of my back, a gentle reminder of her presence.

I straightened, a newfound resolve settling in my gut. "Yeah, darlin'. Let's go home."

As we walked toward the exit, I felt the weight of gazes on me. Some were curious, some respectful, all acknowledging my return. It was a reminder that my place here wasn't gone, just... transformed.

"You know," I said as we stepped into the cool night air, the scent of pine and asphalt filling my lungs, "I think I might have some ideas for the club. Things we could do differently, maybe even better. Of course, it's possible those things are already in place and I just don't remember it."

Ridley's laugh, rich and melodious, echoed in my ears. "There's the Venom I know. Always plotting, always three steps ahead."

I grinned, feeling a sense of myself returning, a piece that had been missing since I woke up and realized I'd missed out on the last thirty years of my life. "Gotta keep you on your toes, sweetheart."

We walked to my bike, hand in hand. The moon cast a silver glow over everything. As I swung my leg over the seat, Ridley pressed against my back, her arms wrapping around my waist.

"Ready for the next chapter?" she whispered, her breath hot against my ear.

I revved the engine, feeling the familiar rumble beneath me. "With you? Always."

As we roared out of the parking lot, the cool night air on our skin, a surge of hope filled me. The road ahead might be uncertain, but with Ridley by my side and the club at my back, I was ready to face whatever came our way. The future stretched before me, a blank canvas waiting for us to paint our own story. And I knew, with absolute certainty, that it would be a story worth telling.

Chapter Six

Venom

The first pale light of dawn kissed the edges of the curtains, outlining Ridley's sleeping form. My gaze lingered on her face, tracing the curve of her cheek, the rise and fall of her soft breaths. A pang of longing, laced with a curious ache, blossomed in my chest. Fragments of memories swirled through my mind, taunting me with their fleeting glimpses, like a half-forgotten dream.

Her blonde hair flowed over the pillow like a silken river, and a deep sense of belonging washed over me, intertwined with a gnawing unease at the vast emptiness where my memory should be.

Carefully, not wanting to disturb her peaceful slumber, I slipped out of bed. My muscles protested with a dull ache, a reminder of the passage of time I couldn't quite grasp. Silently, I padded toward the kitchen, driven by an inexplicable need to understand the broken puzzle of my past.

The familiar aroma of freshly brewed coffee greeted me like an old friend. Coffee maker. Timer. Programmable. That much I remembered, surprisingly. I inhaled deeply, closing my eyes as the smells triggered a cascade of images -- flashes of gleaming chrome, the roar of engines, the wind whipping through my hair as I rode. The laughter of men around a crackling bonfire, leather cuts over their shoulders.

My eyes snapped open, heart pounding in my chest. "Why can't I remember anything since Ridley came into my life? Why are only those years missing?"

With trembling hands, I poured myself a mug of coffee, hoping the warmth would coax more memories to the surface. Recent ones. The familiar feel of the ceramic against my skin grounded me, a small comfort in the overwhelming chaos of my mind.

"Good morning, handsome." Ridley's voice, bright and melodious, broke the silence.

I turned, my gaze drawn to her as she emerged from the bedroom, wrapped in a silken robe that clung to her curves. Her eyes twinkled with a mischievous glint, stirring something deep within me.

"Mornin'," I responded with a gruff rumble, trying to mask the turmoil within. "Sleep well?"

She padded over, her smile lighting up the room as she rose on her tiptoes to plant a soft kiss on my cheek. "Always do when I'm next to you."

Her casual, yet undeniably intimate gesture sent a jolt of electricity through me, a mixture of excitement and confusion. My brow furrowed as I tried to reconcile the warmth of her presence with the chilling void in my memory. After sleeping together, I'd moved back into our bedroom. Didn't seem like there was any point in keeping separate rooms. I'd also hoped it might make me remember things faster.

"You okay?" Ridley asked, her smile faltering slightly. "You've got that brooding look again."

I sighed, setting down my mug. "Just… trying to remember. It's all jumbled up in here." I tapped my temple.

Ridley's expression softened, and she rested her hand on my chest, right over my heart. "It'll come back to you. I promise. And I'll be right here, every step of the way."

I covered her small hand with mine, the fit so perfect it felt like we were destined to be together. "I know, darlin'. I just wish I could remember everything now. It's like looking at a photograph with half the image missing."

"Well," Ridley said, a playful glimmer in her eyes, "maybe I can jog your memory a little." She leaned in, her lips teasing mine.

My body responded instinctively, arms tightening around her waist as I leaned down, the scent of her intoxicating me. Just as our lips were about to meet, a sudden crash from outside the house shattered the intimate moment.

"What the hell was that?" I growled, my protective instincts kicking in.

Ridley sighed, reluctantly pulling away. "Probably just the neighbor's dog getting into the trash again. I swear, that mutt is more trouble than a Prospect on his first run."

Her offhand mention of the club stirred another fragment of memory, a hazy image I desperately clung to.

"Ridley," I said, my voice laced with urgency. "I can't keep living with these holes in my head."

"I'm not sure we should force it more than we already have. As it is, we've done all the things the doctor said not to do. I'm honestly worried. What if this causes more harm than good?"

The rough ceramic mug warmed my calloused fingers as I leaned against the counter, inhaling the rich aroma of coffee. My gaze drifted to a photo on the fridge, catching a glimpse of a younger Ridley. Her blonde hair, wild and windswept, framed eyes brimming with mischief.

"Damn," I muttered, setting down the mug with a soft clink.

The kitchen vanished, replaced by a vivid memory. I was back at the club's gate, witnessing a commotion.

"Is there a problem, Pete?" I'd asked as I approached.

"*Just some fucking whore who insists on seeing Bull,*" the prospect said, twisting the woman's arm a little more and making her cry out. "*Fucking poked my chest and bowed up at me like she's fucking someone.*"

I chuckled. "Is that so?"

I leaned down and met her blue gaze.

"*Venom,*" *she said softly.*

My gaze narrowed. "Just who the fuck are you, sweetheart? Because I sure as hell don't remember you."

"*I'm Ridley Johnson,*" *she said, her voice almost a whisper. I could see the pain etched on her features.*

Shock hit me as I quickly stood. Without pausing, I slammed my fist into Pete's jaw. The woman, now freed from his grip, tumbled the rest of the way to the ground. I wrapped my arms around her.

"*I've got you, baby girl. No one's going to fucking touch you again.*" *I lifted her into my arms and held her tight. Then glanced at the prospect. "Roll that bike up to the clubhouse."*

"*Who the hell is she?*" *he asked, his eyes burning with hate in the near darkness.*

"*Bull's daughter.*"

The fog began to clear when I heard Ridley's voice. Not in my memory, but right in front of me.

"Venom?"

I blinked, the compound fading away to reveal our cozy kitchen. She stood in front of me, a concerned frown creasing her brow.

"You okay, babe?" she asked. "You seemed a million miles away."

I swallowed hard, my throat suddenly dry. "Yeah, I'm... I'm good. Just remembering."

Her eyes softened as understanding dawned in their depths. She reached out, her small hand resting on my arm. The simple touch sent a jolt through me, grounding me in the present while reminding me of all I'd forgotten.

"What did you remember?" she asked softly, her thumb tracing soothing circles on my skin.

"The day you came back," I finally admitted, my voice low and steady. "When that prospect detained you at the gate."

A slow smile spread across her face, and she chuckled. "On that day, I thought Dad was going to have an aneurysm."

My lips curved into a smile, my tension easing as I watched her move around the kitchen. She pulled out plates and mugs, her petite frame graceful and purposeful in the warm morning light.

"Breakfast?" She glanced over her shoulder, raising an eyebrow.

"Sounds good." I nodded, settling into a chair at the small kitchen table.

As Ridley bustled about, the smell of sizzling bacon filled the air. I couldn't help but stare at her, looking over the changes from the woman in my memory just now to the one before me. Her blonde hair wasn't quite as long. Laugh lines framed her eyes and mouth. But she was still as beautiful as ever.

"You're staring, tough guy," she teased, refilling my coffee cup. "What's going on in that head of yours?"

"Just… trying to piece it all together," I admitted gruffly.

She softened as she sat across from me, cradling her own mug between her hands. "You know, most men would kill for the chance to fall in love with their wife all over again."

The words hit me like a punch to the gut. I opened my mouth, closed it again, then tried once more. "Ridley, I…"

She reached across the table, covering my larger hand with hers. "Hey, it's okay. We've got time."

My gaze locked onto hers.

"That day… When I saw you again. It was like… like seeing color for the first time after a lifetime of black and white." I cleared my throat. "I don't remember everything that happened, but I did see a piece of it."

"Venom," she whispered, emotions thickening her voice.

"Even if it's not all there yet, I do know one thing. You scared the shit out of me. I wanted you so damn bad and knew I shouldn't touch you. Even now, I feel the same."

A single tear slipped down her cheek, yet her smile remained radiant. "We'll get there again. One memory at a time."

The shrill ring of the phone shattered the moment. Ridley reluctantly pulled her hand away, rising to answer it. I watched her, my mind still reeling from the intensity of our conversation.

"Hey, sweetie," she said, her voice softening with a mother's warmth. "No, I don't think that's a good idea right now. Maybe in a few days…"

My heart quickened. Was she talking to one of our kids? Maybe our son? A surge of desperate curiosity flooded through me, quickly followed by a wave of shame for not remembering him.

"Hold on," she told who I thought might be Dawson, her gaze flicking to me.

"Tell him to come," I said. Maybe if I saw my son in person, it would help me get more memories back. "I want to see him."

She hesitated for a moment, then nodded. It

confirmed that I'd been right. It seemed she was talking to our son. "Change of plans, Dawson. Your dad wants to see you. Come on over."

The next thirty minutes crawled by like molasses. I ran a hand through my hair, my mind racing with questions. What would Dawson be like? Would there be any spark of recognition?

The rumble of a motorcycle engine cut through my thoughts. My head snapped up, and my body tensed instinctively. I moved to the window and peered out as a sleek bike pulled into the driveway.

The rider dismounted with fluid grace, removing his helmet to reveal a young man. One I recognized from the pictures in the house. My son. As he approached the house, my breath caught in my throat. The set of his jaw, the way he carried himself -- it was like looking in a mirror, but one that reflected a younger, less weathered version of myself.

Dawson stepped inside, his blue eyes -- Ridley's eyes -- scanning the room before landing on me. For a moment, neither of us spoke; the air thickened with unspoken emotions.

I stroked my beard unconsciously as I fixed my gaze on Dawson's smooth, clean-shaven face. The contrast struck me. We were alike and yet so different.

"Hey, Dad," Dawson said softly, a tentative smile dancing at the corners of his mouth.

The word "Dad" hit me like a physical blow, stirring something deep within me. I struggled to find my voice.

"Dawson," I finally managed, tasting the name on my tongue -- both foreign and achingly familiar. "It's... good to see you, son."

Dawson's eyes crinkled at the corners, a flicker of relief washing over his features. "It's good to see you too, Dad. I, uh… I noticed you looking at my face." He ran a hand over his smooth jaw, a wry smile tugging at his lips. "I'm a firefighter. Can't have a beard in that line of work."

I nodded, remembering Ridley had mentioned it before. A swell of pride caught me off guard, surprising me with its intensity. I motioned toward the living room, my movements stiff with an unfamiliar awkwardness. "Let's sit down."

We settled into the worn leather couch, the material creaking softly beneath us. My fingers drummed against my thigh, searching for words.

"Your mother mentioned…" I began, my voice gruff. I cleared my throat, trying again. "Ridley said you're married. Have a daughter."

Dawson's face lit up, his entire demeanor shifting like the sun breaking through clouds. The tension in his shoulders eased, and his eyes sparkled with unmistakable joy. "Yeah, I do. Nora's my wife. She's… she's everything, Dad. And Taylor, our little girl…" He paused, a soft chuckle escaping him. "She's a firecracker. Mom's influence, I think."

"Your mom mentioned a baby."

He nodded. "Yeah. I have a son now. He's so damn tiny I'm afraid I'll break him."

My heart ached for memories that slipped through my fingers like sand. I leaned forward, elbows on my knees, drinking in every word.

"Your grandson's name is Elijah. We thought it might be better to bring him by a different day, so my club president is watching him."

"Congratulations," I murmured, sincerity lining my tone. Even though Ridley had mentioned it before, it hadn't hit me until now. The realization that I was a grandfather washed over me -- joy mingling with a deep sense of loss for the time that eluded me.

Dawson's expression softened; vulnerability crept into his voice. "Taylor... she adores you, Dad. She's always asking when she can see her grandpa again -- drawing pictures of you on that big bike of yours."

The image hit me like a punch to the gut -- my granddaughter eagerly awaiting my return, her excitement palpable despite the distance between us. For a brief moment, I could see her. The memory vanished again. I swallowed hard, battling against the lump forming in my throat as emotions swirled within me like a storm.

I watched Dawson's face, noting how my son's eyes crinkled at the corners when he smiled -- just like Ridley's.

"Taylor's got quite the artistic streak," Dawson said, his voice soft with affection. "Every day she comes home from school with a new masterpiece. And I swear, Dad, nine times out of ten, you're right there in the center of it."

A low rumble of laughter escaped my chest, surprising me. "That so?"

Dawson nodded and reached into his back pocket, pulling out a folded piece of paper. As he unfolded it, I caught a glimpse of bright crayon scribbles.

"This is her latest," Dawson explained, holding it out to me. "See? That's you on your bike, and there's Taylor riding behind you. Not that Nora or Mom let her actually ride when the bike is running. But you often put her on the seat and push her up the driveway, or a little ways down the street."

My throat tightened as I stared at the childish drawing. The stick figure meant to be me sported an enormous beard and an even bigger smile. I traced it with my fingertip, overwhelmed by a longing for a connection I couldn't quite grasp.

Dawson watched me intently, his expression a mix of hope and caution. "Do you... have any questions, Dad? About Taylor or anything else?"

The weight of everything I didn't know pressed down on my shoulders. I wanted to ask a thousand questions and demand every detail of the life I'd forgotten. But the words wouldn't come. Instead, I shook my head and handed the drawing back to Dawson.

His face fell slightly, but he nodded in understanding. "It's okay. I don't want to push too much, too fast. One of the brothers in my club, Logan, is a paramedic. He's actually the one who saved your life, and he's with Akira. He explained about your memory loss and that trying to force it could actually make things worse."

Dawson stood and brushed imaginary dust from his jeans. "I should probably head out. But, uh, there's something else you should know, Mom." He turned to Ridley, who hovered silently in the doorway. "Farrah and Mariah are on lockdown at the Devil's Fury. They tried to leave to come here."

Ridley's entire demeanor shifted in an instant. Her eyes flashed as she let out a derisive snort. "Well, remind your sisters that they're still not welcome at the Dixie Reapers -- at least not until they offer a genuine apology."

The tension in the room skyrocketed as confusion battled with a strange sense of protective anger surging within me -- a feeling I struggled to understand. What the hell had my daughters done to be banned from this place?

As Dawson nodded and headed for the door, my mind raced with questions. The soft *thud* of the closing door echoed through the house, leaving a heavy silence in its wake. I turned my gaze to Ridley, her petite frame taut with tension, eyes stormy with unspoken emotions.

My throat tightened, the urge to ask about my daughters burning on my tongue. What could they have done to warrant such a harsh response from their own mother?

"Ridley," I started, hesitant. "About Farrah and Mariah…"

She turned to me, her blonde hair catching the light, a complex mix of emotions playing across her face. For a moment, I caught a glimpse of the vibrant, outgoing woman I knew she could be, but it vanished beneath something darker, more guarded.

The question died on my lips. Did I really want to know? Ridley had already shared so much with me, at my insistence. But what if the doctor and Dawson were right and it would only make things worse? The things she'd shared so far had been good memories. But if my daughters weren't allowed here, then they'd fucked up in a big way. I wasn't sure I was ready to find out more about the situation.

Instead, I stood tall, my imposing frame filling the room. "I need some air," I muttered, brushing past Ridley and striding toward the front door.

As I stepped onto the porch, the rumble of distant motorcycles called to something deep within me -- a part of my identity that even amnesia couldn't erase.

I took a deep breath, resolve hardening inside me. I might not have remembered everything, but I was determined to piece together the puzzle of my life.

For Ridley, for my children, and for myself. The life we shared was worth fighting for, worth remembering.

As the sun climbed higher in the sky, I narrowed my eyes with determination. This was just the beginning of my journey back to myself, and I was ready for whatever challenges lay ahead.

Chapter Seven

Venom
Three Months Later

My eyes snapped open, the morning light filtering through the curtains and casting a warm glow across the room. My heart raced as memories flooded my mind in a torrent -- vivid, undeniable images that brought sudden clarity to the fog that had clouded my thoughts for months.

The scent of Ridley's shampoo filled my nostrils as I sat up abruptly, my breath catching in my throat. She lay beside me, still sleeping peacefully, her blonde hair splayed across the pillow. The sight of her anchored me as the full weight of my regained past settled over me like a heavy blanket.

"Fuck," I muttered under my breath, running a hand through my hair.

Ridley stirred slightly at the sound of my voice but didn't wake. I watched the gentle rise and fall of her chest, marveling at how young she still looked compared to my weathered sixty-something-year-old ass.

My mind reeled as I sorted through the recovered memories. Flashes of our kids -- Dawson, Mariah, Farrah -- growing up. The day Ridley got her property cut. Stepping down as VP. Taylor running after me, begging to be picked up. And finally, the day I got shot and nearly died.

Pain pierced my brain as everything hit me like a freight train.

How could I have forgotten all this? A mix of relief and regret washing over me. Finally, I could recall all those missing years.

I clenched my fists, feeling the calluses earned

from years of working on bikes and throwing punches when needed. The tough, no-nonsense biker was still there inside me. But so was the devoted husband and father I'd become.

Ridley mumbled something in her sleep, drawing my gaze back to her. Even after all these years, the sight of her still made my heart skip a beat. I reached out, hesitating for just a moment before gently brushing a strand of hair from her face.

My fingers trembled as they grazed her cheek, a mix of awe and disbelief coursing through me. The softness of her skin beneath my fingertips was achingly familiar yet somehow felt brand new. In addition to our past, I still vividly recalled our time together the past few months, as we'd fallen in love all over again. Each delicate curve and line on her face told a story -- our story -- that I was rediscovering with every touch.

"Ridley," I whispered, my voice rough with emotion.

Her eyelids fluttered, and I held my breath as those striking blue eyes I'd fallen for decades ago slowly opened. Confusion clouded her gaze for a moment as she focused on me, her brow furrowing slightly.

"Venom?" she murmured, her voice thick with sleep. "What's wrong?"

I couldn't find the words, overwhelmed by the rush of memories and feelings. Instead, I cupped her face gently, my thumb tracing her cheekbone. Her eyes widened, a dawning realization replacing the confusion as she searched my face.

"You..." she breathed, her hand coming up to cover mine. "You remember?"

I nodded, a lump forming in my throat. "Everything, darlin'. Every damn thing."

The air between us crackled with tension, years of shared history flooding back in an instant. Ridley's eyes welled with tears, her grip on my hand tightening as if she was afraid I might slip away again.

A heavy silence stretched between us, thick with unspoken emotions. The soft morning light cast a warm glow across Ridley's face, highlighting the tears that threatened to spill from her eyes. I could feel my heart pounding, each beat a reminder of the love I'd rediscovered.

"Ridley," I whispered, her name falling from my lips like a prayer. My voice was rough, laden with the weight of restored memories and lost time. "My Ridley."

The dam broke. Ridley's eyes overflowed, tears streaming down her cheeks as she flung herself into my arms. Her body collided with mine, soft curves meeting my chest as she clung to me with desperate intensity.

"Oh God, Venom," she sobbed, her voice muffled against my chest. "You're really back. You're here."

I wrapped my arms around her, pulling her impossibly closer. The familiar feel of her in my arms evoked a flood of memories. Bike rides at sunset, lazy Sunday mornings, the birth of our children -- it all came rushing back.

"I'm here, darlin'," I murmured into her hair, my own eyes stinging. "I'm not goin' anywhere."

Ridley's fingers dug into my back, her body shaking with each sob. I could feel her tears soaking through my shirt, but I didn't care. All that mattered was holding her, proving to both of us that this moment was real.

"I thought I'd lost you," she choked out, her

words punctuated by hiccupping breaths. "Even when you came back, you weren't really... you."

The pain in her voice cut through me like a knife. I tightened my grip, one hand coming up to cradle the back of her head. "I know, sweetheart. I'm so damn sorry. But I'm here now. All of me."

My grip on Ridley remained firm yet tender, as if she might dissolve into mist if I dared to loosen my hold. Her petite frame fit perfectly against my larger one, a familiar puzzle piece slotting into place. The warmth of her body seeped into mine, a soothing balm that eased the ache of lost time.

"Ridley," I breathed, my voice rough with emotion. "My fierce, beautiful girl."

She shuddered against me, her fingers tracing the lines of my back through my shirt. The simple touch ignited sparks beneath my skin, reminding me of all we'd shared and all we'd missed.

"I can't believe you're really back," she whispered, her breath hot against my neck.

Slowly, reluctantly, we pulled apart just enough to lock eyes. The vibrant blue of her gaze, swimming with unshed tears, held me captive. In that moment, a lifetime of shared understanding passed between us -- the triumphs, the struggles, the unwavering love that had seen us through it all.

"Believe it, darlin'," I murmured, lifting a hand to cup her cheek. My thumb brushed away a stray tear, the salt of it a testament to the depth of her emotion. "I'm here, flesh and blood and memories intact."

Ridley's lips curved into a tremulous smile, a glimpse of that vivacious spirit I'd fallen for all those years ago. "Prove it, old man," she challenged, her voice husky.

I didn't need to be told twice. Leaning in, I

captured her lips with mine in a kiss that was both passionate and tender. It was a homecoming, a promise, a reaffirmation of the love we'd rediscovered, and the love we'd had for decades. Her lips were soft, yielding, yet demanding all at once -- so quintessentially Ridley that it made my heart ache.

The kiss deepened, intensifying with each passing moment. Ridley's fingers tangled in my hair, pulling me closer as if she couldn't get enough. The taste of her -- sweet and familiar -- flooded my senses. My hands roamed her back, tracing the curves I'd memorized long ago, rediscovering them anew.

A low groan escaped me as Ridley nipped at my bottom lip, the sharp sensation sending a jolt of electricity down my spine. The fire that had always smoldered between us roared to life, consuming us both. I could feel the heat of her body through the thin fabric of her nightgown, her soft body pressing against me.

"God, I've missed you," I breathed against her lips, barely breaking contact. The words were inadequate, but they were all I had.

Ridley responded by deepening the kiss, her tongue sliding against mine in a sensual dance. The room around us faded away, the soft morning light and gentle rustle of curtains becoming nothing more than background noise. The world outside ceased to exist, leaving only us and the bond we shared.

My hands slid lower, gripping her hips and pulling her flush against me. Ridley let out a soft gasp, the sound music to my ears. In that moment, nothing else mattered -- not the lost time, not the challenges ahead. There was only us, wrapped in each other's arms, rediscovering the passion that had never truly died.

As our kiss broke, we remained close, our foreheads resting together. Our breaths mingled, hot and heavy, as we caught our breath. The quiet intimacy of the moment settled over us like a warm blanket. I gazed into Ridley's eyes, seeing the same love and passion I'd fallen for all those years ago.

"Ridley," I murmured, my voice a low rumble. "I remember everything. Every moment, every touch, every word. I'm so damn sorry for what I put you through. You never gave up on me, even when I couldn't remember us."

Tears welled in Ridley's eyes, but her smile was radiant. "I knew you'd come back to me. I never stopped believing in us."

I pulled her closer, burying my face in her hair. "I love you, darlin'. More than I can ever say. You're my heart, my soul. Without you, I'm nothing but a shell."

Ridley's arms tightened around me, her body trembling slightly. "I love you too, you stubborn old biker," she said, a watery chuckle escaping her. "Don't you dare leave me again, you hear me? I can't go through that again."

I pressed a kiss to her temple, my heart full to bursting. "Never again, sweetheart. I'm here to stay."

The morning sun painted the room in hues of amber, casting a warm glow over our entwined bodies as we settled back into the bed. Ridley's soft curves molded against me, her head tucked under my chin. I breathed in deeply, savoring the warmth of her skin against mine.

"This feels like a dream," I murmured, my fingers tracing lazy patterns on her bare shoulder. "If it is, I don't ever want to wake up."

Ridley's hand splayed across my chest, right over my heart. "It's real. We're real." Her voice was thick with emotion, but I could hear the smile in it. "How are you feeling?"

I took a moment to consider, my mind sifting through the flood of memories. "Like my brain got hit by an eighteen-wheeler. But also like I've been given a second chance at life," I replied honestly. "Everything's so clear now. It's overwhelming, but in the best way possible."

She lifted her head, those beautiful blue eyes meeting mine. "We have all the time in the world to sort through it all. Together."

I couldn't resist leaning in for a soft kiss, relishing the way she melted against me. As we parted, I noticed the sunlight catching the silver strands in her hair, reminding me of how much time we'd lost. But it didn't matter now. We had found our way back to each other.

"I can't wait to see the kids," I said, a hint of excitement creeping into my voice. "To really see them, you know? To remember all our history."

Ridley's smile was tender. "Dawson will be over the moon. And the girls... We may have to go to the Devil's Fury to see them. I'm still pissed as fuck at them, and I know the rest of the club is too. Oh, God! The club! Everyone will be so happy to hear you remember everything."

As we lay there, wrapped in each other's arms, I felt a profound sense of peace settle over me. The world outside could wait. For now, this moment was ours alone.

As we basked in the tranquil glow of our reunion, a distant rumble pierced the morning stillness. The unmistakable growl of motorcycles, a sound that had once been as familiar to me as my own heartbeat, now stirred something primal within my chest.

Ridley's fingers tightened ever so slightly against my skin. "Sounds like some of your brothers are heading out," she murmured, her breath warm against my neck.

I closed my eyes, letting the rhythm of the engines wash over me. "Yeah," I replied. "Funny how some things never change, and yet they do. Not the first time I've heard that sound the last few months, but it's different today."

The rumble grew louder, then faded, leaving behind a charged silence. I found myself torn between the cocoon of our bed and the pull of the open road. The dichotomy wasn't lost on Ridley; I could feel her studying my face.

"You've missed it," she said. It wasn't a question.

I met her gaze, seeing understanding in those eyes I'd fallen for all those years ago. "I did," I admitted. "But I wouldn't trade this moment for anything. I can ride with them later."

She smiled, a hint of mischief playing at the corners of her mouth. "Who says you have to choose? We've got a lot of lost time to make up for, but the club's still out there. Still needs you."

I raised an eyebrow, a slow grin spreading across my face. "You trying to get rid of me already, darlin'?"

Ridley laughed, the sound rich and full. "Not a chance in hell. You're stuck with me, come hell or high water."

As her laughter faded, I found myself marveling at the strength of the woman beside me. She'd weathered every storm life had thrown our way, emerging even more radiant than before.

"We've faced down plenty of both, haven't we?" I mused, running my fingers through her hair.

She nodded, her expression turning serious. "And I'd do it all again if it meant I could be here by your side."

"Love you." I kissed her softly.

"I love you too." She snuggled against me, and for the first time since I woke up in the hospital, everything felt right.

Chapter Eight

Ridley

The golden hour cast a honeyed glow across the living room, softening the hard edges of Venom's face as he sat beside me on our well-worn leather couch. Shadows danced across the planes of his rugged features, highlighting the silver threading through his beard. My heart thundered in my chest.

I drew in a shaky breath, the air heavy with the scent of leather and Venom's familiar cologne. My fingers twisted in my lap, betraying my nerves despite my usual take-charge demeanor.

"There's something I need to tell you."

His dark eyes met mine, intense and unreadable. A shiver raced down my spine at the weight of his gaze.

"What is it, darlin'?" he rumbled, his deep voice sending tremors through me.

I swallowed hard, steeling myself. "These past few months, rediscovering each other... it's been incredible. But I need you to know -- I love you. All of you."

Venom's brow furrowed slightly, a question in his eyes.

"The man you were before," I continued, my voice growing stronger. "The memories we built over decades, the life we created together. But also the man you've become. Your strength, your determination to piece everything back together. I started out wanting to make you fall for me all over again. But..."

My hand reached for his almost of its own accord, our fingers intertwining. The roughness of his palm against my skin grounded me.

"You're still the same at your core," I said softly.

"That fierce protectiveness, that unwavering loyalty. But there was a vulnerability the last few months, an openness that took my breath away."

Venom remained silent, but his grip on my hand tightened. I forged ahead, baring my soul.

"I fell in love with you," I admitted. "And I wouldn't change a single moment of our journey. Even though I've been terrified, I got to see a different side of you. I think this may have actually brought us closer together."

The confession hung in the air between us, charged with potential. My heart raced as I waited for his response.

Venom's expression softened, the hard lines of his face melting into something tender. His thumb traced slow circles on the back of my hand, sending shivers up my arm. The silence stretched, but it wasn't uncomfortable. I could almost see the gears turning in his mind as he absorbed my words.

Finally, he spoke. "Ridley, darlin'… you've been my anchor through all this." He lifted our joined hands, pressing a kiss to my knuckles. "Your love, your patience… it's been everything."

My breath caught in my throat as I saw the glimmer of unshed tears in his eyes. This tough, alpha male rarely showed such raw emotion.

"I've been thinkin'," he continued, shifting closer to me on the couch. "About our past, our present… our future." The last word held a wealth of promise. "Maybe we can take the best of both worlds, yeah?"

I nodded, encouraging him to continue.

"Like… remember how we used to have those Sunday morning rides? Just the two of us?" A smile played at the corners of his mouth. "We could start that up again. But this time, maybe we take a different route each week. Explore new places together."

The idea sparked excitement in my chest. "I'd love that," I murmured, picturing us on his bike, the wind in our hair, discovering hidden gems in the countryside.

Venom's eyes lit up. "And for our anniversary this year... instead of the usual steakhouse, what if we tried that new place two towns over? Something different, but still special."

I couldn't help but grin. This blend of old and new, of cherished memories and fresh experiences, felt perfect. It was us, evolving together.

"We could make new traditions," I suggested, my mind racing with possibilities. "Like... a monthly game night with Dawson and Nora. Or a monthly cookout at the clubhouse during the warmer seasons."

Venom nodded, a slow smile spreading across his face. "Weaving our past and present into something beautiful for our future."

The metaphor, so poetic coming from my usually gruff husband, made my heart swell. I leaned in, pressing my forehead to his. "I love you," I whispered. "Every version of you."

His large hand cupped my cheek, his touch infinitely gentle. "And I love you, Ridley. Always have, always will. Even when I didn't remember you, some part of me still knew you were mine."

My fingers danced across my phone screen, a smile playing on my lips as I tapped out a message to Isabella and Torch. I wanted them to know Venom was completely back now, and that we needed to celebrate.

"You think they'll all come on such short notice?" His voice broke the silence, a hint of uncertainty coloring his usually confident tone.

I looked up. "Babe, when has the club ever

turned down a chance to party? Besides, this is big news. They'll want to celebrate with us."

Venom nodded, his beard trailing down his chest as he leaned back into the couch. "Suppose you're right. It'll be good to see everyone. You know, now that I actually remember who everyone is."

"Speaking of everyone. How do you want to handle telling the kids? Should we wait until we're at the clubhouse? I can tell Dawson he, Nora, and Taylor are invited to a get-together there. I doubt she'll want to bring the baby, but I'll make sure she knows he's welcome too. As for Farrah and Mariah..."

Venom's eyes softened, a rare vulnerability crossing his weathered features. "Might be best to give them a heads-up. Don't want to overwhelm them in front of the whole club."

I nodded, my heart swelling with love for the tough man who always put our children first. I quickly fired off texts to Dawson, Mariah, and Farrah. I asked Dawson to bring his family to the clubhouse, then told Mariah and Farrah we'd make arrangements to visit them.

As I set my phone down, the air around us seemed to crackle with anticipation. Venom stood, offering me his hand. "Ready to face our family, darlin'?"

I took his hand. "With you? Always."

* * *

The floorboards hummed beneath my boots, the bass of a country rock song pulsing through the soles and into my bones. It vibrated in the air, mingling with the scent of leather, whiskey, and something else: anticipation. Excitement. The kind that makes your fingers tingle and sets your heart to a double beat.

Venom stood beside me, his presence filling the

space like a warm, solid wall. His hand was a reassuring weight in mine, his calloused fingers interlaced with mine. I felt the warmth of his breath on my ear as he murmured, "Looks like the whole damn club turned out."

I squeezed his hand, a smile tugging at my lips. "Well, it's not every day the infamous Venom gets his memories back."

The words were barely out of my mouth when the crowd parted like the Red Sea. There stood Torch, his silver hair gleaming under the dim lights, his weathered face etched with a familiar grin.

"Well, well," his gruff voice boomed over the music, silencing the room. "If it isn't the man of the hour. Welcome back to the land of the living, brother."

Venom's hand tightened around mine, a silent communication passing between us. Then, he stepped forward, pulling Torch into a brief, yet powerful embrace.

"Good to be back, old man," Venom said, his voice rough with emotion.

I watched them, my heart swelling with a mixture of gratitude and relief. The bonds of brotherhood that held this club together had helped Venom weather this storm, and now, we were all stronger for it.

Torch turned to me, his gaze softening. "You did good, little girl," he said quietly, his hand resting on my shoulder. "Knew you had it in you to bring him back."

Tears welled up in my eyes, blurring the edges of the room. The faces of our makeshift family swam before me, each one etched with a story of resilience and love.

This night wasn't just about Venom's return. It

was about our collective healing, our shared victory. It was a new beginning.

More of the club gathered around Venom, shaking his hand, giving him a slap on the back. Everyone was eager to see him back to his usual self.

My eyes swept over the crowd, searching for my son and Nora, the missing pieces of my heart. And there they were, Dawson, Nora, and little Taylor, weaving through the throng.

Dawson, the spitting image of his father, reached us first. His voice, rough with emotion, rasped, "Dad, it's good to have you back. Really back."

Venom pulled Dawson into a crushing embrace. "Missed you, boy," he mumbled, his gruff exterior crumbling for a fleeting moment.

Even Nora had tears in her eyes as she hugged my husband, and little Taylor couldn't stop jumping up and down, too excited over seeing her grandpa for the first time in months.

Venom crouched down, his hulking frame seeming to shrink as he addressed the child. "Hey there, princess."

"Do you remember me now, Grandpa?" she asked.

"Of course I do. How could I forget my favorite little troublemaker?"

Taylor giggled, her shyness evaporating as she launched herself into Venom's arms. My chest ached with a bittersweet joy. It was a moment of pure, unadulterated happiness, a gift after a long, harrowing journey.

As the night wore on, the party swirled around me, a kaleidoscope of laughter and light. I found a quiet corner, leaning against the bar, watching Venom laugh with our friends, his eyes crinkling at the edges.

The memory of our journey -- the fear, the hope, the unwavering love that had bound us together -- flickered through my mind like a film reel.

Venom's gaze met mine across the crowded room, and the world seemed to melt away. Our eyes locked, a silent promise, a vow to cherish every moment, to build a future even stronger than our past.

He strode toward me, his presence commanding, his eyes holding a love that was both fierce and tender. "You okay, darlin'?"

I leaned into his touch, my voice thick with emotion. "I'm perfect. Just thinking about how lucky we are."

A smirk played on his lips. "Luck's got nothin' to do with it, sweetheart. We fought for this. *You* fought for us."

As his lips met mine, the world faded away. In that kiss, a promise, a future, a love that would endure any storm. We would face whatever challenges lay ahead, stronger, wiser, and more in love than ever before.

The clubhouse was alive with the pulse of laughter and music, a vibrant heartbeat that resonated through my very bones. In Venom's arms, I swayed to the rhythm as he pulled me onto me the makeshift dance floor, our bodies molding together. His strong hands at my waist were an anchor, a constant reminder of the unbreakable bond that held us together.

"Remember our first dance?" His voice, rough and rich like dark chocolate, rumbled against my ear, sending a shiver down my spine. "Because I do."

"How could I forget? You stepped on my toes three times."

He chuckled, the sound a warm caress on my skin. "And you still married me."

"Best decision I ever made," I murmured, pressing closer.

The night unfolded like a whispered dream. I watched with pride as Venom arm-wrestled with our son Dawson, his muscles rippling beneath his shirt. The other old ladies gathered around me, knowing looks on their faces. Especially Isabella and Darian.

I savored every detail of the night, etching it onto the canvas of my mind. I didn't want to forget a second of this.

As the clock struck midnight, Venom's hand found mine again. We exchanged a glance, a silent conversation passing between us, a language only we understood.

He cleared his throat, the sound cutting through the joyous cacophony. "Listen up, you bunch of degenerates." he called out, his voice a command that held the authority of a man who had led this club through hell and back. The room fell silent after a bit of laughter, all eyes turning to us.

My hand squeezed his, my heart swelling with a love so vast it threatened to burst from my chest. "We just wanted to say thank you. For standing by us, for believing in us, even when we didn't believe in ourselves. Without all your support, I don't know how we would have gotten through the past few months."

Venom nodded, his gaze sweeping across the sea of faces. "This club, this family -- you're the backbone of everything we are. We wouldn't be here without you."

A lump formed in my throat as I looked at the faces around me. "We love you all."

A chorus of cheers erupted, the sound washing over us like a wave of affection. As Venom pulled me close, his lips brushing my forehead in a tender caress,

I knew that this -- this moment, this love, this family -- was everything I'd ever wanted and more. It was the culmination of our dreams, a testament to the strength of our bond, a beacon of hope in a world that desperately needed it. It was our home, our haven, and it would endure, a testament to the power of love, laughter, and the unyielding spirit of the human heart.

As the cheers faded, I sensed a subtle shift in the atmosphere. The night wound down, but the warmth of celebration still clung to the air. I glanced up at Venom, catching that familiar glint in his eye.

"Ready to head out, darlin'?"

I nodded, a thrill of anticipation coursing through me. "Let's go home."

We wove through the crowd, accepting hugs and well-wishes. My heart swelled as I watched Venom exchange a firm handshake with our son Dawson. They shared a moment of understanding that spoke volumes.

Stepping into the cool night air, Venom's arm snaked around my waist, pulling me close. The rumble of motorcycles in the distance mingled with the muffled sounds of the party inside.

"Life's full of surprises, sweetheart. Some of 'em even good." He smacked me on the ass, a light teasing slap. "Tonight was one we'll always remember."

We walked in comfortable silence toward Venom's bike, moonlight casting long shadows across the parking lot. As we reached it, he turned to me, his eyes dark with promise.

"I'm going to make every damn second of our future count. Even if something happens and I lose my memories all over again, I want new ones. New stories for you to tell me, new ways for you to bring me back."

"Promise you'll always come back to me?" I

asked.

"With everything I am." He leaned down and kissed me. As we broke apart, breathless and grinning, I knew this was more than just a new chapter. It was an entire new book waiting to be written, with endless possibilities stretching out before us.

Harley Wylde

Harley Wylde is an accomplished author known for her captivating MC Romances. With an unwavering commitment to sensual storytelling, Wylde immerses her readers in an exciting world of fierce men and irresistible women. Her works exude passion, danger, and gritty realism, while still managing to end on a satisfying note each time.

When not crafting her tales, Wylde spends her time brainstorming new plotlines, indulging in a hot cup of Starbucks, or delving into a good book. She has a particular affinity for supernatural horror literature and movies. Visit Wylde's website to learn more about her works and upcoming events, and don't forget to sign up for her newsletter to receive exclusive discounts and other exciting perks.

Harley at Changeling: changelingpress.com/harley-wylde-a-196

Bad Boys Multiverse

Contemporary MC, Organized Crime, and Crossovers

A Bad Boy Romance
Dixie Reapers MC
Devil's Boneyard MC
Hades Abyss MC
Devil's Fury MC
Reckless Kings MC
Savage Raptors MC
Swift Angels MC
Owned by the Mob
Bryson Corners
Underland MC

Paranormal MC

Devoted Guardians MC
Balor's Saints MC

Print and Audio:

Dixie Reapers MC Print
Dixie Reapers MC Audio
Devil's Boneyard MC Audio
Hades Abyss MC Audio
Devil's Fury MC Audio

Changeling Press LLC

Contemporary Action Adventure, Sci-Fi, Steampunk, Dark Fantasy, Urban Fantasy, Paranormal, and BDSM Romance available in e-book, audio, and print format at ChangelingPress.com – MC Romance, Werewolves, Vampires, Dragons, Shapeshifters and Horror -- Tales from the edge of your imagination.

Where can I get Changeling Press Books?

Changeling Press e-books are available at ChangelingPress.com, Amazon, Apple Books, Barnes & Noble, Kobo, Smashwords, and other online retailers, including Everand Subscription and Kobo Subscription Services. Print books are available at Amazon, Barnes and Noble, and by ISBN special order through your local bookstores.

Changeling Press, LLC

ChangelingPress.com

www.ingramcontent.com/pod-product-compliance
Lightning Source LLC
Chambersburg PA
CBHW051518260626
47170CB00003B/671

* 9 7 8 1 6 0 5 2 1 9 4 9 3 *